FLIRTING
with the
SCROOGE

A GRUMPY SUNSHINE HOLIDAY ROMANTIC COMEDY

GIA STEVENS

Flirting with the Scrooge: A Grumpy Sunshine Holiday Romantic Comedy by Gia Stevens

www.authorgiastevens.com

Published by: Gia Stevens

Copyright: Flirting with the Scrooge: A Grumpy Sunshine Holiday Romantic Comedy by Gia Stevens © 2023 Gia Stevens

Print ISBN: 978-1-958286-16-6

Editor: My Notes in the Margins

Publisher: Wild Clover Publishing, LLC

v111323

This is a work of fiction. Names, characters, places, and incidents either are the products of the author's imagination or are used fictitiously. Any resemblance to actual persons, living or dead, business, companies, events, or locales is entirely coincidental.

For everyone searching for their soulmate…
Be sure to find someone who will write a beautiful song for you.

Or at the very least, fuck you under the Christmas tree.

Merry Christmas!

While this story is a romantic comedy there may be situations that are triggering to some. For a list of those content warnings please visit my website and scroll to the bottom of the page.

THE NEW NEIGHBOR

CHAPTER ONE
★ ⭐ ★

Tatum

Some people love Christmas, but I *love* Christmas. Ever since I was a little girl it was always my favorite holiday. Everything from the delectable smell of vanilla, sugar, and melted chocolate from fresh baked cookies wafting through the air to hunting for the perfectly symmetrical and lush Christmas tree at the local tree farm. And let's not forget decorations galore, inside the house and out. Honestly, it's a holiday that should be year-round.

Rising on my tippy toes, my fingertips scratch at a box sitting on the top shelf in my garage. As I stretch, the step stool scrapes against the cement floor beneath me. Oh, come on, just a little farther. With a one footed hop, I'm able to push the box just enough to expose the corner so I'm able to pull it with my other hand. With both hands I secure the box against my chest. As I step backward, my toe slips off the edge. The box flies from my grasp as my arms flail wildly to regain my balance. The cardboard rips down the side as it hits the floor, spilling plastic ornaments and Christmas lights across the cement. Just my luck. As I tumble backward to the floor, a stack of sharp cornered boxes breaks my fall, instead of the pile of inflatable decorations. A mushroom cloud of fake snow plumes into the air and flutters down around me. It's like I'm living in my very own snow globe. I blow a strand of hair out of my face. The one thing that should bring me joy this year just tried to kill me. Great.

If someone told me a month ago this is where my life would be, I would have laughed in their face. Never did I imagine I'd be lying in a heap of cardboard boxes and fake snow. No one expects to not only get dumped but also fired in a span of thirty seconds. But here I am a month before Christmas, single and definitely not in the mood to mingle.

One day, it was all... gone. The bow on my neatly wrapped Christmas present was catching my ex canoodling with his intern at a charity gala my sister was coordinating. When he told me he was dumping me to focus on his career, it was accurate as long as his career involved a leggy brunette in a pencil skirt. We spent five years together, and he tossed me out faster than an unwanted fruit cake.

My only goal for the next four weeks is to drown my sorrows in tinsel, lights, and ornaments. And clearly, I'm even having a hard time with that. Any other year I would be stringing up Christmas lights and blowing up the inflatable Santa and all his workshop accessories, but this year my bah humbug is at an all-time high. Which I hate. I'm always the first one to put up my decorations, mostly to encourage my neighbors to do the same so I can have some actual competition for the neighborhood decorating contest.

I peel myself off the ground and brush off my jeans. Coffee. I need more coffee. Pushing my way through the door that leads from the garage into my kitchen, I pull a cup off my mug tree, and fill it to the brim with the deep brown deliciousness. While clutching the mug with both hands, I leisurely stroll toward the large picture window that faces the street. By now, a tree would be standing tall in this very spot, but this year is different. It's hard to get into the holiday spirit when your life crumbles to pieces a week earlier.

I lift the steaming cup of coffee to my lips and take a sip. No more wallowing. No more letting my ex consume my thoughts. I need to immerse myself in the one thing I love and forget everything else. Christmas. As my nana would say, "Only let your thoughts be consumed by someone who deserves them. Give everyone else the middle finger." Nana was classy like that.

Whirling around, I stomp across the room and back into the kitchen. It's time to raise some middle fingers. I slam my coffee mug on the white quartz kitchen island a little harder than normal. I'm surprised it doesn't crack. Shoving my feet into the fur lined boots, I throw my coat over my shoulders and tug my knit cap over my hair. Time to make the decorations my bitch.

I press the garage door button. The bright light slowly fills the dark garage as the door rises. I finish cleaning up my previous mess and dig into the other boxes sitting on the cement. I rifle through several boxes, pulling out all the decorations I'll need and move everything else to the side.

A light coating of snow dusts the ground as I drag one box out to the driveway leaving a plowed snow path in my wake. From my back pocket I pull out a piece of paper.

Unfolding it, I glance down at the haphazard diagram of my decoration set up. The blowup Santa and reindeer will be on the left side and the snow globes, Santa's workshop, and the candy cane walkway will be on the right. The twenty-foot maple tree in my front yard is already strung with colorful lights, so I only need to add the over-sized fake presents underneath.

Over the next several hours, I run extension cords, carry out boxes, and set up all the decorations. Once everything is in place, I plug it in for a trial run. I shuffle my way to the end of the short driveway, being careful so I don't slip, and admire the lights as they faintly twinkle to life. Santa rises to his eight-foot height and the snow swirls around in the inflatable snow globe. Now it's not Clark Griswold-esque, but it's pretty close. A triumphant smile covers my face. This may be my best work yet. Maybe getting dumped actually put a little extra pep in my Christmas step.

I tiptoe around the decorations, careful not to disturb the powdery snow as I inspect each light and electrical cord. Once I confirm everything works properly, I pull the plug, cutting off the power.

A large black truck rumbles down the road and slows as it approaches my driveway. Instead of entering mine, it pulls into Mrs. Hendrickson's across the street. My gaze immediately drifts to the California license plate. Soon after, a moving truck pulls in with a storage container on the back. A tall, broad shouldered, dark-haired male steps out from the black truck. He's got a ruggedly handsome lumberjack vibe to him with the green flannel coat and dark beard to complete the ensemble. A duffle bag is in one hand and a guitar case in the other. Another man, older with a graying beard and a beanie, meets him at the rear between both trucks. He must be a new neighbor. But I never saw a for sale sign in front of the house.

I step backward, gaze glued to my new neighbors, when my heel kicks one of the empty boxes, throwing me off balance. My arms windmill and I bellow out a screech as I crash to the ground with a thud. Boxes and tubs fling to the side and skate across my driveway. When I glance up, both men's gazes shoot my way. Heat creeps up my neck and floods my cheeks. I wave them off, yelling, "I'm okay!" Just bruised my ass and my dignity. Without a second glance back, both men turn around and walk inside. Well that's one way to introduce myself.

While still on the ground, my phone rings in my pocket, startling me. I pull it out and *Olivia* flashes on the screen. I press talk.

"Hey. What's up?" I wince, rising to my feet. I can already feel a bruise forming on each ass cheek.

"I've set up a client meeting on Friday." My sister, Olivia, started her own event coordinator business and asked me to work with her, which was perfect timing since I was just fired. I brush the speckles of snow off my butt and thighs. "Okay. Just let me know when and where."

"I've already added it to the shared calendar. So, what are you doing today?"

"Just setting up the last of the outdoor decorations."

"That sounds boring."

Olivia never got into the holiday spirit as much as I did. I loved going to my nana's house and helping her decorate. There was something special about having a cup of hot cocoa and throwing tinsel on the tree and hanging stockings over the fireplace. Nana always had two trees. One for me to decorate, which was home to every ornament I could find. Homemade. Store bought. If it had a hook, it went on the tree. There wasn't a branch untouched once I was finished. And then there was Nana's more elegant and pristine tree. But she always told me she liked mine more. Now that I'm older, I've learned less is more. At least when it comes to my own tree. The outside is another story.

"What if I said I have a new neighbor?"

"Now that could be interesting. Give me the deets."

I stroll back into the garage, careful so no one else can hear me. "Two guys pulled into Mrs. Hendrickson's place across the street with a truck and a moving container."

"Are they cute?"

"One is older. Maybe mid-fifties. The other is harder to tell because of his beard, but he appears younger."

"Get your ass over there and get a closer look. Bring cookies too. Neighbors like cookies. Plus, you'll need to tell him all about the neighborhood decorating contest."

I push an empty box to the side with my boot. "That's true. He can't be the only one with an undecorated house."

"And while you're there, you can tell me if he's hot or not. Perhaps a holiday hook-up is exactly what you need. He can twittle your tinsel. You can deck his balls."

I bark out a laugh. "No twittling. And the only balls I'll be playing with will be covered in glitter."

"I'm sure the glitter can be arranged. Some guys might be into that."

I laugh and shake my head. "No glitter. I just want to spend this holiday with you and our friends."

"Well, you're no fun. Let me know how it goes and tell me if he's hot."

"You have a boyfriend."

"I need to know if he's hot for *you*."

I roll my eyes even though she can't see me. "Alright. You'll be the first one I call."

"You better. In fact, put me on speaker when you go over there. Then I can get the play-by-play."

"That's not happening. Kay. Bye." I press end and shove my phone into my coat pocket.

I stack all the boxes and totes from the driveway and haul them into the garage. While I'm cleaning up, I steal glances across the street. So far, no one has come out and the curtains are closed, so I can't see in through the large picture window.

Once I'm finished, I make my way inside. I glance at the oversized starburst wall clock. It's still early. Maybe baking will get me out of this funk and I can bring them across the street to meet my new neighbor. Two birds. One stone.

SATAN'S BALLSACK

CHAPTER TWO

★ ★ ★

Connor

I toss my duffle bag onto the floor and lean my guitar case against the well worn fabric couch. It's been years since I've been back to Grams' house. Hell, it's been years since I've been back to Harbor Highlands. I guess that's what happens when a record producer stumbles into the bar your band is playing at and offers to sign you. It's been a lifelong dream to play music professionally, but it happened so fast. One minute I'm thirty-four, playing local bars, then the next my band is selling out various halls, theaters, and clubs. We're not filling stadiums, but for a follow up tour, that's a possibility. Unfortunately, the vanity of it all wore off pretty quick. As fast as I entered Hollywood, I was ready to leave. And that's why I'm here.

When I got the phone call saying they were moving

Grams to Whispering Pines Assisted Living and they needed someone to fix up her house so they could sell it, I jumped at the opportunity. I'm not Bob Vila or anything, but I know my way around a toolbox. At the very least, there's always YouTube. Plus, it was the perfect excuse to get away and have some time to myself and contemplate some life decisions about what I want the next step to be.

I throw myself onto the couch and exhale a sigh. "Thanks for all your help, man. I appreciate it." My phone rings in my pocket. Pulling it out, I glance down at the screen, sigh, then mute the call. A second later my phone dings notifying me of a voicemail.

"Anytime." Devon, a friend and former roadie from the tour, sits in a rocking chair next to the couch.

We spent the last two days driving from California to Minnesota. Once we arrived in town, we picked up the storage container for all of Grams belongings. The rest of the family will go through it later.

"How long are you staying?" Devon asks.

"I don't know. However long it takes to clean and fix this place up and get it on the market." I glance around the room. Dated wood paneling covers three of the four walls in the living room. The one mustard yellow painted wall is covered with picture frames that have been there for the last twenty years. I know for a fact when I remove them there will be dark rectangular squares covering the wall from the faded paint. The carpet's color has dulled over time, making it appear like a faded patch of dirt on the floor. This might be more work than I bargained for.

"Are you sure hiding out in Harbor Highlands is what you need?"

Sitting up, I peer around the one room I've seen so far and all the work that needs to be done. I rest my elbows on my knees and scrub my hands down my face. "It seemed like a good idea at the time. I can't take it back now." Even though I'm slightly terrified to find out what kind of state the rest of the house is in.

"You expect to go undetected here in the middle of nowhere Minnesota?"

"That's what the beard is for." I run my fingers over my newly grown facial hair.

He barks out a hearty laugh. "Just add some sunglasses and you'll be incognito."

"Exactly."

"Well, let me know if you need anything. My Uber should be here any minute." He rises to his feet.

"Thanks for everything." I stand and hold out my hand.

His hand firmly grips mine. "Hit me up when you get back to LA."

"Definitely." But truth be told, I don't know if I want to go back.

Devon's Uber pulls into the driveway, and he's out the door. Silence fills the house. The type of silence where you can hear your own thoughts. This is what I wanted. To be left alone. To be by myself, but I'm not ready to deal with all that right this moment.

I toss my duffle bag into one of the spare bedrooms, then return to the living room. I glance around. There's so much shit. I don't even know where to start. My only task was to box everything up and clean the place up. Maybe apply a fresh coat of paint. As I spin around, this place will need more than some paint in order to get a decent price.

Harbor Heights has always been a great, family friendly neighborhood. Growing up, there was never a shortage of kids to play with when I stayed with Grams. The three bedrooms, two baths would make a great starter home for a new or young family. But not in its current state.

I slide on my shoes, throw on my coat, and trudge back into the cold to collect all the boxes in the back of the moving truck. A cloud of breath hovers in front of me and I walk down the stairs. There's a light covering of snow covering the grass, even more in the shadows. The real cold hasn't hit yet, but it will soon. I can feel it in my bones.

Once I reach the back of the truck, I lift the roll up door, and tuck a stack of broken down boxes under my arm. A blistering chilly wind smacks me in the face. Shit. Being away for almost three years, I've forgotten what Minnesota winters are like. If I'm going to be going in and out, I'll need some proper winter clothes. Especially once the snow really comes down. I make a mental note to hit up the local fleet supply store. They'll have all the winter essentials. But I'll go later, right before they close, so there will be fewer people.

Two more trips later, I grab my two other bags and the last of the boxes and drop them on the floor. While I'm here, might as well start with the living room. I grab the packing tape and assemble boxes. I start with the smaller items, wrapping anything that may be fragile with newspaper.

In the middle of taping up one box, my phone rings from the end table. Glancing at it, *Satan's Ballsack* flashes on the screen. Also known as my agent, Spencer, but I prefer Satan's Ballsack. I roll my eyes, but I know I have to at least answer the call, so he doesn't send a search party thinking his payday has gone AWOL.

"Hey Spence."

"Thank fuck you finally answered. I just tried to call you. Did you get any of my phone calls or voicemails?"

I rake my hand through my hair. "Yeah. I've been a

little busy driving across the country. Once I got settled, I was going to call you back." But what I want to tell him is I purposely sent each one to voicemail because I don't want to listen to anything he has to say. And I wasn't going to call him back. Or at least not right away. If he wasn't so good at what he does, I would have fired him months ago.

"So I can expect you back in LA, in what? A week? We need to have a meeting and nail down your schedule. We gotta get the band back into the studio working on the second album. The first tour was a big success, we need to keep the momentum going."

I scoff at his use of *we*. It's more like *I*. He needs to keep the momentum, so the cash continues to flow in. I, on the other hand, couldn't give a damn.

"So, I'll book you a flight back to LA—"

"That's not going to happen." I rub my temples and pace the living room to burn up this anxious energy before I tell him to fuck off and fire him. I inhale a deep breath through my nose, and exhale through my mouth. A technique my therapist mentioned I should try. "I told you I'm taking care of some stuff. I'll be back when it's done."

"Zane told me that you're helping your grandma. What's the big deal? Why didn't you tell me?"

Fucking Zane and his big mouth. That's the excuse, but not the reason. "Does it matter? Do you need to keep tabs on me? Should I call you when I'm taking a shit, too? Since you need to know every facet of my life."

"Yeah. I need to keep tabs on you. You got two weeks to take care of whatever. Then I'm booking you a flight—"

I hang up. My patience is wearing thin. For once, I want to be on my own schedule instead of someone else's. His name flashes on the screen as my phone rings again, but I ignore it. He'll eventually get the hint and stop calling. In the meantime, I go back to packing boxes.

Several hours later, I have three stacks of boxes and a good chunk of the living room cleared. I wipe my brow with the back of my hand. At this rate, I'll finish ahead of schedule. But then that means back to LA.

Suddenly, a knock on my door draws my attention. Who's knocking? Did Devon miss his flight? I stroll to the front door and rip it open.

Holy shit.

Definitely not Devon. Her bright blue eyes sparkle as they gaze back at me, and her full lips pull into a warm smile. Her knitted cap covers her long blonde hair. Then recognition hits. She's the same woman from across the street who fell on her ass while putting up decorations.

"Hi. I'm Tatum. I live in the house across the street." She twists around to point at her house and I get a whiff of her sweet vanilla scent. "I had no idea Mrs. Hendrickson sold her house. I never saw the For Sale sign. Then again, I've been a little preoccupied. But you don't need to know any of that." She chuckles softly.

And fuck me. Her laugh is just as sweet as she smells.

"I want to welcome you to the neighborhood. And I made you cookies as a welcome to the neighborhood gift." She holds out the plate full of cookies toward me. I glance down and then back up. "Now, I know you just moved in, but the entire neighborhood always hosts a decorating contest—"

Not even a half a day in and it's already started. "I don't decorate."

"But it's for charity. I always helped Mrs. Hendrickson with hers. Plus, I've won the last three years so if you need any tips—"

I slam the door.

WHAT THE CRAP?

CHAPTER THREE

Connor

Asshole. If there was one word to describe me, that would be it, and I won't deny it. She didn't deserve getting the door slammed in her face, but I just got to town and barely got my bags inside before someone came knocking, wanting something from me. After I saw it wasn't Devon, my first instinct was that I was outed and a fan was looking for pictures or an autograph. But instead, I got a blonde holding a tray of cookies. Something about that piqued my interest.

Instantly, the sweet smell of sugar and vanilla assaulted my nostrils. I wasn't sure if it was coming from the cookies or her, maybe both, but I was willing to see what she wanted. After she introduced herself and mentioned Grams, I lowered my guard. It warmed my heart knowing

Grams had someone close by to watch out for her. The warm and fuzzies soon died when she mentioned Christmas and decorating. Just like everyone else, she wanted something from me. Well, technically, I never stuck around long enough to see what she actually wanted before I slammed the door in her face.

I peek through the curtains of the living room and watch as she runs down a few of the stairs, stops, and spins around, her hair fluttering over her shoulder, before she leaves again. This time empty handed. I track her all the way until she disappears into her house. Oh shit. Why does it feel like I'm giving off stalker vibes?

Yanking open the door, I peer down at the plate of delicious smelling cookies she left, then up to her house. It would be irresponsible of me to leave them outside and attract any wildlife. So, I'm, in fact, doing the neighborhood a favor. Without a second thought, I bend down and swipe the plate off the ground and close the door behind me.

The bottom of the plate is still slightly warm. She must have just baked these. Unable to resist any longer, I grab one off the plate and bite down. I groan. Son of a bitch. This cookie is fucking delicious. Buttery and soft. The chocolate chips are still warm and melty. These remind me of the ones Grams would make. After I finish one cookie, I grab another and stroll back into the living room, leaving a trail of cookie crumbs behind me.

I don't waste another minute and work on packing up the rest of the nick-knacks and removing all the photos from the walls. After a task is complete, I reward myself with another cookie. Two cookies later, the last of the boxes in the living room are taped up. Just then, my phone rings. My first thought is that it's my agent calling again with some amazing offer I can't say no to. When I glance at the screen, *Zane* flashes at the top. I press the green phone icon.

"Hey man. What's up?"

"Did I thank you for running away and giving us all a break?"

I laugh. "I didn't run away. You make me sound like a teenager. I had some family shit to take care of."

"Family shit. Running away. Either way. Thanks, man. It's nice to have a few days to myself."

Zane's been with the band for the past year since our previous drummer decided he couldn't handle the pressure and temptations of Hollywood. After he bailed, we found Zane. His skills on the kit are comparable to Neil Peart.

"I'm happy to be of service." I run my hand over my beard.

"Did Spence get a hold of you? He's been calling the entire band like a scorned lover."

"Oh yeah and all seven hundred of his voicemails."

He laughs. "Speaking of scorned ex-lovers, have you talked to yours? Apparently, now she's—"

"Nope and I don't care." I don't say anything else because there is nothing else to say. She's nothing but an ex, or maybe more like a mistake, and that's it.

When I don't give him more, he changes the subject. "So, how's the cold? I can't believe you ditched sunny California for what? Canada?"

"Minnesota." I stop pacing and stare out the living room window that lines up with my new neighbor's window. A silhouette of a petite woman moves from one side of the room to the other.

"That's practically Canada. Either way it's cold as fuck and there's snow."

I tug on one panel of the curtain, fully closing it. If I can see her, she can see me and the last thing I need is to get caught staring into her window. "Well, there is more than just snow. A neighbor dropped off some cookies to welcome me to the neighborhood."

"Wait? People still do that?"

"I guess so. If I wind up dead, it's probably from the cookies Tatum dropped off. She lives across the street, dark blue house, white trim. Can't miss it."

"So, a female? Hot?"

"She's alright. But not why I'm here." Fuck. She's more than alright. Her bright blue eyes could warm anyone on the coldest of days.

"I'll check back in later this week. Make sure you're still alive."

"Fantastic. Later." I end the call and stroll into the kitchen. All this cookie talk makes me want another. Blindly, I grab one off the plate and shove half of it in my mouth.

I chew a couple of times. Something doesn't taste right. Maybe she *is* trying to poison me?

I chew again and my teeth sink into something soft that isn't a chocolate chip. I gag as I frantically search for a garbage can. When I come up empty handed, I rush to the sliding glass door, yank it open, and spit out everything. Bits of cookie speckle the pristine white snow. Glancing down at the other half of the cookie in my hand, I see it. What the crap? Raisins. Fucking gross. She is trying to kill me. Okay, maybe not actually kill me, but who disguises oatmeal raisin cookies as chocolate chip? Slamming the door shut, I stomp back to the plate and toss the half-eaten one on top. I rest my palms on the mustard yellow Formica countertop and glare at the cookies as if they did something wrong. Pushing off, I rip off a piece of paper towel and collect the last three good cookies and leave the other vomit patties on the plate. Since I don't want these in my house, there's only one reasonable place for them to go.

I slide on my boots and coat. With the plate of cookies in hand, I mosey across the street and set the plate on her doorstep. Two of us can pass cookies in this neighborhood. Granted mine are the same ones she gave me. But it doesn't matter.

Snowflakes fall from the sky as I trek back to my house. I stifle a yawn. Seeing as this is my first day here, and I already got most of the living room cleared out, I'm calling it a day. Tomorrow I'll work on moving the furniture and ripping up the old carpet. I'm curious to see what's underneath.

As I stroll down the hallway to my bedroom for the month, I lift my shirt off and toss it into the corner of the room. Note to self: find a laundry basket. I shove my pants to my feet and pull a towel from one of my bags. A muffled knock sounds from somewhere in the house and I freeze to listen more closely. It happens again, but louder. With a towel wrapped around my waist, I follow the sound until I'm back in the living room. I peel back a corner of the curtain and peer out the window. Looks like my new neighbor is gracing me with her presence once again. Can't say I'm complaining, though. I throw open the door and prop my forearm on the wood frame.

Her gaze drops from my chest down to where my hand is holding the towel closed. Her plump lips part slightly. A pink blush covers her cheeks and I know it's not from the cold. Interrupting her lustful gaze, I ask, "Can I help you?"

THE SNOW SHOVEL POLICE

CHAPTER FOUR
* ⭐ *

Tatum

The door flies open and my breath hitches. I'm eye level with a very impressive, sculpted chest with a light dusting of dark hair in the center. With a mind of its own my gaze travels down to his bare stomach and over every ridge and valley of his six-pack abs. There's no way it's that defined when he's relaxed. He must be flexing. I'll just stare at his stomach until he relaxes, that's the only way to find out for sure.

"Can I help you?"

Once again, his deep, smokey voice turns my nipples into stiff peaks. Or maybe it's the crisp winter air? I'm going to go with the latter. My gaze jerks up and meets his. Heat spreads over my cheeks, knowing he caught me admiring him.

"Aren't you cold?" Shamelessly, I take another peek down south following a strip of hair that disappears under a towel wrapped low around his hips. Is that his bulge under the towel? Even in the cold? I try not to salivate but I feel like Pavlov's dog. I swallow. Hard.

"Matter of fact, I am, so what do you want?"

His voice jolts me from my gawking. I want to say "lick you like an ice cream cone" but he's a little rude. Any new neighbor has always been so friendly and enjoyed the warm welcome. Everyone except him. "You left these on my doorstep. Including a half-eaten one." I shove the plate of cookies at him.

His gaze drops to the cookies, then back to me and he says matter-of-factly, "I don't like raisins."

"Well you could have thrown them away or given them to someone else."

"I did. I gave them to you."

I scoff.

"If that's all, I'm going to jump in the shower." He pauses for a moment and when I just stare at him dumbfounded, he closes the door on me. Again. Ugh!

I stomp my way back to my house as snowflakes flutter from the sky and slam my door shut for no other purpose than I hope the scrooge from across the street heard. I doubt it, but I'll pretend. Not only did he slam the door in my face earlier and take the cookies I left for him, but then he had the audacity to give half of them back and shut the door on me. And who doesn't like oatmeal raisin cookies? I blow out an exasperated huff. No one has ever done that to me. Perhaps he's busy and didn't want the interruption. There were stacks of boxes behind him, but he didn't need to be so rude about it.

Flustered once again, I sigh. I need to find my Christmas Zen. I turn on my favorite movie, *The Holiday*, in need of a distraction. Maybe I need to swap houses with someone and find true love. Clearly, whatever I'm doing now isn't working. I got dumped and now the grump who hates Christmas lives across the street. This is shaping up to be a great holiday.

While the movie plays in the background, I lug out boxes from the spare bedroom closet filled to the brim with decorations. I start with hanging the stockings on the mantle, then move on to draping pine garland adorned with red bows and ornaments around the doorways, and lastly, I place wreaths on both the front and back door. But my favorite part is setting up my nana's porcelain Christmas village.

While growing up, the first thing I would want to do is help her lay out all the buildings and place the ice skating rink in the center. Christmas music would softly play in the background, and a wide grin would never leave my face. This weekend I'll top off all the decorating by going to Fir Meadows Tree Farm to pick out the perfect tree. I'm ready to transform my house into a winter wonderland.

Two hours later, my heart is full of Christmas cheer once again. When I glance out the window, I notice not only has the sun gone down, but the snow has also gotten heavier. I better do some shoveling before it gets any worse. Peeling myself off the couch, I make my way to the door. I throw on my coat, hat, mittens, and boots. With a flip of a switch, the exterior lights flood the top half of the driveway. Glancing out the window in the door, large snowflakes fall to the ground and by the looks of it, the snow isn't light and fluffy.

My boot sinks into the snow as I close the door behind me, leaving a perfectly shaped boot imprint in my wake. If I don't clear this now, it's going to be ice tomorrow. With my shovel in hand, I start at the top of the driveway and make my way toward the street.

Halfway through, I partially unzip my coat, the heavy snow giving me a workout. With only a few rows left, I glance up and I'm greeted with the holiday grump as he stalks toward the end of his driveway, shovel in hand.

"This your first time shoveling?" he yells from across the street.

I lift my shovel and heave the pile of snow over my shoulder. "No. It's not," I sneer. I don't want him assuming he has me figured out. While I have shoveled before, it was only when there was a dusting of the feather light snow. Never the wet, heavy snow, like now. Growing up, my dad always took care of it or I lived in an apartment where a maintenance crew was hired. Once I got my house, either Adam did it or we hired someone else to do it.

He pushes his shovel, leaving behind a snow free strip across the blacktop. "The way you're doing it, you're going to hurt yourself." When he reaches the edge, he bends his knees and lifts the snow onto the top of the snow pile.

I stop and lean against my shovel. "Who are you? The snow shovel police?"

"I'm just trying to save your back. But you go ahead and continue however you'd like." He pushes another heap of snow across the blacktop.

"You know what? You stay on your side of the street, and I'll stay on mine." I plunge the tip of the shovel into the snow and push it across the driveway. When I reach the end, I lift with my knees and toss it into the yard. Dammit. This *is* easier. Chalk this up as a new learning experience.

"If you say so, but you should watch out."

I stop in my tracks. "Ooh. Watch out from what? You?"

"No. I'm serious. You should step back."

I slam the edge of the shovel into the snow and lean on the handle. "I'm not scared of you. In fact, why don't you come over here and tell me that to my face?"

"Don't say I didn't warn you." He glances at me and shakes his head as he continues to clear the snow at the end of his driveway.

"I want to finish this so I can get away from you." The scraping of metal on pavement catches my attention. A wave of snow races toward me as a large snowplow rounds the corner and barrels down the street. I swivel around, but my feet slip and slide on the slush. The shovel flies from my grip and ends up on the other side of the driveway as I regain my balance. As the snowplow drives past, a mixture of dirt and wet, slushy snow showers down on me at the end of the driveway.

He throws a pile of snow into his yard before directing his attention toward me. "You got a little… something… right there." He brushes his shoulder. "Do you want help with that?"

I glare at him through my snow-covered lashes. "No," I deadpan.

He shrugs then strolls up his snow free driveway. I stand there as he props the shovel against his house and makes his way inside. I huff. Screw it. I'll call someone in the morning.

SCROOGE McASSFACE

CHAPTER FIVE
* ⭐ *

Tatum

"I just got to Roasters. I'm going to grab a coffee and a scone. Do you want anything?" I ask Olivia as I sandwich my phone between my ear and shoulder as I step out of my car.

The past two days have been blissfully scrooge free, even though I noticed his truck coming and going throughout the day. Not that I was watching. No. I'm being a good neighbor and making sure the neighborhood's safe. Someone has to keep a watch out for the new eye-candy… er new neighbor. But the image of him in only a towel is burned into my memory. Who answers the door in only a towel when it's twenty degrees out? Unless he was trying to deter me from knocking on his door again as if I was an unwanted visitor convincing him to follow their religion or sell him a school fundraiser coupon book. If that's the case, he should know his bare chest, in all its man muscle glory, isn't going to do the trick.

I pull open the glass door. The quaint coffee shop buzzes with the low hum of conversations and the soothing hiss of steaming milk. The rich aroma of freshly ground coffee beans intertwines with the warm scent of pastries, causing my stomach to rumble.

"A blueberry scone sounds amazing right now," Olivia says. "Also, we'll have to make plans so I can show you the space for the Christmas charity gala. What are you doing this weekend?"

I stand in line behind a tall, broad shoulder guy in a green flannel coat. "I'll be heading up to the Fir Meadows Tree Farm on Saturday to pick out my tree. But I'm free after that."

"That's perfect. Alright, I'll see you in a bit."

Ending the call, I drop my phone into my purse. The line moves and I step forward. While I wait, I lean to the side to get a better view of the pastries in the display case to see what's for purchase, even though I already know I'm going to get a blueberry scone.

"Give me an Americano. And that blueberry scone." The guy in front of me points at the display case.

The voice. I roll my eyes and cross my arms over my chest, huffing out a sigh louder than normal. "You've got to be kidding me. Are you stalking me or something?"

He spins around and raises an eyebrow. "Seeing I was here first, wouldn't that make it the other way around?"

Dammit. He's not wrong. "Fine. Don't you have someone else you can direct all your scroogeness to this early in the morning? Maybe go throw snowballs at little children. Steal some unwrapped presents from the donation bin. All those seem right up your alley."

He ponders the thought for a moment. "Nah. Why would I do that when you're right here?"

"Ugh! Whatever. Let me just order my coffee and I'll be gone." He shuffles to the side as he waits for his order, and I step up to the register. "I'll have a coffee, black and two blueberry scones."

The barista's face softens. "I'm sorry, we just sold our last one. But we do have some cranberry scones left." Just my luck. Everyone knows blueberry is the superior scone and now my morning is ruined. My lips press into a thin line as my gaze slingshots to Scrooge McAssface.

With a smug smile on his face, he digs into the brown paper bag, pulling out a perfectly baked blueberry scone and opens wide for a giant bite. A few seconds pass as he chews. "This is so good. You should have gotten here sooner," he says around a mouthful of crumbs. "Want some?" He holds the freshly bitten scone toward me.

I narrow my eyes and snarl my lip. "No. I'll pass." I return my attention back to the barista, flashing her a friendly smile. "Just the coffee then."

"I have an Americano for… Connor," a male, maybe in his early twenties, yells. The scrooge raises his hand and strolls to the counter to collect his coffee. The barista's eyes widen in surprise. "Wait. Are you… Connor Ja—"

"No." His voice is stern as he rips the coffee from his hands and storms his way toward the exit, dodging and weaving his way between customers. He shoves the door open so hard I'm surprised it doesn't snap off the hinges. Then he stomps out, leaving the entire coffee shop, including me, perplexed about what just happened.

Well, that was… odd. At least now I have a name to the face. Connor. Though I much prefer Scrooge McAssface. I shake my head. I don't need him occupying any more of my thoughts. If he wants to be moody, he can go do that by himself. I grab my coffee and head out to the parking lot.

I pull into the alley of Olivia and Ledger's house. With my coffee in hand, that would be better if I had a blueberry scone to go with it, I make my way up the freshly shoveled walkway. Before I can get to the door, Olivia's throwing it open. Her blonde hair is plopped in a messy bun on the top of her head. "Did you get a call from Mom?"

My eyebrows pinch together. "No. I don't think so. Why?" Granted, my phone could have rung but I was so busy dealing with a grumpy neighbor, I wouldn't have even noticed.

"She just called me to ask if I got the invite to attend her Christmas charity gala. Under The Mistletoe or whatever." She waves her hand in the air. "I can't believe she has the audacity to think I would want to go after what happened."

Several months ago, Olivia and our mom had a falling out when our parents didn't want her dating Ledger. They constantly tried to set her up with different guys, mostly to further their own agenda. Our father even threatened their relationship by bribing Ledger to stay away. It ended happily for Olivia and Ledger, but the tension with our parents never settled.

With Olivia's no fucks given attitude toward Mom's opinion on who she's dating, all their attention will be on me and my now non-existent boyfriend. I imagine their matchmaking will soon turn to me once they find out Adam dumped me. That'll be a fun conversation while attempting to dodge every single man my mother heaves in my direction. I'll admit it was nice to have all eyes off me while Olivia was single, but now the tables have turned. FML.

I throw myself down on a stool at her kitchen island and with my elbow on the counter, I prop my chin up with my hand. "Do we have to go? Will she really know if we're not there?" It's a stupid question to ask because, of course, she will know if we aren't there. In fact, I'm sure she would love it if we didn't go just so she can gain sympathy from all the other socialites about how her daughters don't support her. She's manipulative like that.

"We have to go. Not because we want to, but to show her we don't give a fuck. Plus, I can't wait to find a dress that shows off my new tattoo." She climbs up onto the stool next to me and pulls down the collar of her boat neck sweater. Inked on her shoulder is a dandelion with the seeds floating away, but a few of the seeds transform into birds that wrap around her bicep.

"That's gorgeous." I trace the outline of a bird with my finger.

"Ledger helped me design it." Her lips tip up into a soft smile when she mentions his name.

To spite our mother's hatred of tattoos, Olivia goes out of her way to display all of her ink at every opportunity.

I drop my hand to my lap. "I know you're right. We have to go, especially since she sent the invite. I wish we could tell her it got lost in the mail."

"Saaame." She releases the collar and lifts one shoulder to adjust her sweater. "But we have a business now. We need to approach this as a business opportunity and do some networking. All the while throwing up our figurative middle fingers at her." We both laugh. "But this also means we have to send her an invitation to our event, otherwise you know she'll try to make us look bad."

I rub my temples. "At this point, the only winners here are the two charities."

"Speaking of charities. I talked to Parisa and she said

The Lilith House is partnering with the local food bank to double their efforts for holiday meals and toys for kids. If we make them our charity, the monies will go twice as far."

Finally, a more neutral topic. "Yes! That's a fantastic idea. I already told her the donations we get for my neighborhood decorating contest will also go to The Lilith House."

"This is going to be the best holiday for all the kids." She glances around. "Where's my scone?"

"Oh. About that." I fill her in about bringing cookies to the new neighbor, how he slammed the door in my face, and criticized my shoveling. "So, while I was in line at Roasters that jerk took the last scone."

"I would have tackled him."

"I mean, he did offer me the scone after he took a bite out of it." I laugh thinking about how ridiculous the situation was. "But it was weird, after he got his coffee his whole demeanor changed and he bolted."

Olivia shakes her head. "Guys are weird."

I spend the rest of the morning and early afternoon at Olivia's house. We decide on a winter wonderland theme for our charity gala and we brainstorm décor and catering ideas.

When I arrive home, I stop and collect the mail from the mailbox before heading inside. I toss the stack of mail on the counter and stroll down the hallway to my bedroom. Pulling my sweater over my head, I lay it over the back of a chair and exchange it for a hoodie. I swap out my skinny jeans for yoga pants. Before I exit the room, I grab my tablet from my nightstand and freeze. Placing the tablet aside, I grip the black picture frame. As I trace my finger over the glass, memories flood back of Adam and me in the picture.

It was one of our first dates where he took me to The

Boat House and then for a nighttime stroll along the
Lakewalk. It was a time when both of us were happy and
in love. Now… one of us has moved on. I stride into the en
suite bathroom and hold the picture over the trash can but
pause. Things should be different. My life should be
different. But it's not. Blowing out a breath, I amble back
to the bedroom and open the nightstand drawer and place
the picture frame glass side down. I pick up my tablet and
go back out to the kitchen.

I flip through the stack of mail. Junk. Garbage. *Better
Homes and Gardens Christmas Ideas* magazine. Yes, please. I
push that one to the side. Garbage. Junk. Connor Tyler? A
plain white envelope addressed to Connor Tyler from
California. When I read the address, I realize it actually
belongs to the new neighbor. The mail carrier must have
delivered it to my box by accident. As much as I want to
rip it up and toss it in his face like confetti, I'd rather not
end up in federal prison. Orange is not my color. First, he
steals my scone, now I have to deliver his mail. I'm getting
shafted. And not the good kind of shaft either.
Begrudgingly, I walk across the street and shove it in his
mailbox. Even though I know his full name now, Scrooge is
still more fitting.

THE CHRISTMAS TREE THIEF

CHAPTER SIX

★ ⭐ ★

Tatum

I open the car door and step out, my boot sinks into the freshly fallen snow. Tilting my face toward the warm afternoon sun, I inhale a deep breath. The crisp, cold air carries the earthy scent of pine and cedar, mingling with the invigorating aroma of fresh baked cookies and hot chocolate. Glancing around, the laughter of children running around all bundled up in their snow gear fills the air along with the muffled chatter of adults. A couple to my right discusses which type of tree they should get. These are my people. Everyone is here to find the perfect tree to bring home and decorate and admire for the next twenty-five days. We really need to normalize Christmas decorations all year round.

Growing up, going to the tree farm and picking out the

perfect tree was always a family tradition. Sadly, sometimes traditions die. But I am determined to keep this, at least for me. A light breeze hits my cheeks and I tug my hat down a little more. My nose follows the lingering smell of hot cocoa and freshly baked chocolate chip cookies. Inside the open barn, I discover two young girls, maybe twelve or thirteen, working the counter of a small stand.

"What would you like ma'am?" one of the girls greets me.

"I'll take a hot cocoa, extra marshmallows, and one of those amazing smelling cookies, please."

I pass my money over to the young girl and grab my goodies. The warm sun hits my face as I step back outside. The loud rumble of a tractor echoes over the field as it rounds the corner from behind the barn. Children race across the open lot toward the entrance to wait for the wagon to pull us around the farm. I leisurely stroll behind the crowd to get in line. Just as I bring the cookie up to my mouth someone bumps into me and I lose my grip and watch it tumble to the white, fluffy snow. Dang it! My smile turns bitter as I mourn the loss of the cookie. I am once again jolted from the back when another person bumps into me and I lose grip of my cocoa, which spills all over my new boots, and discolors the once white snow brown. What is wrong with people? Can't they watch where they are going? My gaze shoots up in hopes of spotting the culprit. Green flannel coat. And he's just walking away without a care in the world. He's not getting away that easily.

"Hey! Hey you!" Realizing that could mean anyone. I try again. "You in the green flannel! Stop!" This time everyone stops and stares at me. Luckily so does the inconsiderate cocoa spiller. FML. I can't get away from him. I stomp toward him, snow kicking up beneath my boots. Any semblance of happiness has left my body and is now replaced with annoyance. I shove my pointer finger at his chest. "You made me spill my cocoa!"

His eyebrows pinch together. "Me? What are you talking about?"

Heat flushes my entire body as I glare at him. "Oh, don't play stupid! You bumped into me, made me spill my cocoa, and didn't even say sorry."

"You want me to say sorry?"

"Yes, that's the polite thing to do. You can't just go around bumping into people."

"And you assume I'm polite?"

Why is this man so infuriating?

"Well, when you bump into someone…" I hold up my hand, palm out, "you know what? Forget it. The wagon is filling up and I don't want to miss the first round." I would have a better chance at a civilized conversation if I were talking to a snowman.

I swivel on my heel and make my way to where a crowd is forming in front of a ramp to get on the wagon. When I'm next in line to get on, an older gentleman holds out his hand to help me over the small gap. With a sigh, I nestle down on the firm, cold straw bales, regretting not grabbing the blanket from my car as a chill runs up my spine. I survey the farm, taking in the rows of evergreens and Douglas firs as I search for the perfect tree. I'll know it when I see it. Finding the perfect Douglas fir requires careful consideration of its height, fullness, and overall shape, ensuring it will be a stunning centerpiece in my living room. It's almost like a superpower. Instead of Spidey sense it's my Dougyfirsense. Upon turning my head forward, I'm met with an unwelcome face beaming a big smile at me.

Once again, my happiness plummets. This time it's to the floorboards of the wagon. "Are you following me?"

"Um no? Did you accuse all these other people of following you too?" Connor waves his hand in front of him.

"Why do you always answer my question with a question?"

"Why do you always ask so many questions?"

"Ugh! I just can't with you."

"So, you've said." He then brings a steaming cup of hot cocoa up to his lips and takes a sip. "This cocoa is so good. You should have gotten a cup."

Under my knit cap, the tips of my ears flame red hot. I cross my arms over my chest and give him a death glare.

With the cup still up to his lips, the crinkle in the corner of his eyes doesn't go unnoticed.

When the wagon is full, it jolts to a start. I secretly pray that it will cause him to lose his hot chocolate, but no luck. Slowly, we slide down the snow covered path that winds around the tree farm. Again, I start glancing around to see if I can spot my perfect tree. The sooner I find it, the sooner I can get away from the jerk across from me. Peering over my left shoulder, I scan all the trees, but nothing catches my eye. When I rotate to glance over my other shoulder, I'm met with a familiar green flannel.

"Why are you sitting there?"

"I like this view better." He crosses his ankle over his knee. His foot coming dangerously close to invading my space.

"Well, at least you didn't answer with a question."

"Would you rather I did?"

"Ha. Ha. You're distracting me from my Christmas tree shopping."

"This looks pretty intense."

"I take my trees very seriously."

"I can see that."

I continue scanning row after row, and then I finally see it, calling to me like a beacon. A gust of wind whispers past me and I swear I hear "Tatum, take me home. I'm yours." That's my tree, with its lush and vibrant green needles. It's going to be so beautiful in front of my bay window. A wide smile covers my lips. Movement from Connor pulls me from my treegasm. His gaze darts to me and then to my tree and then back to me.

Oh, no you don't. That is my tree. I narrow my gaze at him.

He smirks like he knows that's my tree and his only mission is to steal it from me.

Well that's not happening. We continue this back and forth wordless conversation like two gunslingers in the wild west facing off in a duel at sunset.

The wagon stutters as it slows and the operator hollers, "First stop, folks!"

Before the wagon comes to a complete stop, he leaps over the side like he's a professional at parkour. Perhaps he practices on the weekends. I shake my head. Why do I care? He's trying to steal my tree. I shove past a middle-aged couple on the left and then shift to the right to shimmy between a woman with two kids. Politely, of course. With an "excuse me" and a "pardon me."

Once I reach the back, I jump off, skipping a step to save me a few seconds. I round the rear of the wagon and sprint after him. He's ahead of me by about eight feet, but I can catch up. I lift my knees up higher, but with each step down, I sink a little deeper—almost up to my knees. I'm sure if I was an Olympic hurdler, I'd have no issue. But currently the struggle is real. Very real. I find his enormous footprints already in the snow and use those instead of making my own path to gain more ground. Work smarter, not harder. But he's still too fast. His legs are longer than mine.

Refusing to give up, I dig deep and scoop up some of the more wet snow with my fur-lined mitten and pack it tightly into a ball. I wind up and throw. It soars through the air until a cloud of snow bursts as it hits the back of his head.

Oh shit. My eyes widen, and my mittens fly up to cover my mouth.

His steps falter, and he comes to a stop. Slowly, he turns to face me, his eyes meeting mine. "Did you just hit me with a snowball?"

I only have two seconds to assess his anger. Is he Hulk furious, or stub your toe annoyed? But then I remember everything he's done to me. Slammed the door in my face twice. Returned my cookies. Distracted me from the snowplow. And took the last scone. He will not get my tree. I prop my hands on my hips. "You're trying to steal my tree!"

"It's not your tree. You don't get to call dibs on a tree."

"Yes, I can, and I saw it first. Dibs!" I take a step. "Dibs!" Another step. "Dibs!" Now we are standing toe to toe. His tall frame towers over me, but I don't back down. I crane my neck up to meet his gaze. "You're just being a scrooge and trying to steal my tree."

"So, you assault me with a snowball?"

"I didn't assault you. Stop being so dramatic."

"Now I'm being dramatic?"

"There you go with the questions again." I step around him. "I don't have time for this. Or you. Now if you'll excuse me, I have a tree to claim."

"I don't think so." He steps in front of me.

"Yes, I do." I brush him to the side.

He stumbles, almost falling into the snow. "You just pushed me."

"I barely grazed you. Get over it."

"No, that was a push. I had no idea you were so violent."

"I'll show you a push." This time, I shove him with both hands. His arms spin like a windmill and a cloud of snow billows in the air as he makes impact. I puff out my chest in triumph. As I saunter past him, my foot catches on something, causing me to lose my balance and fall face-first into the fresh powder. The cold crystals melt on my tongue and face. I spit out a mouthful of snow and drag my mitten down my face. I swivel my head around and I'm met with his cocky grin.

"You tripped me! What's wrong with you?" I scoop up a pile of snow in my cupped mittens and throw it at him.

"Wrong with me? You pushed me!" He gathers a handful of snow and tosses it at me.

Back and forth the snow continues to fly between us along with a few expletives until a voice pulls us from our scuffle.

"Mommy! Daddy! That one is perfect!" A little girl's voice echoes off the trees.

"It sure is, sweetie. Let's go get the guy to tell him we want this one," the mom says.

Still sitting in the snow, I exhale an exasperated sigh. At least she has good taste in trees.

"Are you going to push them in the snow, too?" Connor asks from a few feet away.

I glare at him, but all he does is laugh. Rising to his feet, he brushes the snow off his long legs and broad shoulders. Like a gentleman, he holds his hand out to help me up but he's more transparent than a crystal vase. His intentions are anything but gentlemanly. I'm sure he'll let go once I'm half way up causing me to fall on my ass in the snow. Hard pass. I snarl my lip and bat his hand away like it's diseased.

"Suit yourself." He spins around, leaving me in the snow, hiking his way back to the wagon.

Mumbling incoherently, I wobble in the unstable snow as I stand. Maybe I should have tampered down my pride and taken his assistance. But then he would have the upper hand and that can't happen. Following in Connor's oversized footprints, I trudge back to the waiting crowd.

The second stop was a complete bust. Luckily, Connor kept his distance. If he didn't, I might have thrown him off the wagon. Here I am trying to be the friendly neighbor by bringing him cookies, and how does he repay me? Tries to steal my tree. The more I think about it, the higher my blood pressure spikes. By the third stop, I'm feeling a little desperate. Or a lot desperate. My only goal for today is to find a tree. I can't leave here without one.

From the corner of my eye I spot one with potential. One side is nice and fluffy but a little balding in the back. It's the mullet of Christmas trees. There aren't even enough extra branches to attempt a comb over. Maybe I can hang some extra ribbon to cover it up. Even the ugly trees need love, too. I peek out of the corner of my eye to make sure he isn't watching me so he can treenap me, again. Or maybe I do want him to steal this one. When the wagon comes to a halt, I jump out and make a mad dash to my tree so no one else can claim it.

Arriving back to the wagon, I find my seat feeling good. A smile graces my lips. Christmas tree checked off the list. My lips level to a thin line as soon as Connor sits next to me, almost too close.

"Find a tree?"

"Yep. You?"

"Yep."

"Good."

"Good," he parrots.

He stretches out his legs in front of him and rests his arms along the railing behind us. I cross my legs, one knee over the other, and curl away from him. As more people gather on the wagon space starts to become more limited. Soon he has to sit up straight and scoot closer. His thigh brushes up against mine. His heat radiating through me. I won't admit this to him, but it feels kind of nice on this chilly afternoon.

Pretty soon the wagon is moving again, the ride slightly bumpier than before. With each bump he gets a little closer, rubs a little harder. The friction sends a lightning bolt of heat to between my legs. Traitorous body. His gaze is trained forward on the path in front of us and I fight not to stare at him. For a brief moment I'm distracted with two kids playing Slap Jack as their laughter fills the wagon. All of a sudden, my left side goes cold. When I peer over my shoulder Connor is missing. I glance up to see where he went, and he's moved to an open seat across from me. He's facing the front of the wagon but staring at me from the corner of his eye. His beard making it hard to read him. I tilt my head and give him a quizzical look. Why did he move? Tired of rubbing up on me?

A second later, a giant pile of snow comes crashing down on several unsuspecting riders, including myself. My shoulders scrunch to my ears as snow tumbles inside my jacket and down my back. My eyes lock shut, and a shiver runs through my body. Shrills, shrieks, and laughter fill the wagon. Glancing behind me, a pine tree branch bounces as leftover snow flutters down. No longer cold, but instead burning with rage my gaze darts to Connor as laughter racks his body.

An icy bead of freshly melted snow trickles down my back and I glare at him. "You knew that was going to happen."

He just laughs harder.

I mouth "I hate you."

"Did I ruffle your tinsel... Tinsel?" A slow smirk spreads across his lips.

Ugh! He's been permanently upgraded from Scrooge to Scrooge McAssface.

CHRISTMAS MULLET

CHAPTER SEVEN

★ ✦ ★

Tatum

Ever since the tree incident, I've been doing everything possible to keep Connor off my mind. But that's easier said than done when every time I look out the window he's there. Not in a Michael Myers kind of way, but while I was setting up my tree, he just so happened to be shoveling his driveway. Then he proceeded to chop wood on the side of the house. Of course, he was in a spot where I had a crystal clear view of him. It was like he knew I was watching… er… could see him. But damn, when did a guy heaving an axe over his shoulder become so hot? I lift the collar of my hoodie and sink my teeth into the fabric, needing to distract myself from running across the street and sinking my teeth into something else.

A car horn beeps, pulling me from my thoughts.

Olivia's waving at me through the window of her SUV sitting in my driveway. When she steps out, she peers over her shoulder at my neighbor's house. She swivels back to face me, picks her jaw off the driveway, and fans herself.

I nod, then lift my wine glass to my lips and swallow a gulp.

Olivia pushes through my door. "What the hell? Is that your neighbor? Why didn't you tell me your neighbor is a hot lumberjack mountain man?" She shrugs off her coat and hangs it up on the hook behind her. "This is the kind of information you can't keep to yourself."

I shrug and pass her a glass of wine. Right now, I'm torn between hating him and hating myself because with so little effort, he can make me wetter than an otter's pocket. "It would have been better if he never moved in."

"Why? Then you would miss out on this view." Olivia sips her glass of wine as she stares out my bay window.

"For the past two days, he's been going out there to chop wood. Of course, he gets too hot and needs to strip out of his coat. Somehow, he can make taking off a coat sexy. And don't get me started on what he has on underneath. His long sleeve shirt forms to his body like a second skin. Muscles bulging and flexing with each swing of the axe." I leave out the part where he's entered my dreams for the past two nights. Like the dream where he has to chop down a tree in order to save me, Tarzan style. Obviously, the only way he can do that is shirtless. In my dreams there's no smart mouth, glaring looks, slamming doors in my face, or stealing Christmas trees. In fact, he doesn't even speak a word. If only he were like that in real life.

"Two days! And you're just telling me this now!? I see how it is, saving all the good stuff for yourself." She softly bites down on the rim of her glass.

"What are you talking about? You have a boyfriend."

"Ledger knows whose bed I'll be crawling into tonight. Plus, this is recon. For you." She nudges me with her elbow, pulling out her phone and snapping a picture.

"What are you doing?"

"Taking a picture."

"You can't just take photos of people."

"I'm not going to post it on the internet. Parisa wanted to see what he looks like." She shrugs.

"Yeah okay. Whatever you say." Simultaneously, we spin around, swallowing a sip of our wine as we stare out the window.

"Damn. He's going inside. Guess that fun is over." She does a half turn away from me and freezes. She tilts her head to the side. "What's wrong with your tree?"

"Nothing." I grit my teeth.

"No, something is definitely wrong." Olivia bends down and twists the base, spinning the base of the tree. "Oh. My. God."

I guzzle the last of my wine.

She bursts into laughing tears. "Your tree has a mullet! It's all party in the back." She waves her hand over the tree. "And it's balding in the front," she screeches between fits of giggles. She doubles over, almost falling to the floor as she tries to catch her breath.

I roll my eyes. "It's not that bad." Truth be told, it's worse than bad. Not even the extra pine garland I wrapped around the branches helped. It now resembles a bad comb over.

"Oh yes, it is!" she spits out between laughs.

"Fine." A ghost of a smile plays on my lips. "It's terrible. My tree belongs in the eighties. I should just decorate it in a florescent track suit."

"You can get a leg warmer for the trunk."

"And a sweat band instead of a star."

"Instead of Christmas music you need a montage of Madonna, Cyndi Lauper, and The Bangles." Olivia dances around my living room while singing "Girls Just Want to Have Fun." When she's done, she drops onto the couch. "How did this happen?"

Plopping down next to her, my wine sloshes in the glass but doesn't spill, and I exhale a sigh. "When I was at the tree farm, Connor got me so flustered I just grabbed the first one I saw so I could get out of there. I knew it wasn't perfect, but I wasn't expecting it to be this bad." I wave my hand over the tree.

She bolts upright. "Wait? Connor? Your ridiculously hot neighbor? You went tree shopping with him?"

"No! I went by myself, and he just so happened to show up, too. Like a stalker."

"Isn't that like the third time he's just showed up where you are?"

"Fifth. But who's counting." Besides the shoveling incident, the tree incident, and getting coffee at Roasters, I've also run into him at the gas station and while getting my mail. I scrunch my nose and tap my chin as I get a lightbulb moment. "I should get him back."

"Get who back for what?"

"Connor. For stealing my tree."

"And what are you going to do? TP his house?" She laughs. "Oh! Are we going to build a snow dick in his yard?" A wicked grin spreads across her lips.

"No, but since he's so averse to having any holiday spirit, I could give him some of mine. And I have pink spray paint." I swipe the can off the counter. The little ball rattles inside as I give it a shake.

A mischievous glint sparkles in her eyes. "Whatever it is, I'm in."

"Are the ski masks necessary?" Olivia trails behind me as I climb over a snowbank. Her white parka and fur lined boots are an obvious telltale sign we're not very good at being stealthy. If anyone drove past, we'd look like a couple of drunk girls stumbling through the yard. Which is kinda true. Yes, we're two bottles of wine in, but we know exactly what we're doing. Maybe.

I freeze and hold up my mitten covered hand over my mouth to shush her, but the mitten makes it less effective. "Yes. What if he comes out and sees us?"

"And how are we going to escape in knee deep snow?" She pulls the bottom of her ski mask up, exposing her face. "I can't breathe in this thing."

"I don't know. I haven't thought that far ahead. My only plan was to not get caught." A light toward the side of the house flickers to life and my heart jumps to my throat. I twist around and motion for Olivia to pull her mask down. Even in the dark, I can see her roll her eyes. She tugs the ski mask down but loses her balance and topples to the side. She's basically face down, ass up. My hands fly up to muffle my laugh. Once I regain my composure, I whirl around to zero in on the closed, curtained window, watching for any silhouettes moving. My eyes go dry from not blinking. After the light shuts off and the room goes dark, I exhale a sigh of relief.

I hike up the wreath and hold it close under my arm. We trudge a few more feet in the deep snow, trying to be as quiet as possible. I toss the wreath to the side. A plume of freshly fallen snow floats up into the air and sparkles in the moonlight as it flutters down. "Alright. This is the perfect spot."

Over the next hour or what feels like an hour, but was more like twenty minutes, we haphazardly collect all the snow in the surrounding area. The recent snowfall makes it a little harder, but the snow underneath is perfect for constructing our masterpiece. Once we're finished, we step back and admire our handy work.

"Why do people do this? I now have snow in my bra." Olivia pulls at the front of her coat. "You know this would have been more fun if we built a giant dick instead of a snowman."

"It's a family neighborhood." I hold up a can of hot pink spray paint. "Now to add the finishing touch." Rounding the three balls of snow, I put my graffiti skills to the test. This should get my point across. I rise to my feet and puff out my chest.

Olivia moves to stand next to me, a hand on her hip. "Well, that will show him exactly how you feel. What are you doing with this?" She holds the wreath toward me.

"Oh yes! Can't forget that." I trudge out of the snow, following our original path, and tip toe my way up the sidewalk to the front door. I pull out a sticky clip from my pocket. With my teeth, I remove the paper backing, stick the hook to the door, and hang the wreath. I take a step back and make sure it's straight. A wide grin spreads over my face and I whisper, "Merry Christmas Scrooge McAssface."

HOT PINK DICK

CHAPTER EIGHT
★ ⭐ ★

Connor

I stir awake and roll onto my back. I stretch my legs and wince. Everything hurts, including my eyelids as I struggle to open them. All day and well into the evening, I was busy working. First, I wanted to rip up the old, musty, dated carpet in the living room. Since I've never ripped up carpet, I wanted to make sure I knew what I was doing, so I watched a couple of how-to videos. An hour later, I was YouTube certified.

It was a pleasant surprise to find real maple flooring underneath, and it was in good condition. Maybe a quick sand and a new coat of lacquer and it'll be as good as new. I pray it's the same under the laminate flooring in the kitchen, then it will create a nice flow between the two spaces.

I groggily roll out of bed, still half asleep. To my left there's a chair with a t-shirt draped over the back. I pick it up, do a sniff test and determine it to be okay, then yank it over my head. I rake my hand through my hair and drag myself to the kitchen, weaving in and out of stacks of boxes.

I drop a scoop of coffee into the basket, fill the reservoir with water, and press the button. Five agonizing minutes pass before there's enough coffee to fill my mug. My phone buzzes on the counter next to me. Glancing down, *Satan's Ballsack* flashes on the screen. I groan. Spence is like the ex-girlfriend who just doesn't understand you don't want to talk. If he's not calling, he's sending text messages. At least those are easier to ignore than the incessant calls.

Reluctantly, I press the talk button. "Hey Spen—"

"Finally, you answer. Everyone's asking about you. This 'I'm away' will only fend them off for so long."

Finally? I talked to him yesterday. I scrub my hands down my face. "Tell everyone I'm taking some personal time. Don't I get some personal time?"

"Whenever someone says they are taking some personal time it's usually another way of saying they're in rehab. Wait. Are you really in rehab?"

"No."

"It's okay if you are. You should get the help you need. We'll just have to find a way to spin it—"

"I'm not in rehab."

"So, what do we tell them? That you're spending time with your grandma."

"No. Then people will come looking and I don't need that."

"After the success of your last tour, everyone in Hollywood wants you to make an appearance at their birthday party, their launch party, movie premier, you name it. This is the perfect opportunity for more exposure. Keep the momentum going."

"That's not going to happen."

"If you don't show up somewhere, people will come looking."

I rub my temples with one hand. "Fine. I'll send you some old vacation pictures and you can leak them to the press. Tell everyone I'm vacationing in Cabo or some shit."

"You need to figure out your shit sooner rather than later. This might buy you a little extra time, but people will get restless."

"Yeah, yeah. I'll worry about that when it happens."

"Are you at least working on some new music? Get a jump start before you get in the studio."

"Yeah," I lie. Music is the last thing on my mind. I'm not feeling it. And if you're not feeling it, you create shit. But clearly, that's what he wants to hear. "Speaking of which. I better get back to working on those songs."

"Wait. That sounds like sarcasm. Connor you better—"

I press end. That's not how I wanted to start my day. When you hit rock bottom, the only way to go is up. Let's hope that's where this day goes.

Scratching my beard, I stroll into the living room. The bright sun warms my body as I stand in front of the large picture window. As I stretch an arm, I take a small sip of my hot coffee. When I open my eyes, coffee spews out of my mouth, spraying across the living room window. Nope. This is rock bottom. What the fuck?

In my front yard is a lopsided snowman, with stick arms, a scarf, and a giant pink dick painted on its back. I stomp to the entryway and shove my feet into my boots. I'm opening the door before I can throw my coat over my shoulders. The brisk morning air hits my face, but it barely fazes me since a fire is coursing through my veins as I run down the short sidewalk. My gaze is locked on the snowman but a noise from across the street draws my attention and Tatum steps out of her front door, a big smirk on her face.

The snowman is now forgotten. The sound of my boots slapping against the blacktop echoes through the silent neighborhood as I stomp down the driveway. "What the hell is this!?" A cloud from my warm breath forms in front of me.

She saunters down hers, like she doesn't have a care in the world. "That's for stealing my Christmas tree." She comes to a halt directly in front of me in the middle of the road.

"I didn't steal your Christmas tree. Go find the ten-year-old girl who staked claim to it and build a snowman with a giant dick painted on the back in her yard!"

She lifts her chin in an attempt to reach my height, but she's not even close. "If you didn't distract me, it would have been mine!"

A car slows and honks as they swerve around us. I grab her wrist and tug her to the end of my driveway. "You're going to take this down!"

She yanks her hand from my grasp and rests it on her waist as she pops her hip. "What? It's just a snowman."

"With a giant dick painted on the back!"

Two women, maybe in their thirties, walk by, smiling and snickering to each other.

"What are you looking at? Did you come by to see my dick?" I yell to the passersby.

Tatum huffs. "Oh my god. No one wants to see your penis."

"Except you. You're drawing them in my yard. I only have to assume."

She blushes but doesn't say anything. Shit. Has she thought about my dick?

"Y-y-you're so full of it." She spins, her blonde hair floating around her as she storms away. Halfway across the street she stops and stomps back. "You know what, you're nothing but a scrooge! A holiday fun sucking scrooge! God forbid other people enjoy the holiday season."

I just stand there and let her get all her hurt and anger out because I know I deserve it. It was a dick move to steal her tree or let someone else steal it. It's not my intention to be an asshole to her, but right now I'd rather feel her hatred than a fake nice only to get what they want.

Out of the corner of my eye a car careening around the corner, barreling straight toward us catches my attention. Don't they realize the roads are icy? Tatum continues to yell at me, but I'm not even paying attention anymore. I'm focused on the car and if they're going to slow down. Then I stop thinking and react. I grip her wrists and yank her toward me and out of the street. Everything else happens in slow motion. She yelps as the toe of her boot trips over a chuck of ice and she face plants into my chest. The force of her body knocks me off balance, causing my feet to slip from underneath me. She grips my arms so I'm unable to regain my balance and we tumble backward. I smack down on a snowbank, and she falls on top of me. A sharp pain shoots up my spine and I wince.

"Slow down, asshole!" I yell to the road as I flinch. I'm sure they didn't even hear me.

Her breathing is heavy as she lies on top of me. Several seconds pass before her eyes flutter open. "You saved my life." Her voice is low and soft.

"I don't know about that, but I did spare you a few broken bones. Maybe a concussion." A breeze passes over us, and I get a whiff of her familiar vanilla scent but now it's mixed with something floral, like lavender. Suddenly the pink dick and the dick in the car are both forgotten. Even in pain, I don't hate the weight of her on me. Shit. This isn't supposed to happen. With a mind of their own, my fingers dig into her hips wanting to relish in this moment for a second longer.

She lifts the top half of her body. "That guy almost hit me."

"Yep." I pinch my eyes closed, no longer in pain from hitting the snowbank but something else.

"Oh my God. Are you alright?" Her gaze roams my body as her hand brushes over my chest, searching for an injury.

I wince again. "Your knee is kinda pinching my testicles."

"Oh!" She jumps off me as if she touched a hot stove.

I attempt to sit up but grimace and fall back to the snowbank. "I'm just going to lie here for a moment." Partially because of the pain but I also need to collect my thoughts with how much I enjoyed her body on mine.

"What can I do? Ice? Do you need ice?" She frantically collects snow into the palms of her mittens.

"Well… There is something you can do." The corner of my lips pull into a slight smile.

"Anything. What is it?" Her distraught gaze meets mine.

I sit halfway up so I can see her face. "You could always kiss it and make it better."

Her face falls. "You're such a dick." She shoves at my chest.

My back hits the snowbank as a half laugh, half groan escapes me. "You asked."

"I thought you were going to be serious."

"And who says I wasn't?"

She throws the snowball at me and it crashes into my shoulders, bursting into a plume of snow dust. With a hand on her hip, she rolls her eyes before looking both ways and crossing the street.

"Hey, where are you going?"

"Away from you!" she yells over her shoulder.

"You're just going to leave me here wounded in the snowbank?"

"Yep. And if I'm lucky, a snowplow will come by and bury you."

"That hurts." I laugh and, shit, it really does hurt.

She holds up her mitten covered hand like a stop sign. "If you can't tell, I'm giving you the middle finger."

FUCk XMAS FRANK

CHAPTER NINE
* ⭐ *

Tatum

Later that day, Olivia steps out of her SUV and onto my driveway, garment bag in hand. "I bring you dresses."

Before she can close the car door, I'm greeting her with a hug. "You're a lifesaver. I had no idea what I was going to wear to the gala and zero desire to go shopping."

"Gasp." She feigns shock with a hand to her chest. "You didn't want to go shopping?"

"Not for a dress anyway. I've been… preoccupied." Daydreaming about my neighbor, which should not be a thing, but it's totally a thing. Ever since the snowbank incident he's been on my mind. Did he get hurt? Besides his testicles? Then I'm thinking of his testicles, which leads to something else in the general vicinity, like the prominent bulge in his sweatpants. Maybe someone needs to smack *me* in the face with a snowball.

Olivia glances across the street into Connor's yard, as if she knows who's been occupying my most recent thoughts. "I see he kept the snowman. And added extra accessories."

"Yeah. I'm pretty sure he found the ugliest tree at the tree farm to put in his yard." A Charlie Brown looking tree is perched next to the snowman we built.

"Did he add a stick hand? Wait. Is it..."

A woman holding hands with a little boy stroll passed the house on the sidewalk. The boy yells out, "Look Mom, that snowman is waving!" The little boy enthusiastically waves at the snowman.

I lean in toward Olivia. "I'd hate to disappoint him, but it's not waving."

Olivia busts out laughing. "Oh my God! The snowman is flipping you off!"

All I can do is press my lips into a tight line, holding back my smile as I frantically nod.

She doubles over with laughter. "Did he crown the snowman with your wreath, too?" She wheezes.

"Sure did."

Olivia gasps for air next to me.

After our argument and brush with death, we went our separate ways. An hour later he came back outside and collected some sticks and used twine to MacGyver a makeshift stick hand. "At least he kept it festive. Perhaps he's found a tiny sliver of Christmas spirit. I've named him Frank. Fuck Xmas Frank. Because I'm sure if he had two hands, he would show all of us exactly how many fucks he gives about Christmas."

"Fuck Christmas Frank," she says.

"No. No. Fuck Xmas Frank. He can't be bothered to use the full word." I shrug.

A chuckle escapes her. "Wait, we gave him two stick arms. What happened to the other?"

"A neighbor's dog wandered through his yard, gnawed on his arm, and then ripped it off his body. But he didn't leave without marking his territory. Maybe that's why he's so bitter about Christmas."

"Oh! Poor Frank got peed on!" She laughs, almost hyperventilating. "Usually, that only happens after too many shots of tequila. I need to come over to your house more often. This is pure entertainment."

"I'm glad you're finding my neighbor from hell experience entertaining." I grab the garment bag from her arms and walk toward the house. "I, on the other hand, just want to go back to before he got here. When my life was calm and peaceful."

Olivia's hot on my trail. "And when you were sulking over Adam?"

I whirl around, hand on my hip. "I wasn't sulking."

She rolls her eyes. "Oh, please. There was so much sulking. I could practically hear you sulking from across town."

"You can't hear someone sulking," I say, mostly to myself.

"I know you put on a good front when everyone was around, but I know you. At the end of the day, you came home, alone, and polished off a glass or two of wine and beat yourself up over why he broke up with you."

Some nights it was three glasses, but who's counting? We were supposed to be each other's forever, at least that's what I thought. I did everything to be the perfect girlfriend, and what did I get in return? Tossed to the side for someone else. "There is nothing wrong with a little alone time. It helped me reflect." And agonize about what I did wrong and what I could have done to make it better. Dammit.

"There is when you're doing it for the wrong reasons." With her hands on my shoulders, she spins me around so I'm facing her. "Adam's an idiot and you deserve someone better than him. Someone who will give up everything to be with you and not mold you to fit his perfect life." She uses air quotes on the last two words. "And Fuck Xmas Frank agrees with me with his one finger salute."

Deep down, I know she's right. I've been beating myself up over this, but it's still hard. I force a smile and give her a curt nod. All my life I tried to be the perfect daughter, girlfriend, employee, and what has it gotten me? Dumped, fired, and alone for Christmas. Maybe I need to take notes from Frank and fuck it all.

Over the next hour, I try on the three dresses she brought over and pair possible shoes and accessories. Not once did Adam or Connor enter my thoughts. I focused on me. Perhaps spending time with someone besides myself was the exact distraction I needed. After the dress is picked out, along with the perfect accessories, Olivia leaves and once again I'm left with only my thoughts.

I curl up on the couch and toss a blanket over my lap. The TV comes to life as I scroll through a streaming app to find the perfect Hallmark movie to watch. Thirty minutes pass and I have no idea what's happening. Something about a farm. An arch nemesis. It's as if I've been staring at a blank screen the whole time. Picking up the remote, I turn off the TV and reach for my tablet instead. Maybe if my eyes are busy, I won't get lost in my own thoughts.

After I read the same paragraph three times, I know it's useless. Each time I stop, my mind wanders to Adam and if I could have done something different in our relationship. Maybe if I tried a little harder, we'd still be together.

I slam my tablet on the cushion next to me and huff. Instead of sitting here, stewing in my own thoughts, I do the only surefire thing that will keep me occupied. Jumping up from the couch, I stride into the kitchen. I pull out my nana's homemade cookbook and flip to her cookie recipes. I trail my fingers over the soft, worn paper and make a mental note of all the ingredients I have and which ones I'll need. Chocolate chips. I don't have chocolate chips.

My gaze flits to the clock on the wall. Nine o'clock. The store's only open for another hour. I can make it. I dash to my bedroom and stand in front of my vanity. With a tug on the hair band, my hair falls from the messy bun and cascades over my shoulders. I stare at myself in the mirror. Hours have passed since I removed my makeup and traded my jeans for comfortable yoga pants.

My mother always told me I couldn't leave the house unless I was looking my best, stating, "You never know who you'll need to impress." I know for a fact yoga pants and a t-shirt are not looking your best. Screw it. I'm not in the market to impress anyone. So far impressing people has gotten me nowhere.

I yank a hoodie from the hanger and tug it over my head, feeling the soft fabric against my skin. This will at least keep me warm. Hastily, I shove my feet into my boots and throw my coat over my shoulders, not bothering to zip it up. As soon as I open the door to the outside, cold air blasts through me, reminding me why I should just stay home. But I can't, I'm now on a mission. The door slams behind me.

NUT BUTTER

CHAPTER TEN

★ ✿ ★

Connor

Why does there have to be so many varieties of peanut butter? There's crunchy, creamy, organic, and natural. If I'm not eating natural peanuts, am I'm eating artificial peanuts? Lab made peanuts? Is that a thing? And don't get me started on whatever nut butter is. That sounds like something I shouldn't be putting in my mouth. I yank a container of creamy off the shelf and toss it into my cart. Now I better go contemplate my life decisions in front of the many varieties of jelly.

I picked up a lot of essentials as soon as I got to town, but I was in and out. I wasn't going to spend too much time shopping around since that would lead to the chance of more people seeing, and possibly recognizing, me. When I poured the last drop of milk into my cereal, I knew grocery shopping was necessary. Instead of shopping in the daylight, I ate my dry cereal for breakfast and carried on with my day. Now I have thirty minutes before the grocery store closes and I'm trying to throw as much shit in my cart as possible. So far, the foot traffic has been minimal, so I haven't had to duck and run yet.

As I'm about to leave, a familiar scent wafts past me. Vanilla with a hint of lavender. I remember it from when her body was flush against mine in the snowbank. Twisting my neck, I catch sight of blonde hair under a knit cap and navy coat. She walks past me as she talks on the phone. Thankfully, she's not on speaker while she shops. Those people are annoying as fuck. I have the urge to walk up next to them and start screaming obscenities. Maybe they'll get the hint that I don't need to hear their conversation, but probably not.

She rounds the corner at the other end of the aisle, and I turn my cart around and follow her. The jelly can wait. I eavesdrop on her conversation as she talks to someone about a party and Christmas decorations. Then it dawns on me, she briefly mentioned something about a neighborhood decorating contest. That was until I slammed the door on her. I feel bad about that. But she caught me in a bad mood. I have to admit the cookies she made were fucking delicious. They reminded me of the ones Grams would make, except for the oatmeal raisin. Those shouldn't even be considered a cookie. Disgusting pucks of crap is more like it.

As I trail behind her, like the stalker I guess I'm becoming, a piece of black fabric falls from under her coat and flutters to the floor. She continues her power walking around the corner to the next aisle. I hurry to see what it is. Bending down, I scoop it off the epoxy resin flooring. The silky fabric is smooth between my fingers. Son of a bitch.

These are her underwear. Quickly, I glance around to see if anyone else saw anything, and then I shove them into my coat pocket.

I race out of the side aisle and down the center aisle, shifting my gaze down each one to see if I can find her. The cart slides to a halt when I finally spot her. She's no longer on the phone, instead she's tapping her chin with her finger, staring at the shelves of candy. She tosses a box of candy canes into a basket looped around her arm.

I stroll down the aisle, careful to not draw attention to myself until I'm standing almost directly behind her. "Excuse me, miss?"

She jumps and spins around. "Oh!" As soon as her gaze meets mine, her tone changes and she props her hand on her hip. "Oh. It's you."

"It's funny how we keep running into each other." I flash her a sly grin. Now that I have a closer view, something is different about her. She's not all dressed up, hair perfectly styled, face covered in makeup. She's more relaxed and comfortable in a hoodie that must be three sizes too big for her. I could get used to seeing her like this.

"Or not so funny, since you're stalking me. What do you want? Are you here to tackle me to get the last bag of chocolate chips? Since I don't have snow, I'll have to use this jar of caramel sauce instead." She reaches into her basket and holds up a glass jar.

"Are you telling me you want to pour caramel sauce over my body and lick it off? Normally, I require a first date, maybe hold hands, but if you want to get right to it—"

"No, you scrooge. I'd throw it at your head—never mind. What do you want? I don't want to exchange pleasantries with you." She narrows her gaze at me.

"What happened to 'Oh, Connor. You saved my life. I

owe you so much'," I say in a high-pitched falsetto voice.

She pops her hip. "I didn't say that. And right now, I kinda wish the car would have hit me. It would have at least saved me from this conversation."

"Nah. I would have visited you in the hospital."

She shakes her head. "I was afraid of that. What do you want so I can get back to my shopping?"

A slow smile spreads across my lips. "I have something for you." I shove my hand into my pocket, grab the panties, and hold my balled fist toward her.

Her eyebrows knit together as she eyes me and then my fist. I nod for her to hold out her hand. Slowly she lifts her open palm under mine. I drop the fabric into her hand. Confusion covers her face until she opens the crumpled ball of fabric. Two seconds later, her cheeks flush a cherry red and fuck, the color looks good on her. Quickly, she clenches her fist and shoves her hand into her pocket.

"Where did you get those?" She leans in and whispers. "Did you break into my house and steal my underwear?"

I bark out a laugh. "Wow, you think very highly of me. But no. You dropped them a few aisles back. Must have been the static."

"Oh my god." She pulls open her jacket to see if anything else will fall off her. Then she glances over one shoulder and then the other, probably hoping to not find anything else stuck to her.

"I was just being a gentleman and returning this before some creep found them and took them home. Sniffed them. Maybe touched himself while—"

Her hand flies up and covers my mouth. "Don't finish that sentence." She drops her hand and her body trembles as her face scrunches in disgust. We share a moment of silence before she says, "Thank you. That was nice of you... I guess." A small smile flirts on her lips.

Her smiles are becoming the favorite part of my day. Moments like this, two people having a conversation, is exactly what I crave. Granted, it's a conversation about her panties, but it's still a conversation, and it's real. No hidden agenda. No favors being asked. Only two people talking in the candy aisle.

"No one said I was nice." A few seconds of silence pass between us. I don't want this conversation to end so I spit out the first thing that comes to mind. "I'm surprised to see you out looking like that."

Her expression goes from friendly to hurt. She glances down, then tugs her coat closed. "What do you mean? Are you saying I look like a heaping pile of trash?"

Shit. Open mouth, insert foot. "No. That's not what I meant. Usually, you're all dressed up and perfect. It's refreshing to know you can be… relaxed. It's a good look on you."

Her face softens a fraction. "Um… Thank you?"

Over the loudspeaker someone announces that the store will be closing in fifteen minutes and to bring all your items up to the check out.

I glance to Tatum. "Enjoy the rest of your evening." I push my cart past her, not wanting to make eye contact. When I reach the end of the aisle, I glance back and she's still standing in the same spot I left her, like a statue. Slowly she lifts her head and her lips part when our gazes meet. I flash her a wink. I've seen the little telltale signs she doesn't completely hate me by the way she brushes her hair behind her ear to the slight color change in her cheeks when we talk. But the biggest sign is the subtle way her lips fall open a fraction of an inch as if she's waiting for a kiss. From that look alone, I know she'll be thinking about me later tonight, and it won't be about how much she wants to strangle me.

YOU LIIIIKE HIM

CHAPTER ELEVEN
★ ★ ★

Tatum

I've been sitting at a table across from Olivia at Porter's for the past two hours. We've been going over paperwork full of rules and guidelines for a New Year's party we're coordinating. Being in the middle of the afternoon, Porter's is much quieter than normal, plus they have food.

As much as I'm trying to concentrate, my head's not in it. I've read the same paragraph three times and each time the words smash together. I glance out the window next to our table as snowflakes flutter down from the gray sky. It's almost hypnotizing as they dance around before they land softly on the ground. Suddenly, a gust of wind causes a pile of snow to tornado across the parking lot as. A shiver runs down my spine. The snow reminds me of Connor shoveling, then it drifts to our run in at the grocery store the other night. I still can't believe he found my underwear. I've never been so embarrassed, but surprisingly, he wasn't a jerk about it. He didn't swing them over his head and make a crude joke about getting into my panties. But he did joke about me pouring caramel sauce on his body and licking it off. I won't lie, after I got home and crawled under the covers that exact image filled my thoughts. A heat creeps through my body as I rehash it all over again.

"Hello? Tatum?" Olivia's hand flashes in front of my face and I startle. My gaze flits to hers. "So, what do you think?"

"Yeah. Yeah. That all sounds good." I flick my wrist.

"Oh my God. You have no idea what I just said." She laughs. "Are you bored already? Because we still have about five more pages to go through."

"A little. I wasn't expecting snow today." Quickly, I change the subject so I don't blurt out I've been daydreaming about Connor.

"Me either. I thought it was going south."

"Yeah, that's what the meteorologist said. I really should've become a meteorologist so I could get paid to be wrong all the time. I could say that there's a fifty percent chance of snow in the middle of July and no one can be mad at me because it will either snow or it won't." I push the papers away. "Time for a career change."

Olivia laughs. "I'm not sure that's how it works."

"But it's the truth." My gaze drifts between the snow falling outside and the TV to see if there're any new updates. It's been coming down all day and doesn't seem to be letting up either.

"They're saying it could be one of the biggest snowstorms of the season. So far, they're predicting ten to eighteen inches are possible."

"If you ask me, there's a big difference between ten and eighteen inches."

"Even more so when we're not talking about snow."

We both laugh. I've lived in Harbor Highlands my entire life, so I'm used to the snow. Somedays I like the winter more than others. Mostly when I'm at home snuggled with a big, fluffy blanket and cup of piping hot coffee, watching the sun rise and how it causes the snow to sparkle like a sea of diamonds. And I hate it when I have to drive. There's always some jerk who thinks just because he has a big truck with even bigger tires he can go as fast as he wants. Even big tires are no match against icy roads.

The server drops off two burgers and fries at our table. The comforting aroma of a toasted bun and melted cheese causes my stomach to rumble. I dip a french fry in ranch and pop it into my mouth. We eat in silence for a few minutes. The farther the sun dips toward the horizon the harder the snow falls and again my mind wanders to Connor.

"Do you find beards sexy?" I ask between bites of my cheeseburger.

Olivia taps her chin, pondering the question. "I do like a little scruff. Nothing too big or bushy. And definitely not one that hangs to his chest, but I love the rough, scratchy feeling, especially when he's going down on you. Ledger has the perfect amount of scruff." There's a small sparkle in her eyes.

"You and Ledger are complete opposites. He's grumpy, you're bubbly. Did you find it hard to navigate?"

"Honestly, it fueled our connection. We fed off each other and it kinda brought us together more than pushed us apart. Plus, it's a lot of fun." A bright smile covers her lips as I'm sure thoughts of her boyfriend flit through her mind. The tell-tale sign is when her eyes gloss over like they are doing now. She swallows a bite of her burger. "Why do you ask?"

"Oh. No reason." Quickly, I dip another fry and shove it in my mouth before I say anything else.

She swallows a sip of her drink. Her eyes go wide and light up like a Christmas tree as she fights to not spray liquid all over the table. "Wait! Are you talking about your neighbor?"

"No! I'm not," I spit out entirely too fast.

"Omg! You like him!"

"No. I don't." I keep my eyes trained forward and bite the inside of my cheek to prevent the smile that wants to take over.

"Yes! You do! I know that look! You liiike him." She throws her hands up in the air. "How did I not see this earlier?"

"I'd like him to drown in a vat of fruit cake batter. That's it."

"Come on. You're talking about beards, which he has. You both seem to take pleasure in getting under each other's skin at every opportunity. You two hate flirt!"

"No, we don't. That's not even a thing."

"Oh yes, it is! And you two are totally hate flirting the hell out of each other. You're constantly at each other's throats, but then when he's not around, you casually bring him up in conversation. Have some fun and go for it." She shrugs her shoulder, but a sly smirk spreads across her face. "Also, he gave you that cute nickname. What was it again?" She taps her finger against her chin as if she's thinking, but she knows exactly what it is. She just wants me to say it.

I blow out an exasperated sigh. "Tinsel." However, I have to bite the side of my cheek to hide my smile.

"See. Cute nickname. And you can't tell me you hate it." She raises a perfectly sculpted eyebrow.

Ugh! She's right. I don't hate it but I should. Same goes for liking him. It's not possible. I hate him. Or at least strongly dislike him. A relationship between us would only work if he didn't talk. But there is no relationship. There's nothing. Why do I keep thinking about this? Thinking about him. I've never been the wishy-washy person. If I see something, I go for it, but Connor has me tied up in knots. I need to go home and sort through my thoughts because Olivia isn't helping.

"Let's call it a day. The snow's coming down pretty good and I'd hate to drive in it as it continues to get worse. I'll take these home and go over them." I grab the stack of papers and shove them in a folder.

"Yeah. You're probably right." We pay our bill and say our goodbyes to Rylee and Jake behind the bar before heading out.

After I come in from shoveling the three inches of snow that's already accumulated on my front step, I flop down onto the couch and tug a blanket over my lap. The soft glow of the Christmas tree creates a warm ambiance. I bring the cup of hot cocoa to my lips and take a sip. My mind flits back to the conversation earlier with Olivia. Hate flirting. That's not even a thing. There's a lot of hate, but definitely not flirting. Why would I flirt with him? Sure, he's semi attractive... fine, he's sexy as hell and I don't know why I find him so hot. One minute he's a jerk, but then there are teeny tiny moments when he's sweet, so it tells me he's not a complete asshole. He seems averse to people in general. When I've run into him in public, he always has his hat pulled down and sunglasses on. And the time at Roasters when someone asked about his name, he was out of there faster than when Christmas decorations go on sale after the holidays. I swallow another sip of my cocoa. It makes me even more curious about him.

The lights on the Christmas tree flicker briefly, then shut off. Silence fills the house. I wait a few minutes, expecting the electricity to spring back to life, but it doesn't. Climbing off the couch, I peer out the window. I can't see anything. It's pitch black out. In fact, the entire neighborhood is without power. Crap.

VANILLA AND ASS

CHAPTER TWELVE
★ ★ ★

Connor

I strum the strings on my guitar, loving the way the music flows all around me. Through me. The soft melody fills my soul. This is the first time I've picked up my guitar in over a week. I'm pretty sure this is the longest I've ever gone without playing. Sadly, I didn't have a desire to play anything until recently when I ran into Tatum at the grocery store. There was a glint in her eyes that sparked something inside me. So here I am on a cold and snowy evening doing what I love again. Since I was a kid, I knew I wanted to play music. Eventually it became the air I needed to breathe. Too bad, it's also the very thing that nearly destroyed me.

I strum a few more chords, the soft melody almost like a lullaby while the snowflakes dance across the sky to the music I'm playing in my living room. Suddenly, everything goes black, and I freeze. Rising to my feet I find the nearest lamp to twist the knob, but nothing. That's when I notice the streetlights are off as well. In fact, the power's out for the entire neighborhood. Shit. I set my guitar down in the case. If the power is out, then that means the furnace is as well.

Since Grams keeps everything, I found a drawer full of flashlights and two unopened packs of batteries. I pull them out and set them on the counter. Not knowing how long we'll be without power, I throw on my jacket and shove my feet into my boots. Outside the backdoor is a small covering where I stacked some firewood I chopped earlier. No better time to use it than now.

Snow swirls around me as a gust of wind smacks my face, sending a chill down my spine. Quickly, I load my arms up with as many pieces as I can carry. Back inside, I stack them next to the fireplace in the living room and go back out to get another arm full. Once I have enough wood for a few hours, I stack a few pieces inside the fireplace and light some paper for a fire starter. It crackles and pops from the temperature change, but eventually evens out to a warm glow. I sit cross-legged in front of the flames, mesmerized by the way they shimmer and dance. Something so simple, yet it can be so destructive. Much like my career.

An hour passes and we're still without power. I open my phone and check the power company's website and sure enough the power is out for twenty thousand customers. A third of the city is without power, in the middle of a snowstorm nonetheless. Rising to my feet, I make my way to the kitchen but freeze when I pass the picture window. Across the street, through Tatum's window, I can make out a silhouette carrying around what appears to be a candle. As I glance around, I spot several dots of light scattered around her living room. She's going to burn her house down with all those candles. A pang of guilt hits my chest. If my furnace isn't working, then I'm sure hers isn't either. The fire in the fireplace crackles, drawing my attention from my neighbor.

I trudge toward the door and shove my arms into the sleeves of my coat and tie my boots. I yank a knit beanie over my head and open the door. My boots sink into the freshly fallen snow. My tracks practically fill in as soon as I step out from the blowing snow. With my head down to block my face from the snow and wind, I trek down my driveway and across the street. Once I'm at her door, I raise my fist and knock. Several seconds pass before Tatum answers, a big comforter wrapped around her.

"What do you want?" She pulls the blanket tighter.

"The power's out."

"Well duh. Half the city is without power right now."

"Come to my house. I have a wood burning fireplace."

"You've come here to save me?" Her shoulders drop a fraction.

"If by saving, you mean keeping you from freezing to death, then yes. I'd hate for that to be on my conscience."

A smile flirts on her lips and fuck if it isn't sexy as hell.

"Aww, you were thinking about me."

"The offer expires in five. Four. Three. Two."

"Okay. Okay. Spending the evening with you sounds better than freezing to death. Let me get my things. Come in."

She steps into her house, and I follow her lead. I stay on the small rug inside the door, so I don't track snow everywhere. "What's that smell?" I cover my nose with my hand.

"What smell?" She dumps the blanket onto the couch and throws her coat over her shoulders.

"I don't know. It's a mix between vanilla and ass."

She chuckles. "Well, the vanilla is probably from a couple of the candles. But I'm not sure about the ass. I don't have an ass smelling candle."

"Oh God, I'm going to be sick." I gag. "I threw up a little."

"Help me blow out all these candles, then." She blows out two on an end table.

I point down at my boots that are still on my feet.

"It's fine." She continues to blow out a few more on the coffee table and I help her.

"Oh shit." I retreat from the offensive odor. "I figured it out."

"What is it?"

"It's a mixture of that pine tree smelling one, mixed with that rosemary one, mixed with pumpkin." The little wisps of smoke fill the room, making it even worse. "Why did you think it would be a good idea to light every single candle you have?"

She steps into her boots and laces them into a bow. "I needed light, plus I figured maybe it could keep me warm."

"Yeah, when your house goes up in flames, I'm sure that would keep you warm."

She narrows her eyes at me.

Crossing my arms over my chest, I shake my head. "Don't look at me like that. I'm saving you right now from either freezing to death, nasty candle smell inhalation, or burning yourself alive."

She stands to her full height, which is still half a foot shorter than me. "I don't need saving. I'm only going because you offered, and it sounds better than staying here. But if you keep talking, I might take my chances."

"Your call." I yank open the door and a blast of wind and snow smacks me in the face. Clearly, the weather hasn't let up any. I step outside, the snow already several inches deeper.

"Wait for me!" Tatum rushes after me while tugging her hat on her head. She fumbles to close and lock the door with her mittens on, so I give her a hand.

We trudge our way back across the street. My previous boot prints are barely visible anymore. I lead the way while she follows in my tracks. Once we've reached my doorstep, I open the door for her to move past me and I follow her inside.

She unzips her coat. "Wow. You've done a lot of work in here."

"Yeah. It's kept me busy." I pull my jacket off and offer to take hers. I open the closet next to the entryway and hang both of them up. She toes off her boots, and I do the same.

"The last time I was in here, three out of the four walls were covered in that old, dated wood paneling. You've really brightened it up in here. This looks like all of Mrs. Hendrickson's belongings. Did it come fully furnished?"

"Yeah." She doesn't need to know Mrs. Hendrickson is actually Grams. The less we know about each other, the better. Unsure of what to say or talk about next, I glance around the room. "Um, you're welcome to take a seat." I grab a log from the rack next to the fireplace and toss it onto the fire.

She curls up on the couch, her legs tucked under her. "It's actually cozy in here. The fireplace puts off a lot of heat."

"Yeah. I'm glad it's still functioning. Definitely saved us tonight." I stoke the fire.

"Do you know when the snow is supposed to let up?"

Rising to my feet, I flop down on the opposite end of the couch. "When I checked the news, they said it will taper off after midnight, but it's expected to pick back up tomorrow."

"So, we're in it for the long haul. At least until the power comes back."

"Sounds like it."

She huffs and props her chin up in her palm. The warm glow from the fire illuminates her face. I don't know what it is, but I'm drawn to her. I want to be near her. Feel her presence. If I move one cushion over, we'd be touching. I could run my hand up her denim covered leg. Feel her warmth under my palm. She'd glance up at me, the most beautiful, hypnotic blue eyes meeting mine. Fuck. This isn't why I invited her over.

I jump to my feet. "Do you want something to drink?"

She lifts her head, eyebrows raised. "What do you got?"

"Beer, hard cider, maybe a bottle of water."

"I'll have a hard cider."

I nod as I stroll out of the living room and round the corner into the kitchen. I need to get away from her. Give myself some room to breathe. With a hand gripping the handle of the fridge, I pause, needing a moment to clear my head. After exhaling a deep breath, I open the door and pull out a beer and a bottle of hard cider. When I close it and spin around, Tatum's standing there. My hand bumps into her arm, causing me to lose my grip on the bottle and it crashes to the floor. Shards of glass and cider scatter across the linoleum.

"Shit."

"Oh my God! I'm so sorry!" Her hands jump to cover her mouth.

"It's okay." I set the beer on the counter and reach for a dish towel hanging on the stove. I toss the towel on to the floor to soak up some of the liquid.

"Let me help you." She bends down and picks up pieces of glass.

"Be careful. Don't cut yourself."

"I got it. I'm not going to cut myself." She continues to pick up small shards of glass while I grab another towel. "Shit," she mutters under her breath.

"You cut yourself, didn't you?"

"No…"

I tug on her elbow, forcing her to stand. Flipping her hand over, a streak of red stains the tip of her thumb and runs down to her palm.

"We should get this cleaned up." Before she can respond, I step over the mess and lead her to the garbage can. She tosses the pieces of glass from her other hand into the trash. With my hand still wrapped around her wrist, I guide her down a narrow hallway and flick on the light switch in the bathroom.

"Shit. No lights."

"I have my phone. You could use the flashlight." She reaches for her phone with her other hand, but I stop her.

"Wait. I'm sure you have glass fragments on your other hand too. Where's your phone?"

Her gaze meets mine. "In my back pocket."

"Oh." My chest tightens. I never got to the touching her ass portion of my fantasy earlier, but apparently now it gets to play out in real time. The hairs on my arms rise as if a current of electricity is coursing between us. In fact, I'm sure it's so strong it could power its own light bulb. Hell. It could light up the entire city right now.

Slowly, I reach behind her. My palm drags down the back of her sweater and over the curve of her ass. My fingers run along the seam of the pocket before I dip my hand in. Finding her phone, I pull it out and hold it between us.

"If you swipe up, you'll see the flashlight icon."

I do as she says, and a light on the back illuminates the floor. I usher us the rest of the way into the bathroom and set the phone flashlight side up, so it brightens the small room.

"We'll have to make this quick. I don't know how long we'll have water pressure and it's best to conserve it for emergencies since we don't know how long the power will be out." I guide her hands under the running water to wash away any glass slivers, along with the blood from her cut. Once her hands are clean, I direct her to sit on the closed toilet seat.

"You know I can do this myself."

I don't want to admit that I enjoy touching her, so I go with something else. "I feel responsible. I dropped it."

"It was an accident."

My gaze meets hers, but I don't say anything. Instead, I continue holding her wrist as I pull open a drawer in the vanity. As fast as I can, I push a tube of toothpaste to the side, along with a bottle of shaving cream and disposable razors until I find a few loose Band-Aids. I shut the drawer with my hip and use my teeth to pull off one side of the paper backing.

She chuckles. "You know I could help you."

I spit it out and it flutters to the floor. "Nah, I got this." Then I do the same with the other side. Finally, I'm able to peel back one side and wrap it around her thumb and then do the same with the other. With her hand in mine, I press down the sides making sure it's secure. "There."

"Now I feel like you should kiss it to make it feel better." Her soft, full lips tip up into a smile.

My gaze locks on hers and I bend down, pressing my lips to the pad of her thumb over the Band-Aid. Her breath hitches and her hand slightly trembles as soon as I make contact. If I wasn't so close to her, I would have missed it. Slowly, I lift my head. "There. All better."

"It is." Her words are barely a whisper.

A few silent seconds pass as we stare at each other, waiting for the other to make a move. When she doesn't say or do anything, I pull away. "What do you say we get out of the bathroom and go back to where it's warm."

She nods.

Our gazes linger on each other's for a brief moment longer. I wanted to kiss her again, except not on her fingers. I'd start on her wrists, her pulse would thump under my lips as I press down on her delicate skin. Then I'd trail kisses up her arm and across her shoulder until I reached the side of her neck. I would nip at her sensitive skin, then move up to her jaw and across her cheek. When I reach the corner of her mouth, her breath would hitch, showing me she wants it too. I would cup her cheek with my hand and drag my lips to meet hers. Soft and sensual at first, then growing more ravenous with each passing second. Her little moans and whimpers would spur me to continue. Then I—

"Connor? Hello? Connor?"

Tatum's voice pulls me out of my daydream. I blink once. Twice. Even with the poor lighting, her big, blue eyes shine bright. "Yeah?"

"You can let go of my hand now."

"Oh. Shit. Sorry." I drop her hand and step away as if she's a raging hot fire and I just got burned. If she knew the thoughts that just ran through my head, I'm sure she would light me on fire.

We make our way back into the kitchen and finish cleaning up the mess. I grab her a new drink and manage to not drop this one. When we get back into the living room, she curls up on the couch at the end closest to the fire. I settle down in the rocking chair across from her. It might be best if I'm not within arm's reach of her right now. Discreetly, I adjust myself in the chair.

She lifts the bottle of hard cider to her lips, swallowing a gulp. The bottle rests in her lap as she asks, "So, what brought you to town?"

"Really? Small talk?"

She huffs. "What else are we going to do? Sit here in silence?"

Yeah, that's what I was hoping, but I keep that to myself. The reason I'm here is not to make friends. All I wanted was time to myself. To be alone. To realize there's more to life than being someone else's puppet and being told what to do, when to do it, and how to do it. Instead, I'm sitting in my living room across from a woman who's unknowingly implanted herself into my life and my thoughts. The same woman I steal glances at while she gets her mail like some kind of creepy stalker.

"I needed to get away for a while."

"From California?"

"Yeah. How did you know?"

"I saw your license plate, and I got a piece of your mail by accident. Connor Tyler." She flashes me a snarky smile.

Fuck. I fight to keep my expression neutral. Now that she knows my full name, hopefully she hasn't Googled me. While I've done my best to keep everything hidden, I'm sure if she searches hard enough, she can connect the dots. "I needed to be somewhere quiet. Figure some shit out," I say to keep the conversation going so she doesn't get suspicious.

"Harbor Highlands is kind of an obscure place to buy a house just to figure out some shit."

I lift one shoulder and let it drop, not wanting to correct her.

"What are you running from? Scorned lover? Rob a bank? Are the cops going to bust down your door any minute? Shit. Does me being here make me an accomplice?" She presses her finger to her lips and scans the room as if she's planning her escape route.

A twinge of a smile plays on my lips. "None of that."

"Then what?" Her hand falls to her lap. When I don't say anything for a second, she responds, "Sorry. It's probably personal. You don't have to tell me." She swallows another drink from her bottle.

I do the same. The fire crackles in front of us as a moment of silence passes. "Have you ever had someone demand the world from you?"

She glances up at the ceiling as she ponders her response. "There are a few people who've done that to me."

"That was me back in LA, but it wasn't just one person. It was everyone."

"What do you do in LA?"

Do I tell her the truth? She hasn't figured it out yet, which is refreshing. Instead, I go with the half-truth. "I'm in the music industry."

I keep my answer vague. The moment people find out that I'm the guitarist and lead singer for one of the nation's fastest-growing rock bands, they swarm like flies on shit. That's the last thing I want. So far, my beard has been a great disguise, that and I rarely leave the house. But coming back to Harbor Highlands is like being in a small town, especially when compared to LA. I knew it would be the perfect spot to hide out while I figure out my life. But shit would go south fast if word got out. Everyone would know in two point two seconds, and I would have to leave. Before she can pry further, I ask, "What about you? What do you do?" Then I inwardly cringe.

Dumbass. Why are you trying to get to know her more?

"I work as an event coordinator. With my sister, actually. She started the business and asked me if I wanted to work with her after my ex-boyfriend fired me."

"Oh shit. That sucks. Did he become the ex and then fire you or vice versa?"

"Actually, it was more like a two for one special." She presses her lips together into a firm line as her gaze drifts to the fire.

"No shit." I take a swig of my beer. "So, is that why you do the whole neighborhood Christmas decorating thing?" I mentally scold myself. *Why do I keep asking her questions? There is no reason for me to get to know her.* She laughs and it's so sweet, just like her. Fuck.

"Actually, no. I've been doing that on my own for years. I've always enjoyed Christmas and decorating and baking. As a kid, I was always in the kitchen or decorating with my nana. She always made Christmas extra special for me. After she passed, I make sure to put out two of her outdoor angels every year. You might have seen them in my yard next to Santa's workshop."

"Yeah. Also sorry to hear about your nana."

"Thanks." Her gaze drops to the floor.

"Those cookies you made were delicious." She peers up at me, a small smile plays on her lips. "Except the nasty raisin things."

She sits up straighter on the couch as her lips pull into

a full fledge grin. "I love oatmeal raisin cookies! I can't believe you don't like those."

"I can't do them. Little shriveled prunes. It's not right." I shiver in disgust.

She laughs again. "So, when you moved in, I saw you had a guitar. Do you play?"

I take a long swig of my beer, swallowing the cold liquid. When I lower the bottle, her curious gaze meets mine. "I know a song or two."

She nibbles on her bottom lip a moment before asking, "Would you play something for me?" When I don't say anything, she continues, "Only if you want to, of course. But I would love to hear something. But no pressure. I know some people don't like playing in front of strangers."

The way she rambles is cute. Wordlessly, I rise from the chair and stroll across the living room to where my guitar case is. I sit on the other end of the couch, bend over, and lift the latches. Opening the case, I pull out my Gibson 1942 Banner acoustic guitar. I rest it on my lap as I contemplate what song to play. It would be easy to do one of mine but I fear it would give me away.

Tatum sits up on the cushion with all her attention directed at me. I strum a few chords to test the sound. I make a quick adjustment to the pegs. With my calloused thumb, I play the chords to "Don't Let Me Down" by The Beatles. She inches closer to me on the couch. Softly, I sing the lyrics to the song as I keep my gaze trained on my fingers. I don't dare spare a glance at her. Not because I'm nervous about playing, but because I don't know what I'll do if I see her expression. By the end of the song, her warm thigh presses against mine.

"That was so good. You should be a musician. Performing on stage."

I can't help but laugh. "Thanks."

"I'm serious. I wish I could play an instrument. For a hot minute, I played the violin in middle school. But then I realized that wasn't the cool instrument to play. Plus, I wasn't very good at it." She leans her shoulder against the back of the couch.

"I'm sure you were great."

She laughs, and it's the sweetest melody. "No. I was terrible, I promise." She fidgets with her fingers resting in her lap. "Maybe you could teach me something?"

"Yeah? You want to play the guitar?"

She nods.

"What do you want to learn?"

She purses her lips, the corner of her mouth tips up to the side as she decides on her answer. "'Love You Anyway' by Luke Combs. I love that song."

"Country?"

She bobs her head up and down.

"I don't do country."

"Oh." Her face falls.

"I got a song I can teach you." I pass her my guitar and she holds it in her lap. Rising to my feet, I move to kneel in front of her. "Wrap your hand around the neck like this." I move her fingers so they're over the strings. "And then rest your arms here and let it hang down. Keep it loose." I move her other arm over the guitar body. "This is the C chord." I grip her hand softly in mine and a jolt of electricity courses through my body. Her breath hitches and I know she felt it too. Our gazes meet for the briefest of seconds before I glance away. I move her finger to the correct string and then I hand her a pick from my pocket. "Strum this string while pressing down with your other hand." She does exactly what I say. "Now this is G." Again, I move her finger to the correct string, and she strums it. "Now try them together."

Her tongue peeks out as she remembers where to place her fingers and strums the two chords. We continue this way for a few more chords. Sometimes she makes a mistake but starts over.

When I introduce a new chord, she tries to play it all back but messes up. "I can't do this. My fingers aren't that coordinated."

"Here, let me try something. Scoot forward." She does as I say, and I move to sit behind her. My front is pressed against her back. For a moment her body stiffens, but then she relaxes into me. I lean past her shoulder, her sweet vanilla scent invading my senses. What I wouldn't do to nuzzle into her neck, savoring her delicious smell, and press my lips to her soft flesh. Quickly, I shake the thought from my head. Reaching around the neck, I set my fingers on the strings. "Put your fingers on mine. Then you can get a feel for the movement." Her delicate fingers graze mine, barely touching me as if she's afraid because she'll feel the same current of electricity as I do.

I play the intro chords and then lead into the first verse. Her fingers brush against mine as I move over the strings. With my mouth next to her ear, I croon the lyrics to "Patience" by Guns N Roses. When I reach the end of the chorus, she releases a small giggle.

She tilts her head to face me. "'Patience'. How fitting."

I flash her a small smile but continue playing. Her gaze searches mine, then falls to my lips. Her hands fall to her sides as she inches her face closer to mine. A river of lust and desire flows between us. Her lips part and I stop singing when she sinks her teeth into the corner of her bottom lip. I'm itching to feel her soft bottom lip between my teeth. Then her lips crash to mine.

ONLY ONE FIREPLACE

CHAPTER THIRTEEN
★ ☆ ★

Connor

Holy shit. She's kissing me. Without breaking our kiss, I set my guitar off to the side. With my hands free, I guide her to twist around and straddle my lap. Wrapping one hand around her back, I hold her close as I thread my fingers through her golden locks that shimmer in the firelight. She clasps her hands on my cheeks and slowly rocks against me, the friction causing me to grow harder. Her little moans and whimpers increase when I thrust my erection against her. Before I can deepen the kiss, she pulls away, but her hands never leave my cheeks.

She catches her breath for a moment as her thumb brushes over my beard. "I'm sorry."

My hands glide up and down her spine. "I'm not." I sit up and angle my head to kiss her soft and tender lips. The warmth of her body presses against mine. Fuck. I don't remember the last time I've felt like this. All I know is that I don't want it to stop.

She deepens the kiss, grinding her body against mine. All I want to do is flip her onto the couch and worship every inch of her body. But I refrain. I want her to take the lead… for now. Her hand brushes over the side of my head and combs her fingers through my hair. She latches on to a few strands and tugs, forcing my head back, and a deep groan rumbles from my chest. Her tongue slides across the seam of my lips and I open for her. Our tongues caress each other's, slow and seductive, as we continue to grind against each other like a couple of teenagers alone for the first time. Oddly enough, that's exactly what it feels like. I'm afraid if I stop touching her, I'll lose her and that's the last thing I want.

I wrap my arms around her waist and slide them under her shirt and up her bare back. She's so soft under my calloused fingers. Her back arches as I continue to nip and suck on her heated skin.

"Oh. God," she drawls out, followed by a whimper when I bite down.

"I want to taste you. All of you." She nods. My mouth skates up her neck, leaving a trail of kisses in my wake. Then I'm working my way across her jaw, until I meet her lips, capturing them in a searing kiss. With my patience wearing thin, I wrap my arms around her waist and lift. She releases a surprise squeal as I lay her down on the couch. It's time for me to take the reins.

She laughs. "I wasn't expecting that."

"I'm full of surprises," I mumble against her cheek. While keeping my full weight off her, I pepper kisses along her jaw and continue down her neck. A breathy moan escapes her as I suck on her soft skin. She spreads her legs wider, inviting me in. I nestle in between, my now iron-hard dick pressing against her core. Her breath hitches, but then she's lifting her hips to rub against me. She runs her hand around my back and dips her fingers under the hem of my shirt. As the fabric inches higher and higher, I pull away and sit up. With one hand, I reach behind me for the collar and tug it over my head. Her lustful gaze rakes over my bare chest. Her hands start at my shoulders, dragging her fingertips down and over my pecs. She stops to trace my tattoo for a second before continuing down my abs.

She licks her lips. It's subtle, but it doesn't go unnoticed. "This is what you get when you chop wood?"

"Amongst other things." Goosebumps spread over my skin as she continues to run her fingers over every dip and valley of my abs. Then she's following the same path back up over my ribs and up my chest as if she's memorizing my body. She can do whatever she wants, as long as she doesn't stop touching me. *What am I doing? Don't get attached. You're not fucking staying.* But I know this is a battle I won't win.

I glance down, her hair fans out across the couch as a warm glow from the flickering fire illuminates behind me. Bending down, I press my lips to hers. With one hand, I pull at the hem of her shirt. She sits up, and I break our kiss so I can pull it over her head. My gaze roams down her pink lace covered chest. The swells of her tits heave in anticipation. I bend down and place open mouth kisses on one, then the other. My lips brush along her pebbled nipple before I place my mouth over the lacy fabric and suck. Then I repeat the process on the other side. Her moans and whimpers spur me to continue. With one hand, I pull down the lace, exposing her to the cool air. The hardened peak stands at attention, begging for my mouth. I swirl my tongue around her nipple and then softly bite down. She moans and writhes beneath me from the sensation. Then my attention is on her other breast and I do the same.

"You are absolute perfection." I continue to nip and suck while I massage the other with my hand, pinching her nipple, creating a double sensation. With my mouth still on her, I drag my hand down her stomach until I reach the waistband of her jeans. I flick the button open and tear down the zipper. Her nails dig into my shoulder as she lifts her hips, meeting my hand. I grip the waistband of her jeans and she lifts her butt off the couch. Slowly, I peel them down her legs and discard them on the floor. I run my fingers along the band of her lace panties before tugging them off. I trail my middle finger down her slit. "Fuck. I've barely even touched you and you're so wet for me."

"Yes! Don't stop. Touch me more." She bucks her hips, wanting more. *Needing* more.

I dip a finger into her needy opening, and she whimpers. I push all the way to my knuckle, as a low gasp escapes her. Pulling out, I thrust back in over and over again. This time when I pull out, I add a second finger. "You're gripping me so tight. Imagine if it was my dick inside you. Stretching you. Can you handle it?"

She squeezes my fingers. "Yes! Oh! Yes!"

I continue to spear her with my fingers, harder and faster as her moans grow louder. With my lips wrapped around her, I flick my tongue over her nipple, and she detonates. My name a breathy whisper on her lips as she clenches down on my fingers. When her breathing evens out, I pull out of her and lift my hand to my mouth, sucking her orgasm off both fingers as she watches me with hooded eyes.

"I'm not through with you yet. Spread your legs. Let

me see your pussy." Following my directions, she drops one foot to the floor, opening herself up to me. My dick strains against my zipper. I reach down and adjust myself, but it's useless. I'm hard as fuck and it's not going away anytime soon. Best to occupy myself with something else.

I slide down her body, alternating between licking and kissing her inner thigh. A shiver runs through her body as my beard brushes against her sensitive skin. I slide my hand up her other silky smooth thigh until my fingers reach her pussy. With two fingers, I spread her open and run my tongue up her slit. Her back arches off the couch and she moans.

"Oh God. That feels so good." She bucks her hips, wanting more.

Of course, I'm here to please. I continue my assault on her pussy. Licking. Sucking. Kissing. Her fingers thread through the hair at the back of my head, holding me in place. I'm feasting on her like a goddamn all you can eat buffet and, fuck, I never want to leave. Her pants and moans grow more carnal with each swipe of my tongue. I spear her entrance before sucking on her clit. A sharp sting comes from my scalp as her fingers tug on my hair, but I don't stop. Honestly, I wouldn't be surprised if she has a fist full of lose hair right now. But that's okay. It only encourages me to go faster and harder. I run my hand up her stomach until my fingers graze over her erect nipple. I massage the soft flesh as she writhes beneath me.

"I'm so close. Yes! Connor! Yes!" Her breathing increases along with her moans.

I bite down, then suck at the same time as I pinch her nipple between my fingers. Her body spasms beneath me. She screams out my name as another orgasm obliterates her body. When she comes down from her high, I kiss my way down her thigh until I reach her knee, then I sit up.

"Oh, shit." Her chest heaves as lust swirls in her irises.

"Fuck. I could eat your pussy all night." I run a hand down my beard, wiping off her orgasm.

"My turn." She sits up and unbuttons my jeans and tugs down the zipper. She hooks her thumbs into the waistband and tugs my jeans down. My cock springs free and juts out.

She stares at my dick that's bobbing in front of her and licks her lips before glancing up at me. "Commando?"

I shrug a shoulder. "It eliminates a step for times like this."

A slow smile spreads across her face. "I like less steps."

She wraps her hand around me, pumping once, then twice. Her tongue peeks out as she licks the head. I throw my head back and groan. As she continues to stroke me, she runs her tongue along the underside of my cock before sucking the tip into her mouth.

"Fuuuck." I fight against thrusting into her mouth, but her lips wrapped around me is a little slice of heaven. I reach down and unhook the back of her bra. Without taking her mouth off my dick, she shimmies the straps down her arms and, with my assistance, she tosses it to the floor. She pulls off my dick with a pop and glances up at me through her lashes.

"Come here." With my hand on the back of her head, I lead her up to her knees and crash my lips to hers in a bruising kiss. It's rough and intense and even better than I imagined.

She pulls away a fraction of an inch and mumbles, "Do you have a condom?"

"Are you sure?"

She nods as a seductive smile tugs at her lips. Hurriedly, I grab one from the bathroom and within seconds, I'm back in the living room. I lower myself to the couch, rip open the foil packet, and roll the condom down my length. My fingertips dimple her hips as I guide her to kneel on the couch and straddle me. Her hands rest on my shoulders for balance. With one hand, I grip my dick and tease her entrance with the head. Her teeth sink into her lower lip as she makes small circles with her hips. When she can't wait any longer, she slowly slides down my shaft. Inch by inch, she sucks me in, enveloping me in her heat. I exhale a low groan as she inhales a sharp breath.

Once she's fully seated, she pauses. Her mouth falls open as she adjusts to my size. Her hair falls to the side of her oval face like a curtain as she peers down at me. Holy shit. She's utter perfection. I'm surprised I didn't instantly come as soon as she slid down. But, right now, I'm a ticking bomb waiting to detonate.

"I'm going to need you to move, Tinsel." I buck my hips up and she gets the point.

The corner of her mouth tips up as she slides up and down on my dick. Then her lips part as she increases her speed with each upward stroke. Her breathing gets heavier as her moans and whimpers increase. Grabbing both her wrists, I bind them behind her back with one hand. I run my other hand up her thigh and grip her waist to help control her movements. With her chest pushed out, her tits bounce in front of me, teasing me. Unable to control myself any longer, I wrap my mouth around a hard nipple and swirl my tongue around the peak. She whimpers grow louder as she arches her back even more, pressing into my mouth.

I release her nipple with a pop. "That's it Tinsel. Take everything you need. Ride my cock."

"Oh god! Connor. I'm. Going. To. Come."

"Take it. Fuck. Take all of it." My fingers dig into her waist as I push her down on my dick. Her pussy clenches around me, sending a jolt of electricity straight to my balls. "I'm right there with you. Fuck. Yes." Both our moans and grunts grow louder and more strangled with each stroke. I unclasp her wrists from behind her back and bring my thumb to her clit, rubbing in small circles.

"Yes! Connor! Don't stop!" Her hands rest on my chest, her nails dig into my skin. Her pussy grips my cock as her orgasm rips through her.

I continue to thrust into her from below, seconds away from my own release. My balls tighten as a tingle spreads from the bottom of my spine and jolts through my entire body. My hands grip her hips, my fingers digging into her soft skin as I roar out my orgasm into the condom. Tatum's name a whisper on my lips.

ORGASM TRIFECTA

CHAPTER FOURTEEN
* ⭐ *

Tatum

I collapse forward, resting my forehead on his shoulder. With a feather light touch, Connor runs his hands up and down my back as I collect my breath.

Then it hits like a two by four to the face. Oh my God. I just had sex. I just had sex with my deliciously hot, grumpy neighbor. Mind blowing, earth shattering, amazing sex. Did I lose my mind? Out of body experience? It wasn't that because I remember every scrape of his beard between my thighs. Every lick of his tongue. Every stroke of his cock.

I don't know what came over me. One minute he was teaching me to play the guitar and the next we were kissing. Being close to him. Him touching me. Him softly singing in my ear did something to me. I felt something like

I've never felt before and I couldn't help myself. I just… reacted. A grin spreads across my face.

Suddenly, a lamp flickers to life, illuminating the entire room. No longer are we shrouded by the soft glow of the fireplace. And I'm naked. So much nakedness. And pressed up against Connor. Our little sex bubble bursts into a million tiny pieces.

His hands freeze. "Looks like the power's back on."

"It is. I suppose I should…" I rise off the couch, attempting to be as graceful as I can while not wearing any clothes.

"Get home?"

Not meeting his gaze, I continue searching for my underwear that's somewhere on the floor. "I was going to say find my clothes, but yeah, I should probably get home too." Where is my underwear? Did a gremlin come and steal them? When I spot a piece of black fabric behind an end table, I grab it and say a silent prayer that it's what I'm searching for. Thankfully, it is. I step into the leg holes and shimmy them up.

"I wasn't saying you had to. It was more of a question." He finds his jeans and pulls them up but doesn't button them. That shouldn't be so hot, but it is.

"No. No. I should probably make sure everything is okay at home." I yank my bra off the lampshade and hook the latch in the back.

"Let me walk you home, at least." He bends down and yanks his shirt off the floor on the other side of the room and tugs it over his head.

"It's okay. It's only across the street. I can make it." I point out the window to my house as if he doesn't know where I live.

"Are you sure? I don't mind."

"Yeah. Then you'd have to get dressed. Don't worry

about it." I wave him off but don't realize he's stepped closer and my hand smacks his chest. "Shit. Sorry. I'm just going to go." I don't need to make this anymore awkward than it already is. Rushing to the door, I slide my feet into my boots, then pull my coat out of the closet and throw it over my shoulders. "Thanks for... everything. I'll see you... around."

He chuckles. "Yeah. See you around."

I yank open the door and step outside, a blast of arctic wind cools my heated face. Closing the door behind me, I pause and rest my back against the wood. That was awkward as fuck. Chalk it up to the worst walk of shame ever. Probably the worst in history. The porch light flicks to life and I tilt my head up. Then suddenly my back is no longer pressed against the door and I'm stumbling backward. I pinch my eyes shut, preparing for impact, but it never happens. Instead, a pair of strong hands grip under my arms, stopping me before I hit the ground.

Slowly, I crack one eye to find a pair of whiskey colored eyes staring back at me. "Hi. Again."

"Hi." A sexy smirk plays on his lips.

"I guess we get to see each other sooner rather than later."

"I guess so." He lifts me so I'm standing on my own. "You forgot this." He holds up my t-shirt.

I peek down the front of my coat and only see a lace bra. Well, shit. I pluck it from his grasp. "Thanks. I'm going to go throw myself in the snowbank over there," I hike my thumb behind me, "and pray this is all a bad dream." Without a second glance back, I race down the snow covered stairs, down his driveway, and across the street to my front door. It's only then I spare a glance back. He's propped against the doorjamb, watching me. Offering a small wave, I push open my door and step inside. I close it behind me and exhale a sigh of relief. I can't believe that happened. All of it. I press my fingers to my still swollen lips. A part of me is itching to go back over there and cut the power so we can do it all over again. Except I'll make sure to have a more graceful exit. I groan and push off the door.

Strolling through my house, I shut off all the lights that came on when the power was restored and make my way to my bedroom. Throwing myself onto my bed, I stare at the dark ceiling. I don't remember the last time I had sex like that. Rough, wild, and spontaneous. The ache between my legs is proof of that. I unbutton my pants and pull them over my hips. Tiny Connor size fingerprint bruises dot my hip. My teeth sink into my bottom lip, so my smile doesn't widen into a full fledge grin. Screw it. I deserve to smile. The sex was ah-maz-ing. His kisses were soft, but then he fucked me like… a rock star. Maybe that's it. He put some voodoo curse on me while he was playing the song like a subliminal message.

Kiss me. Take off my clothes. Ride my cock.

It was sweet and tender, but then he took control, and it became raw and carnal. He let it be known the pleasure was mine for the taking. And boy, did I take it. I wanted it so much.

Needing some sleep, I rise out of bed and strip out of my clothes and throw on my pajamas. I crawl under the covers, but the night plays on repeat in my head. Eventually, I fall into a restless sleep filled with sweet dreams of Connor.

The following day, I finish cleaning up after dinner and pour myself a glass of wine. I haven't spoken to Connor all day. I saw him leave in his truck, but he didn't even spare a glance my way, not that I was watching. Okay, I was totally watching. But why didn't he look? That only tells me one thing... he regrets it. Everything. It was all a huge mistake.

Olivia's SUV pulls into my driveway. Before she can fully step through my front door, I blurt out, "I slept with Connor."

She halts in her tracks. "Repeat that. I don't believe I heard you correctly."

"I slept with Connor." Lifting my glass to my lips, I fill my cheeks with wine like a chipmunk to avoid answering any further questions.

She drops a box to the floor. "Shut the front door! You slept with your ridiculously hot neighbor, who you claimed to hate?"

"I wouldn't say hate, per se." I flip my wrist in front of me. "Maybe strong dislike. More annoyed at times. But now I don't know what to do."

"How was it? Good?" She wiggles her eyebrows while a Cheshire grin covers her face.

"Honestly... the best I've ever had. It was an orgasm trifecta. Fingers. Tongue. And cock." I hold up a finger for each one I tick off.

"Damn, he really wanted to impress you. Well, why are you here talking to me? Get your ass over there and do it again!"

I flop onto the couch without spilling my wine. "It all feels so complicated."

As she walks into the living room, she sets the box on the end table and drops to the cushion next to me. "Why is it complicated? You're both adults."

"Okay. Maybe not complicated, but awkward." I take a

sip of my wine and then rehash all of yesterday's events. Starting with the power outage, him inviting me to his house, talking, the kiss, the sex, and then the most awkward goodbye known to man.

"If you ask me, the best way to get over an awkward situation is to go do it again, so you stop thinking about the awkwardness."

"Maybe." But I can't deny all I want to do is kiss the scroogeness off his face. Again.

"No maybe. Just do it. But I gotta go." She rises to her feet. "Dinner with Ledger's fam. Also, those are all the invites to our Christmas party. Thanks for stuffing them." She points to the box on the end table.

"No problem. I don't have anything else to do anyway." Besides sit here in self-pity and fantasize about my neighbor. I climb off the couch and walk her to the door.

"We'll chat later." The door softly clicks behind her.

I eye the box. Might as well put on a movie and get to work. While Hallmark Christmas movies play in the background, I sit cross-legged on the floor stuffing all the invites for our charity gala. Stuff the envelope. Wet the flap. Seal it closed. Repeat. With each action, my mind wanders. Stuff. The way his long, thick cock stretched and stuffed me full. Wet. How aroused I was when Connor spread me out on his couch. The scrape of his beard on my inner thighs as his tongue lapped at my pussy. Seal. How he crawled up my body and sealed his lips to mine in a scorching kiss. Repeat. And I want a repeat. All of it. I continue to daydream while stuffing the rest of the invites.

When I'm finished, I lay down on the floor. Ugh! This is sexual frustration at its worst.

WHO'S THE STALKER NOW?

CHAPTER FIFTEEN

* ⭐ *

Tatum

Twinkle lights dance in front of me as I come to a stop. My gaze travels from the base and zigzags over the gold, red, and green sparkly ornaments all the way to the bright gold star at the top of the fifteen-foot Christmas tree. One of my favorite things to do when I come to the mall during the holidays is stop and admire the tree. Next to it is a smaller tree with Stocking Wish Lists where local kids get to wish for presents and community members fulfill those wishes. I pluck two tags off the tree. Since I'm buying toys for The Lilith House toy drive, might as well buy a few more.

The gleaming holiday lights and tinsel fill every storefront window, casting a warm and colorful glow down the walkway. Iridescent white and blue snowflakes hang from the ceiling, simulating falling snow. Echoes of laughter and joyful chatter are accompanied by the festive melody of Christmas music playing in the background as children race from one side of the walkway to the other in a race to get to the next toy store. Most people hate the mall during the holidays, but I love it. This is my happy place. Nothing can ruin it.

"Tatum?"

I whirl around and all the holly jolly drains from my face. This isn't what I need right now.

"Adam. Hi." Damn it. Why does he have to look so good right now? Why can't he be wearing sweatpants and a hoodie instead of pressed slacks that pair perfectly with his wool peacoat? While I'm not wearing pajamas, if I knew I would run into him, I would have picked something better than leggings and knee-high boots. Especially since I know how much he hates them.

"It's good to see you." He flashes me his dazzling half smile. It's the same one that made me fall for him all those years ago.

"You too." I tuck a strand of hair behind my ear. "You look good." I inwardly cringe. Really, did I just tell him that?

He chuckles. "Thanks." There's an awkward pause. "So, we got your mom's invite to her Under the Mistletoe event at the office, but we can't make it."

"We?"

"Me and Lindsey. Her parents are in town for an early holiday."

"Oh, gosh." I wave my hand between us. "Don't worry about it. It's only one of many events. Speaking of which, you must come to the event my sister and I are hosting." I mentally punch myself. What the hell am I thinking? Am I having an out of body experience and it's someone else who's talking? No way in my right mind would I willingly invite both Adam and Lindsey to my event.

"Oh, yeah?"

"Yes. Both of you. You and Lindsey." I pull open my purse and pull out an invitation. "You definitely have to come." What the hell? Why can't I stop talking? More importantly, why isn't there anyone around to supervise me right now?

Lindsey strolls up behind Adam, wrapping her arm around his waist. "Hey honey. What do you have there?" Her voice is smooth and seductive and perfectly matches her flawless skin.

I tug my coat tighter around me.

"Oh, Hi Tatum. I didn't even see you there."

I give her a wide grin. "Hi Lindsey."

Adam glances to Lindsey. "Tatum invited us to her charity gala. Since we can't make it to the other one, we should go."

"That's such a great idea." She glances at me, and I flash her another bright smile. "We should double date?" Her gaze flits between Adam and me. "Surely, you're seeing someone, or at the very least bringing a date."

"Oh. Uh. Um." My heart plummets to my stomach.

"I'm sure Tatum will be too busy with the event for all that," Adam says.

"Oh. No. Not at all. I'll be there. Of course, I'll be there, I'm hosting. But I'll be there with a date." I hike my purse higher on my shoulder. "Well great. I'll see you two then. You'll be there together. I'll be there with my date. It'll be a great night. Okay. Bye." I sidestep them and race past, needing to get away from them like yesterday. What is wrong with me? Why did I invite them, let alone tell them I have a date?

I weave in and out of various customers milling around

the mall, finishing their holiday shopping. Not paying attention since my focus is on what happened, I sidestep one customer and bump shoulders with a familiar green flannel coat.

"Whoa." Connor's hands firmly grip my shoulders, preventing me from falling on my ass. His gaze meets mine, then drops. "What's the rush? Christmas decoration sale somewhere that I don't know about?"

"Sorry about that." I pull my coat tighter around me as if he might have x-ray vision and can see what I'm wearing underneath. "My mind's a little preoccupied."

"I can see that by the way you almost tackled me to the ground."

"Bye Tatum!" Lindsey yells and waves from the opposite side of the concourse.

I give her a wave and a sheepish smile. When they pass, my face falls and my hand drops to my side.

Connor's gaze flits from them and back to me. "Friends of yours?"

"Ex-boyfriend and his shiny new girlfriend."

He releases a low whistle. "Is she younger than you?"

"Thanks for the reminder, ass face." I backhand his bicep.

"Ouch." He rubs the spot. "But I'm sure you're much stronger than her. In fact, I know you're much stronger."

I cross my arms over my chest and glare at him.

"The look on your face tells me you're not quite over him." He pauses. "But then that brings up a lot of questions about our night together." He taps his finger to his plump, kissable lips.

My gaze lingers entirely too long to not be noticed. "I don't want to talk about it." Turning on my heel, I make it only a few steps before his hand grips my wrist.

"Not so fast. What don't you want to talk about? The

ex-boyfriend? Or the night on my couch where you rode me—"

Quickly, I slap my hand over his mouth. "Could you be any louder? The people in line at the Roasters kiosk didn't hear you." A deep rumble of laughter comes from his chest and I drop my hand to the side.

His eyes crinkle in the corners. "No one's even paying attention."

We both glance around and sure enough, everyone's preoccupied with their own shopping to even notice two people standing in the walkway. If anything, we're just in their way as they weave around us.

"So, which is it?" He tilts his head to the side.

I don't know if he's more concerned about me and my ex or if he's curious if I'm thinking about our night together. Now *I'm* curious if he's been thinking about our night together.

Reaching for his wrist, I tug him to a bench that's next to an indoor fountain. I plop down on the wood and he sits next to me. "Since you must know," I dramatically roll my eyes, "it's the ex."

He glances over his shoulder before tugging his knit cap down. "So why are you still hung up on him?"

"Just dive right in, don't you?"

He shrugs.

"I thought he was my end game. He was supposed to be the guy I grew old with. I did everything for him. He'd have a guy's night, and I would make him snacks and make sure there was enough beer in the fridge."

"Wait. Did you say snacks? Do you want to be my girlfriend?"

I roll my eyes. "I'm serious. I wanted to be perfect for him and in the end, it wasn't enough."

"Maybe instead of being perfect, you just needed to be you."

I don't say anything. Instead, I stare at the ground, avoiding eye contact with him because I'm guessing he'll see right through me. But I was being me, wasn't I? I wanted to show him I cared both in our relationship and at work.

"Anyway, the guy looks like a tool with his 'I work a nine to five behind a desk' haircut." Connor's gravelly voice breaks me from my thoughts. "You can do way better than him."

I huff out a breath. "You're a guy. You don't understand."

He leans forward, rests his elbows on his knees, and tilts his head toward me. "Well, I do understand you deserve better. Especially, more than someone who did what he did." When I don't say anything he continues, "One of us that thinks so, anyway."

A teenage kid wearing a black band t-shirt does a double take and stops. "Hey, are you—"

Connor jumps from the bench and grabs his shopping bag. "Nope." Then he bolts in the opposite direction.

Standing up, I spin around. Within thirty seconds, he's blended in with the crowd and is out of sight. That's been twice now someone's asked him if he's someone and each time he left abruptly. Something is off, but I can't pinpoint exactly what it is.

My head has been a jumbled mess between running into Adam and then Connor. Shortly after I arrived home, he backed into his driveway and into the garage. He started unloading something from the back, but then he shut the garage door, and I could no longer see what he was doing. Shit. Maybe I am the stalker?

Olivia's SUV pulls into my driveway. Before she can reach the door, I'm throwing it open.

"I'm so glad you're here. I ran into Adam today."

"Whoa! What? You need to give me a heads up before you drop a bomb like that. Like a text that says, 'Ran into the ex. Get here stat.'" Olivia shrugs out of her coat and steps out of her boots. "What happened?"

"I was at the mall getting presents for the toy drive for The Lilith House and I ran into Adam with his new girlfriend."

"Nooo!" she gasps.

I vigorously nod. "I wish that was all but then things got awkward and I..." my gaze drops to the floor, "may have invited them to our Christmas charity gala."

"No! You didn't!" Olivia shrieks.

My nose scrunches as I nod. "I did. The words just tumbled out of my mouth, and I couldn't stop them. That also included handing them an invitation." My head falls to my hands. "But then I ran into Connor, and he was even more awkward. It's been twice now that someone's asked him if he was someone and he immediately denied it and took off. It happened once at Roasters and then today at the mall."

"That is weird." Olivia strolls into the living room and stares out the window. "Speaking of your hot neighbor, he's out chopping wood again. I need to tell Ledger we need a fireplace just so I can watch him wield an axe."

I stare at her gawking out my living room window. "Of course, he's chopping wood. Is he wearing the long sleeve Henley or the flannel?" Who am I kidding? I wouldn't kick him out of my bed if he wore either.

"Henley," Olivia deadpans. "Who needs TV when you have this to watch all day?"

"He doesn't do it all day. Just..." I cover my mouth with my hand. "Every other day from three to five."

Her gaze shoots to me and I drop my head to avoid eye contact. "For someone who doesn't like their neighbor, you certainly know his schedule."

"Oh, come on. It's hard not to notice something like that." I wave my hand toward his house.

"Only if you're watching." She rocks on her heels, playing coy.

I don't want to admit to Olivia that I tend to watch him. Hell, I don't want to admit it to myself and saying it out loud would definitely be an admission of guilt.

"But I have to get going. Thanks for stuffing all the invites." She ties her boots, throws her coat on, and tucks one box of invites under her arm.

"Of course. Let me help you." I grab the other box, slide my boots on, and tug on my coat. Olivia opens the door and I follow behind her. She places her box in the back seat and I put the other box next to it.

She stares across the street where Connor is still chopping wood. "Good luck with that one." She wiggles her eyebrows.

I shake my head. "Thanks."

I stand off to the side of the snow covered asphalt and wave as she reverses out onto the street. Her taillights fade out of sight and my gaze lingers where her SUV was, and it just so happens to be in the direct line of sight to where Connor is standing.

With focused determination, he swings the axe overhead and brings it down with a resounding thud that reverberates between the houses. Each strike showcases a rhythmic precision that's almost hypnotizing. Wood chips and splinters fly in all directions with each strike of the blade. My boots are rooted into the snow. I cross my arms over my chest, my finger runs over my bottom lip as I remember what it was like having his lips on mine. The way his muscles flexed and moved as he hovered over me. The axe rises above his head and slams down on a log, but slips.

My heart stops as a gut-wrenching howl echoes through the neighborhood.

WILL YOU STAY?

CHAPTER SIXTEEN

★

Tatum

My heart pounds like a bass drum in a too small of space as I sprint across the road, not bothering to check for traffic. When I get to him, he's doubled over, wheezing in pain.

"Are you alright?" Panic laces my voice.

He lifts his head and glares at me. His nostrils flaring as he breathes through the pain.

"Yeah. Sorry. Stupid question. What happened?"

"The blade of the axe got my foot," he says through gritted teeth.

My gaze drops. An axe blade size slice cuts through the leather of his boot.

"I need to get the boot off," he says.

"Okay. Um." Frantically, I glance around to find

something for him to sit on. Off to the side, I find a large log. "Got it."

Quickly, I rush over to the log, kick it over, and roll it. Once it's close to him, I wrap my fingers around the end and tip it up so it's standing on the end. He hobbles to it and lowers himself down while I hold his arm for assistance. Once he's seated, I kneel in the snow in front of him and rip open the laces, loosening them as far as they'll go. With my hand on the heel, I slowly peel the boot off. He winces in pain as I finish pulling it off his foot. My heart stops. His entire sock is stained red. I've never seen this much blood.

"Oh shit. We need to get you to the hospital."

He winces as he tries to shift his weight on the log.

"I'll be right back. I'm going to get my car." Pushing to my feet, I rush back across the street and inside to get my keys and a couple of towels for his foot. Within minutes, I'm parking in Connor's driveway. I wrap his arm around my shoulders, and we hobble to the open passenger door. Once he's seated, I wrap one towel around his foot and do my best to tie it as tight as possible. That will have to do until we get to the hospital.

I sit in the waiting room. My leg bounces nervously as I standby to hear any news about Connor. My mind wanders to all the possible worst case scenarios. What if he did more damage than we thought, and they had to amputate his foot? What if he gets an infection that leads to sepsis? I jump to my feet. Sitting and waiting is making me anxious. I pace back and forth, chewing on my thumbnail.

A set of double doors open and my gaze darts to an older gentleman in a white lab coat. "Connor Tyler," he calls out.

I rush toward him. "Yes. That's me. Is he okay?"

"Yes. Mr. Tyler is doing just fine. He's in recovery right now. We put some stitches in his foot but there doesn't appear to be any serious damage. We just need to finish up some paperwork and then he can go home. Would you like to see him?"

"Yes. Please."

He nods and directs me to follow him back through the double doors. We walk down a couple of different hallways. Nurses and doctors float around between the different rooms. The doctor enters a room and my pace slows as I approach. The last time I was in a hospital was when I was visiting my nana after she got sick. She seemed so small and fragile as she lay in the bed. Fortunately, I got to see her one last time before she passed. Even though this isn't the same, all the same feelings wash over me as soon as I see Connor lying in the bed.

"Hi." My voice is soft.

His head rolls my way, and a weak smile plays on his lips. The edges of my lips spread into a comforting smile. I want him to know I'm here for him. Whatever he needs.

"How are you feeling?" I lower myself to a chair and pull it up next to the bed.

"Like I sliced my foot with an axe."

A small laugh bubbles out of me. "That's fair. Is there anyone I can call for you?"

"No, but will you stay?"

"Of course." I rest my hand on his, mostly so he knows I'm here and maybe for comfort. "The doctor said he's finishing up your paperwork and then you can go home. I got all the papers and cleaning instructions for you."

"Thanks." He rolls his head so he's not looking at me anymore and instead at the ceiling.

I back my SUV up into my driveway. That way, he'll be closer to the front door. I get out and round the hood and open the passenger door.

"This isn't my house." Connor's voice is still groggy from the pain medication they gave him.

"It's not. It's mine. I wasn't going to carry you up your stairs." I wrap one of his arms around my shoulders for balance. He towers over me while I guide him up to my front door. Digging into my pocket, I shuffle and shift my weight to prevent Connor from toppling over so I can unlock the door. Once inside, we wobble our way past the living room and down a short hallway. Since my bedroom will be the most comfortable place, that's where I lead him.

"The doctor said you should limit movements for a day to let some of the swelling go down."

"You're really pretty." His words slur.

A laugh mixes with a grunt as I maneuver him through the doorway. "Thanks."

"No. You're like really fucking pretty."

I bend over and his butt flops onto the mattress.

A smile teases my lips. "You already said that."

He releases a long, deep sigh. "I'm an idiot."

I untie his one boot that's still on and slip it off his foot and glance up at him. "Why's that?"

"Because I slept with you."

So, the truth comes out. I spent so many hours replaying the night we shared, and he regrets it. I'm really the one who's an idiot. "So, you're an idiot because you slept with me?"

"Yeah." He sighs. With jerky movements, his hand cups my cheek. His thumb gently brushes back and forth, and I can't help but lean into his warm palm. "Because I want to do it again."

I freeze. Did he just say what I think he said? He wants to have sex again. Would it be weird if I asked him to repeat what he said? Shit. Now, too much time has passed for me to ask, and it will most definitely be weird. I rise to my feet, maybe a little too fast. "I'm going to get the rest of the things out of the car."

I rush out the door, but before I get no more than two steps down the hallway, I stop and lean against the wall. He's been thinking about me. Or he's just saying all that because of the pain meds. This would be better if he wasn't drugged up. I'm sure by tomorrow he won't even remember what he said. I blow out a heavy breath and push off the wall.

After I collect his hospital paperwork from the car, I head back to the bedroom. He's lying on the comforter, and his chest slowly rises and falls as his feet dangle off the edge. My gaze wanders up and down his large frame. There is no way that position is going to be comfortable in a couple of hours. I lift his arm and it drops back to the bed. And there's no way I'm moving dead weight either.

Gently, I push his shoulder to wake him. "Connor." I give his shoulder a shake. "Connor. Let's get you up on the bed more."

He moans and groans before his eyes blink open.

"Let's get you more comfortable."

He doesn't say anything, but he nods.

With his help, I'm able to get him scooted up the bed. I grab the corner of a light blanket and tug it over him. His eyes flutter closed. Spinning around, I step backward but his hand on my wrist stops me.

"Stay." His voice is low, and his eyelids are fighting to stay open.

I nod. "Okay."

I strip out of the hoodie and crawl onto the bed next to him. He lifts the corner of the blanket, inviting me in. A clock ticking is the only sound in the room. In the darkness, his calloused fingers brush against mine under the blanket. It's a gentle touch, like maybe he was just moving his hand and it bumped mine. Then he links his fingers with mine and hauls it to his chest. A warm smile covers my lips and I close my eyes.

NURSE TATUM

CHAPTER SEVENTEEN
* ⭐ *

Connor

You know what's great to work out frustration? Splitting wood with an axe. You know what's not a good idea when you're angry and frustrated? Splitting wood with an axe. And I have the fifteen stitches to prove it.

After the mall, I did the first thing that came to mind to work out my frustration and look where it got me. I don't know why it bothers me so much that Tatum had sex with me while still secretly pining over her ex. It was a heat of the moment thing. But fuck. I wouldn't be opposed to doing it again.

If I didn't go to the mall yesterday, I would have been none the wiser about the entire situation with the ex and I wouldn't be laying in her bed with a throbbing foot while she plays nurse. But I needed to do a little Christmas shopping.

Once I started making good money from my music, I always made it a priority to pay it forward by buying gift cards to local music stores to donate to various music programs for kids for Christmas. Being in Harbor Highlands wasn't going to stop me from doing that.

So far this morning she's been in the room three times. The first time was right when I woke up. I barely had an eye cracked before she was at my side, asking me how I was feeling. She changed out of her clothes from yesterday and she looked absolutely beautiful, and her sweet vanilla scent smelled even better. Every time she asked me a question, the only thing I could do was to grunt out an inaudible response.

Sometime mid-morning, she came in carrying a small tray with a plate of toast and eggs. She bent down to set the tray on the bed, and I felt like an asshole as I stared down the front of her shirt at her exposed cleavage. Now, a montage of her prancing around in a sexy, completely impractical, nurse's costume with white knee high boots as "Pour Some Sugar on Me" plays on repeat in my mind. I grumbled a thanks before she left me to my own devices. I took a few bites of food, but mostly just pushed it around the plate.

A soft knock sounds on the door before she enters. "Hey." Her voice is quiet. "I went over to your house to get you some fresh clothes. Everything is still in suitcases. Is that because you're renovating?"

"You went into my house?" I spit out.

"Yeah. So you don't have to wear the same clothes you had on yesterday." She tosses the pair of sweatpants and t-shirt on the bed, landing next to me. "It's not like I snooped through all your things."

"You had no right to do that. I didn't need new clothes."

"No. You're right." Venom laces her tone. "Sorry, I'm just trying to help you feel more comfortable."

"Maybe I don't need your help. Did that ever cross your mind?" I seethe. All the color drains from her face. Her eyes go wide and glossy, like she's about to cry. Fuck. Once again, I'm the asshole. If I'm not mad at her, then I want to kiss her. If I kiss her, I'll want to touch her. If I touch her, I'll want a repeat of the night of the snowstorm. I make a mental note of everything in the house, and off the top of my head there isn't anything in sight that would indicate who I am. Plus, she hasn't mentioned anything... yet. Maybe I'm safe. My shoulders deflate. "I'm sorry. You don't deserve my shitty attitude."

She inches closer to the bed, then sits on the edge by my hip. "I know you're not feeling the best right now, but can you go back to being nice for like five seconds? Like the guy last night. The grunts and grumbles are getting old. All I want to do is help you."

"If I'm being honest, that's the issue."

Her eyebrows knit together in confusion.

I huff out a breath and stare at the ceiling because there is no way I can look her in the eyes with everything I'm about to say. "Every five seconds you're in here making sure I'm comfortable. Fluffing my pillow. Touching me. And every single time you do, my dick gets hard. I'm doing everything in my power to not masturbate while in your bed, because I would need your help to clean up the mess. So yeah. The tension is running a little high right now."

"Oh. Oh!" Her gaze shifts from side to side, then she jumps to her feet as if the bed is on fire. "I'll get you a wet washcloth and some Kleenex, or maybe just a towel. I don't know. And a garbage can. Then you can... you know… do that." She motions over my crotch. "And then no worries about a mess." Pink covers her cheeks as she frantically searches her room for all the items.

I scrub my hands over my beard. "I can't do it knowing you're in the other room waiting for me to finish."

"Good point. Then I can leave." She pauses. "Wait. But what if you need something and I'm not here."

"It's fine. I'm fine." Fuck. I can't believe I told her all that.

She runs around the room and gathers all the items and places them on the bed next to me. "I have clean sheets so I can change bedding later. I'll let you… get to it."

"I'm not—"

She covers her ears and singsongs, "La la la la. I don't need to know anything." Then she's across the room and the door closes behind her with a click.

I continue to lie on the bed in silence. My gaze drifts to the towel and bottle of lotion she threw next to me. Reaching over, I grab the bottle and read the label. "Sunshine Kisses." Flipping open the top, I inhale a whiff. Smells like the beach with coconut and hints of vanilla. Then I snap it closed and toss it to the side. I'm not doing this. I close my eyes and conjure up every possible thing that would not be sexy.

Chords to a new song I'm writing.

The rest of the remodel I need to finish.

Math equations.

Once I'm feeling… better, I swing my legs off the bed and stand. I strip out of the clothes from yesterday and put on the clean ones Tatum brought me. I hobble to where my crutches are leaning against a chair in the near corner of the room. With them situated under my arms, I limp out of the bedroom and down the hallway into the kitchen.

Tatum's standing at the sink washing dishes. She glances up when she hears the pads of the crutches squeak against the linoleum.

"You changed. I mean, your clothes." She points a sudsy hand at me.

"Yeah. Thanks for getting them for me. I appreciate it." My gaze falls to the floor as a wave of awkward crashes through the room. "Would you like help with anything? I need something to do. I'm getting restless."

She chuckles. "It hasn't even been twenty-four hours yet."

Shifting my weight to the crutches, I inch closer to her, careful to not put too much pressure on my foot. "I don't have the patience to sit around all day. I'd rather be doing something. Anything."

"Um." Her lips press together. "You can help me rinse off these dishes."

"Done." Slowly, I move to stand next to her and lean the crutches on the counter next to me. The hum of the refrigerator and swishing of water as she washes the dishes is the only sound in the kitchen. She runs the sponge over a plate in circles. If she keeps going, she might rub a hole through the ceramic.

"I think it's clean."

"Oh. Yeah." She passes it to me.

After rinsing the plate, I run a towel over the front and back before stacking it on the counter. "You seem a little preoccupied. Something on your mind?"

"Well… I'm just curious… did you?" She presses her lips together as if she's afraid to say more.

A beat passes as I digest what she's asking. Then it hits me, but I want her to say it. "Did I? What?"

"You know…" She gestures to my crotch.

"Did I… put on pants?"

"No." Her laugh fills the air. "You're going to make me say it, aren't you?"

"Say what?" I feign innocence, but a smile pulls at my lips.

"I hate you," She whispers. Her gaze drops to the floor before meeting mine. "Did you… touch yourself?"

I drop my hands to my sides and frown. "Really? That's what you give me? Did I touch myself?"

"Yeah." She shrugs as a giggle escapes her.

I flash her a half smile and shake my head. "I didn't. Your sheets are safe."

Her gaze drops to the sink as she concentrates on washing the mug in her hand. "I wasn't worried about that. I don't know why I even asked. It's none of my business."

"Well, it is your bed, so it's a fair question."

"Before I make this conversation any more awkward, let's move on. Since you don't want to rest, what do you want to do?" She finishes washing the last mug and passes it to me.

"Maybe go for a hike. Shovel snow. Chop some wood."

She side-eyes me, but the edges of her lips pull into a smile.

I huff out a laugh. "I don't know."

"We could watch a movie. But it has to be a Christmas movie. That's my December ritual." She dries her hands on a towel and rests her butt against the counter.

"Fine. *Die Hard*." I dry my hands with the towel she just used.

"*Die Hard* is *not* a Christmas movie."

"It is one hundred percent a Christmas movie. In fact, it is the greatest Christmas movie of all time."

"If you take the Christmas out of the movie and make it any other day, the plot would be the same. If it took place during Easter, then it could be an Easter movie," she counters.

"But it doesn't. It takes place during Christmas, so it's a Christmas movie."

"Ugh. I can't with you." She rips the towel from my hands and playfully smacks me in the chest with it.

"Let's flip for it. Winner picks the movie."

She whirls around, resting a hand on her hip. "Really? A coin? We're going to let a coin pick the movie?"

"I was going to say arm wrestle, but that seemed unfair."

She rolls her eyes but giggles. "Fine. But if I win, we're watching *Love Actually.*"

I groan. "That sounds terrible."

Shoving off the counter, she saunters to the dining room table on the other side of the kitchen to where her purse is sitting. My gaze drifts down to the way her hips sway back and forth. Fuck. *C major seven to G. E minor to D. C major seven to G. E minor to D.*

"Call it in the air." She flips the coin, and it rotates end over end.

Her voice yanks me from my thoughts. "Heads."

She catches it in one hand and slaps it on top of her other hand. Slowly, she peels away. "Best two out of three."

"No. No." I grab my crutches and limp toward her until I'm standing directly in front of her. "Can't change the rules now. I won, didn't I?"

"Traitorous quarter." She slaps her palm against my chest. When she pulls away, the coin slides down and she pouts all the way into the living room.

"Thank you, Mr. Washington," I whisper to myself. I slide the quarter into the pocket of my sweats and use the crutches to follow her into the other room. She's already sitting on the couch with her legs tucked under her and a blanket draped over her lap, but something else draws my attention.

I limp toward a tall table next to her tree that showcases an entire porcelain Christmas village. "Whoa. Is this your way to take over the world?" I glance over my shoulder at Tatum.

She jumps to her feet and moves to stand next to me. "What are you talking about?"

I point to the tiny village in her living room. "Is this how you map out your holiday takeover?"

She laughs. "No. It's just one of my holiday decorations. It's a little Christmas village. It belonged to my nana."

"What goes here?" I point to a vacant spot between a toy store and a pet shop.

"It's a spot for a bookstore to complete the set-up. Every year I keep it open with hopes that I'll find it at a reasonable price."

"What does it look like?"

She grabs her phone from the couch and pulls up a picture. "Unfortunately, four-hundred dollars is a little out of my price range."

"Holy shit. That much for a little porcelain building?"

"It's basically a collector's item now. They stopped making them years ago so now the only way to get them is second hand. I've spent hours scouring the internet in hopes of finding one at a reasonable price. So far, no luck." She sighs, tucks her phone in her pocket, and makes her way back to the couch.

I tap my finger against my crutch before turning around and taking the empty spot next to her. She searches for the movie on a streaming app and presses play.

After an hour, my mind wanders. Not because I don't like the movie. I love this movie, but I've seen it so many times. I stretch out my legs in front of me and throw my arm over the back of the couch. Glancing over, Tatum picks up her phone and a picture of her and someone else on her home screen catches my attention.

"Who's that?"

"Huh?" She twists to look at me.

I nod toward her phone. "On your home screen."

"Oh." She shuts the screen off and places her phone down on the blanket. "It's no one."

"With a reaction like that I doubt it's no one. Also, most people don't keep *no one* on their home screen. That's like sacred ground. If you make the home screen, that's official shit. So, I don't believe it's *no one.*"

"You're just going to keep going until I tell you, aren't you?"

"Possibly."

She presses her lips together, before raising her eyebrows. "Would it be bad if I said it was my ex-boyfriend?"

"You still have a picture of your ex-boyfriend on your phone?" I rub my chin. "Wait. The douche at the mall? You still want to be with him?"

She fiddles with her phone case, ignoring me and not saying anything. That confirms my answer.

"You still want to be with him even though he dumped you for his younger intern?"

"Thanks for the reminder, asshat." She throws her phone at me and it lands in my lap. "Yes. No. I don't know. I can't just flip a switch and have my feelings magically disappear. We were together for years and then out of nowhere he dumped me."

"Don't forget he fired you too," I remind her. Not that she needs a reminder, but it doesn't make sense to me. "Why would you want to be with a guy like that?"

"Because I'm a glutton for punishment." She huffs out a humorless laugh. "He wasn't supposed to dump me and then move on so quickly."

"If he's moved on, maybe you should too?"

"I know."

"Let's change this right now. Unlock your phone and pass it to me." She eyes me wearily but does it anyway. I drop my arm from the couch to around her shoulder and tug her to my chest.

A sweet laugh bubbles out of her. "What are you doing?"

"Taking a picture." I hold out her phone in front of us. "Smile." I snap a picture. I tap the screen a few times and save the new picture as her home screen. Then I pass her phone back to her.

"This picture is actually cute." She stares at the screen.

"So, what happened?" Her head shifts to mine and her eyebrows pinch together, so I elaborate. "With the ex?"

She drops her phone to her lap. "I'm not entirely sure. Everything was fine. Or I thought it was fine. We were together for five years, so to me it seemed natural the next step of our relationship would be marriage. One night he wanted to go to dinner at Le Uve—"

"What's Le Uve?"

"It's an upscale Italian restaurant."

"Oh shit."

"What? What's wrong?" Her voice is frantic.

"He was giving you your last meal before your execution."

Her eyebrows knit together. "What do you mean?"

I sit up, readjusting myself, but keep my arm around her. "Like how prisoners get a last meal, usually it's something fancy like steak and lobster, before they're executed. He was giving you a last meal before he dumped you."

"Oh shit." She parrots my words.

"It's a textbook move. He was hoping you wouldn't hate him too much because at least you got a plate of spaghetti out of it."

"Pesto Frutti Di Mare, actually." She pauses. "That son of a bitch. I should have sprung for the one hundred-thirty dollar bottle of Vinate Tunina instead of just a glass."

"You should have." I run my finger up and down her shoulder.

Her wide-eyes flit to mine. "Wait. How do you know about this? How many girls have you dumped at dinner?"

I drop my gaze, avoiding any and all eye contact with her. "I may have done it once… maybe twice."

She sits up straighter, amusement written on her face. "Oh my god! That's such a jerk move!"

"I know, but it was a long time ago. It sounds like maybe you didn't get any closure."

"Yeah. Maybe." Her gaze drops to her lap before directing her attention back to the TV, apparently not wanting to continue with the conversation.

We watch the rest of the movie in silence, but I never remove my arm from around her shoulders, and she never makes a move to pull away either. As the credits roll, I stretch my legs out. My right side goes cold from the loss of her as she sits up.

"Not a terrible movie, but it's still not a Christmas movie." She flashes me a smile.

I throw my head back against the couch. "We can watch it again to convince you."

She shakes her head. "Not happening."

"Suit yourself."

"What should we do next? Another movie?"

"Actually, I'm going to go home. That way, you can have your bed to yourself tonight."

"Are you sure? I don't mind. I just want to make sure you'll be alright."

"I'll be fine." I sit up and rise to my feet. There is no way I'll be able to stay another night in her bed and not kiss her. Not wrap her in my arms and hold her. Make her forget all about her ex-boyfriend because he didn't cherish her. She deserves to be cherished. I want to be the guy to do that for her, but I can't.

"Let me drive you. It'll be easier than trying to walk with crutches in the snow and ice."

All I can do is nod.

FAKE DATE

CHAPTER EIGHTEEN
★ ★ ★

Tatum

My heels echo off the polished porcelain tile floor of the Dashiell Ballroom before coming to a stop in front of a podium where a young woman is standing. I pass her my invitation as she welcomes me to Under the Mistletoe. I give her a warm smile and nod, but what I really want to do is bolt out of here. It's not that I don't want to be here, but I don't want to be here. I would be a terrible sister if I left Olivia hanging though. I inhale a deep breath, knowing I'm here for at least a couple of hours. My entire morning was spent prepping myself for the nine billion questions I'm going to get about Adam and why he's not here and I'm still not ready.

Peering to my left, the ballroom is filled with lavish dark green and deep red decorations that radiate elegance and festive charm. A giant, glistening chandelier hangs from the ceiling, casting a warm glow over the room. A ten-foot Christmas tree covered with intricately designed ornaments and twinkling lights stands along the back wall. Wreaths and garlands swoop around the perimeter, adding a touch of festive sophistication. Luxurious linens and shimmering candle lit centerpieces cover all the tables. I have to give it to my mom. She didn't spare any expense for this event.

I barely have time to remove my coat and pass it to the coat check before my mom is swarming me.

"Oh Tatum! You look so beautiful." She rests her hands on my shoulders and presses her cheek to both of mine. "Where is Adam?" She glances over my shoulder, expecting to see him close by.

No "How are you? I'm glad you came." She's more concerned about my boyfriend, or ex-boyfriend, but this really shouldn't surprise me. She did it to Olivia so it's only fitting she does the same to me. "Adam. So, about that—"

"Tatum!" Olivia wraps her arms around me and whirls me around. I'm thankful for the interruption. "You'll never guess who I heard back from!"

My eyes go wide. "No way!"

"Yes! We are going to have the most amazing food at our event. It will trump all foods at any event." Olivia's wide grin never leaves her face.

Our mom clears her throat. "Hi, Olivia."

Olivia twists around. "Hi Mother. I didn't see you there." She flashes her a fake, snarky smile. Olivia totally saw her, but purposely ignored her, which has been going on since the whole Ledger and our parents' debacle.

"So, you got Chef Louis-Paul to cater your event," our mom says very matter of factly.

"I did. And I did it all on my own." Olivia holds her

head up high. She's worked her ass off to get her event coordinator business off the ground. With each event she does, she gets new clients and with each party, she finds new connections. Pretty soon, every party in Harbor Highlands will be organized by Olivia with me by her side.

"Congratulations. I've heard he's a hard chef to commit to events." While she may have said the words, her congratulations are anything but. Then she returns her attention to me. "So, you never said anything about Adam. Is he coming?"

I was hoping she would have moved on from the question, but I guess not. With my shoulders squared and my head held high, I inhale a deep breath, knowing it's time to rip off the proverbial Band-Aid. "Actually, he's not."

"Is he busy with work again?" She raises a hand and fusses with a strand of my hair. "I swear he works so much I wouldn't be surprised if he has a cot at the office." She cackles to herself.

I move my head and step away. "No. He's not coming…" I inhale a deep breath, preparing myself for what she'll say next. "Because we're not together anymore."

She gasps and rests her hand on her chest. "What happened?" Leaning in so no one else can hear, she whispers, "Did he break up with you?"

My heart plummets to the ground, leaving a Tatum sized heart shape indent in the floor. I laugh to myself. Of course, her first reaction would be that he broke up with me. Even though he did, it still stings. "What makes you think he broke up with me? Never mind. It doesn't matter. We're no longer together."

"While this isn't ideal, I was hoping we could add a lawyer to the family to go with the mechanic we got." Her gaze narrows at Olivia as sarcasm laces her voice. "But this works out perfectly. Dr. Berkshire has a newly single son. I'll have to introduce you two."

"Don't do it," Olivia softly sing-songs into her wineglass.

My gaze flits to her, and she discreetly shakes her head. I shift my attention back to our mom. "That's not a good idea. It's a recent breakup. I'm not sure I want to date again so soon."

"Nonsense." She flicks her wrist in the air. "You can't go to your own event without a date. It's not a good look. Come with me, I'll introduce you." She tugs on my hand.

My eyes go wide as I stare at Olivia. I don't know what to do right now. Being set up by my mom is the last thing I want. After everything that went down with Olivia, I know her wanting to set me up is only to benefit her and her alone.

Olivia's hand reaches out and grips my other wrist and spits out, "She already has a date."

My brows furrow in confusion because I certainly don't have a date.

"She does?" My mom twists to face me. "Is that true?"

Now, it's like I'm in a tug of war match with my body being the rope. And I need Olivia to win. "Um, yes?"

She drops my wrist. "I can't wait to meet him next weekend." With a tight lipped smile, she saunters away. I'm sure to talk or flirt with Dr. Berkshire's son herself.

As soon as she's out of earshot, I grip Olivia's elbow. "What the hell? I don't have a date!" I whisper yell. "Who am I going to find to be my date in less than a week?"

"I was saving your ass. You're welcome. But also, perhaps a certain hot new neighbor can be your date." She tips back her glass of wine, swallowing a sip.

"Connor? No way! Not happening."

"Why not?"

"Because…" Shit, I don't know why. The short span of our relationship, if you can call it that, has been a rollercoaster ride. Asking him to do me this favor seems like a major disaster. Plus, Adam will be there. Ugh! My life is a hot mess. An explosive disaster.

"See. You don't have a reason why you shouldn't. You know Adam is going to be there. Don't give him the upper hand in thinking you're still pining over him."

With one high heeled foot crossed over the other, I hold a tray of cookies in my hand like a server. Softly, I knock on his door. When it flies open, his heated gaze rakes over my body in nothing but a white lace bra and panties. He doesn't say a word, the lust in his eyes says it all. Not wanting to waste another second, he rips the cookies from my hand. His arm wraps around my waist and drags me inside. He walks me backward toward the roaring fireplace and lays me down on a plush makeshift bed. Without saying a word, he proceeds to eat cookie crumbles off my half naked body, starting on my chest and then working his way down to my stomach. My fingers thread through his dark hair as he makes his descent toward my pussy.

I jolt awake, jackknifing out of bed, fingers still clenching the blanket. A sheen of sweat covers my entire body. My heart hammers in my chest. I blink a few times as I smack down to reality. I'm at my house and not in Connor's living room. What the hell was that? The dream was so real. And the ache between my legs proves it.

All through the night, ever since Olivia planted the seed, I thought about Connor and asking him to be my date. Apparently, he not only occupies my daytime thoughts, but also my dreams. Now, not only am I sexually frustrated but I'm still without a date. Groaning, I flop down onto the mattress and drape my arm over my eyes. At the very least, I wish I could have seen the dream to the end.

Since I can only make one of these things a reality, I roll out of bed and throw a robe over my shoulders. Once I'm in the kitchen, I pull out bowls, measuring cups, flour, eggs, butter, and chocolate chips and I set out to bake my bribe.

After the first batch didn't rise how I liked, I toss them out and start again, meticulously following the directions to ensure the next batch is perfect. When one good batch is done, I bake another, and another. There is something therapeutic when it comes to baking. It helps me clear my head. Plus, flipping through the pages of my nana's recipe book fills me with a sense of calmness. I know she's watching over me each and every time I bake one of her recipes.

Once all the cookies are baked, I set them on racks to cool. The water is hot and soothing as I jump into the shower and prepare myself to talk to Connor. When I step out, I wrap a towel around my body and another over my hair. Yanking open my dresser drawer, I pull out a black bra and pause. My mind flits back to the dream I had this morning. A slow smile tugs at my lips and I put it back, grabbing a white lace one instead. I finish getting ready, pile cookies onto a plate, and head across the street.

When I'm standing in front of his door, I inhale a deep breath and knock. While I wait, I rehearse what I'm going to say because I'm not sure if he's going to be up to this. He wasn't my first choice. He wasn't a choice at all. In fact, this entire ordeal wasn't even a thing until Olivia made it a thing. Now, I just have to go for it and hope he says yes because there is no backup option. It's all or nothing.

A few seconds later, the door opens and Connor's broad shoulders fill the doorway. Before he says anything, I spit out, "I need a favor." All he does is stare at me, forearm resting against the doorjamb. Then I remember about the bribery cookies and shove them at his chest. "And I baked you cookies. There are no raisins this time. I promise. In fact, I removed all the raisins from my house, so there is no way for cross contamination."

He eyes the cookies, then me. "So, we're the doing favors for each other kind of friends now?"

I pause, searching for the right words to convince him to say yes. Because what are we? Are we friends? Just neighbors? Two people who've slept together one time?

When I don't say anything, he steals a cookie off the plate and takes a bite. "What kind of favor?" he asks around a mouth full of cookie.

Here goes nothing. "I need you to be my fake boyfriend." I flash him a wide, nervous grin.

Cookie crumbs fly out of his mouth as he half chokes, half coughs from my words. Then he's spitting the rest out off to the side of the steps.

"Hey! There're no raisins. Why'd you spit it out?" I prop my hand on my hip.

He wipes away any residual crumbs from his face and beard. "Say that again? I don't think I heard you right."

My shoulders fall and I glare at him. "You heard me just fine. I need you to be my fake boyfriend or just a fake date. There's a holiday party I'm hosting, and Adam and his new girlfriend will be there, plus my mom is expecting me to show up with a date. If I don't, she'll try to set me up with some doctor's son, or lawyer friend, or someone who I have no interest in."

"Wow. That's a lot to unpack." He swallows another bite of the cookie as he contemplates his answer. Under his beard, his strong jaw clenches as he chews. I can't help but stare as his Adam's apple bobs up and down when he swallows.

"Let me get this straight. You want me to make him jealous?"

"Not jealous. But make him realize that he gave up the best thing that ever happened to him, and he's missing out. And I've moved on to bigger and better things." I rush out all the words so maybe he doesn't get the real motive behind my ask.

He raises an eyebrow, seeing through my lie.

"Okay jealous." I huff. "So, can you help me out? Pretty please?"

His beard twitches as he presses his lips together. "What's in it for me?" He steals another cookie off the plate and shoves it in his mouth.

"I'll do anything," I plead.

"Anything?" He wiggles his eyebrows.

"Almost anything. You perv." I playfully slap his chest.

He raises his hands up in defense. "I didn't say anything. You're the one who went there." He takes a bite out of his cookie and chews. "So, I'm making an ex-boyfriend jealous, and I need to play nice with the parents. This seems like a lot of work. I don't know…"

"Please. I'm begging you. I'm all out of ideas. I need you."

"You need me, huh? Could you say that again, maybe softer and more seductive?"

I glare at him.

He releases a hearty laugh. "Okay. Okay. I need to think of something good. How about an IOU?"

"Great!" My lips split into a wide grin. "So, I need you to dress nice. Suit and tie—"

He holds his hands up, palms out. "Whoa! You never mentioned a suit."

"It's a very formal, Black tie event."

He runs a hand over his beard. "Who attends these types of events?"

I tap my chin. "A lot of business professionals, doctors, lawyers, entrepreneurs. Basically, anyone who's anyone got an invite." He glances at the clouds. My stomach turns with each passing second that he doesn't say anything. "Please help me. I need your help." I flash him the sweetest smile I can, hoping he'll take pity on me.

His head falls and his gaze meets mine. "Fine, but the suit's going to be extra."

"Yes!" I wrap my arms around his waist in a quick hug. His hand runs up and down my back before I pull away. "What do you want?"

"Another IOU."

"Done." I pivot on my heel. Mission accomplished.

"Hey! What about the cookies? Those are mine."

I spin around, holding up the plate. "What? These cookies?"

"Yeah. Aren't those for me?"

"You can have them for an IOU." I flash him a devilish smile.

He pauses. His gaze flits between me and the cookies. "You drive a hard bargain, Tinsel, but deal."

With the cookies in my hand, I stretch my arm out and he snatches them from my grip. "I'll let you know the details."

"It's a date." He winks at me while shoving the other half of the cookie into his mouth before closing the door.

What did I get myself into?

MAKE HIM JEALOUS

CHAPTER NINETEEN
★ ★ ★

Connor

This isn't a big deal. I'm just doing a favor for a friend. Then why are my palms so sweaty? We're friends right? Friends who fuck, maybe? Well, fucked once, but I certainly wouldn't be opposed to making it plural. I run my hands down the sides of my black slacks. It's been years since I've been on a date. But is this an actual date? No. I'm just a friend doing a favor for another friend. At the end there will be no kiss good night. No lingering glances at each other. Even if she bites her lower lip in that sexy way that makes my dick twitch. No. None of that. I scrub my hand down my beard. Fuck. I'm more worried about being her date than I am about anyone finding out who I am. When she told me their occupations I felt more at ease. If I had to guess, they don't listen to a lot of rock music.

Her use of the words "fake date" flash in my mind like a neon sign. So this isn't actually a date. That's all she wants. No feelings. So then why am I disappointed she didn't call it a date? Once again, I have to remind myself I'm not staying. This is only temporary.

Since I didn't bring a suit with me because I wasn't expecting to be asked to a charity gala, I went out and bought one. Luckily, I found a seamstress who could hem the pants for me on such short notice.

When Tatum told me the time of the event, I insisted I'd pick her up at her house since I was her date and all, so I jump in my truck and back it out of my driveway right into hers. Leaving my truck running so it stays warm, I climb out, grab the gift I bought for her, and stroll to the door. I lightly knock and only a few seconds tick by before it opens. One look at her and I forget how to breathe. She's absolutely stunning in the deep navy dress that hugs all her mouthwatering curves. Somehow, it even makes her blue eyes shine even brighter. Everything about not kissing her flies right out the window. My hand twitches to grab her and claim her as mine. Make her forget about her ex-boyfriend. Instead, I shove my hand into my front pocket to restrain myself and use my words. "You're so beautiful. Perfection."

A pink blush covers her cheeks. She brushes a lock of hair behind her ear. "Thank you. You look pretty handsome yourself. Let me get my shoes on."

She slides her feet into her heels that now give her an extra three inches. She's still shorter than me, but now I don't have to bend down as far to kiss her. I imagine what her plump red lips would feel like against mine. My dick twitches in my slacks. Shit. *Stop thinking about kissing her.*

"I got you something. A friendly gift. No big deal." I hold out the gift bag to her.

Her gaze flits from me then to the bag and back to me. "You didn't have to get me anything."

I inhale a deep breath, unsure of why I'm so nervous. "I know. But I saw it and knew you'd like it."

Her fingers slide under the ribbon handle. With her other hand she pushes tissue paper to the side as she peers inside. A small gasp of surprise escapes her. When she glances up at me, her eyes are as wide as her smile. "Oh Connor…" She pulls out the exact porcelain bookstore figurine she showed me previously. "This is too much. This costs too much. Let me give you something." She moves to grab her purse, but I stop her.

"No. I don't want anything. I couldn't bear the idea of you having an incomplete Christmas village. It's not very Christmas of you. So really, it's more of a gift for me."

She exhales a small laugh. "You're so full of it." She stares down at the figurine for a moment then up at me. "Thank you." Rising on her tippy toes, she presses a kiss to my cheek, just above my beard.

I'm a step behind her as she strolls into the living room. After she sets the bookstore in the empty space of her Christmas village, I freeze, holding my breath.

Her eyebrows knit together. "What's that look for?"

My eye shift left and then right. When nothing happens, I exhale. "I was waiting for a Christmas portal to open up and swallow us whole like some sort of Christmas voodoo. Transport us to a three hundred and sixty-five day Christmas extravaganza. Christmas all day, every day."

She barks out a laugh while the brightest smile covers her face. I live for her smiles. They make me forget about everything else.

"I won't lie, that would be my jam. But we should get going or I will have to conjure up some of that Christmas voodoo." She wiggles her eyebrows.

I grab her coat and hold it up for her as she slides her arms inside. After she collects her purse, we step outside as a gust of cold wind flutters past us reddening my cheeks. Luckily, the beard keeps the rest of my face warm.

At my truck, I open the door for her and with one foot on the rail, I grip her waist and help her all the way in. Mostly, it's just an excuse to touch her. Once she's in, I round the hood and climb in.

Before shifting into drive, I glance her way. Even in the darkness, she sparkles. "You look stunning."

"You told me that already."

"Shit. I did, didn't I? I can't give you too many compliments. They might go to your head."

She laughs and it's the sweetest sound. I flash her a wink before pulling out of her driveway. The entire way to the hall, we make small talk. She asks me about the progress on the house and I ask her about the Christmas decorating and neighborhood contest. I was a little shocked when she told me she tried to get real reindeer, but they require a lot of different permits, and she didn't want to deal with that this year. Actually, I shouldn't be shocked. That would be exactly something she would do.

I pull up to the curb of the ballroom and pass the keys to the valet. Before Tatum steps out, I'm opening her door. Her warm fingers clasp around mine as she climbs out. Snowflakes flutter down from the sky like glitter that matches the sparkle in her bright blue eyes. My mission for tonight is to make sure she has a good time and forgets all about the ex. By the end of the night, I want her to forget all about Adam. Forget his name. Forget he even exists.

When both her feet are on the sidewalk, I hold out my elbow and she loops her arm with mine. She glances up at me, a warm smile covering her lips. And fuck me, it's a smile that can melt my icy heart. And it's everything I don't need right now. I shake the thought away and focus on the task at hand.

Before we walk through the door, I stop us. "Can I make one stipulation on the evening?"

"What's that?"

"Can I just be your date? Nothing else? Like if anyone asks about me, I'm only your date."

Her eyebrows pull together as she peers up at me. "Why's that?"

"Tonight's your night. I want the focus to be on you. No one needs to know who I am."

"Oh. Um. Sure. But also, that's your last IOU." She flashes me a bright smile, pleased with herself that she came out unscathed from the IOUs.

"Again, you drive a hard bargain, Tinsel, but deal." Her eyes light up at her nickname and she holds out her hand for me to shake. When I clasp my fingers around hers, I lift her hand and place a soft kiss on the back of it. Even in the dark evening sky, I can see the slight tinge of pink in her cheeks. And I know it's not from the cold.

We drop our coats off at the coat check and stroll side by side down a long hallway that opens to an elegant ballroom. Shimmering silver and tranquil blue drapes fill the room, simulating the perfect winter wonderland. Delicate silver ornaments dangle from the ceiling in staggered lengths, while intricate snowflake ornaments cover the walls. Icy blue linens with silver runners cover the tables, creating a frosty opulence. The ambiance is complete with faux snow accents that lend a romantic touch to the entire space.

"You did all this?" I ask Tatum.

"I didn't do it all by myself. I had some help."

"This is amazing. You're amazing." A light pink blush covers her cheeks. I grip her chin and force her to meet my gaze. "I'm serious. Don't let anyone tell you otherwise."

She nods, but I'm not sure she truly believes me.

"Tatum! Look how amazing everything turned out." A girl who shares an uncanny resemblance to Tatum wraps her in a tight hug. "And this must be your date?" Her gaze shifts to me and then back to Tatum.

"Yes. Olivia, this is Connor." Tatum waves her hand toward me. "Connor, this is my sister, Olivia."

I hold out my hand to Olivia. "Nice to meet you."

"Likewise. It's great to finally put a face to the name." Tatum elbows her in the ribs. Olivia tilts her head at Tatum and mouths "ouch" while rubbing her side.

A tall, muscular guy with tattoos that peek from the cuffs of his button-down shirt and up his neck strolls up to us and throws an arm over Olivia's shoulders. His tattooed hand rubs over her bicep. Olivia whirls around in his arms, rises to her tippy toes, and kisses him. When they're done with their mini make-out session, Olivia turns to me. "Connor, this is my boyfriend, Ledger. Ledger, this is Tatum's date, Connor."

We shake hands and exchange pleasantries. When Olivia and Ledger continue to make their rounds around the room, I bend down and whisper in Tatum's ear, "So, you've been talking about me, huh?"

"Don't think too much about it. I told her how annoying you are." She smirks.

I bark out a laugh. "Like how annoyingly charming? Annoyingly good looking? Annoyingly funny?"

"No. Just annoying." Her hand grips mine as she tugs me along to welcome the new guests.

Over the next hour, Tatum introduces me to practically everyone in the room. Lawyers. Bankers. Doctors. Business owners. When I'm asked what I do, the only answer I give them is "I'm Tatum's date." No one asks any more questions. They only politely nod and move on to the next person for conversation. For a moment, I forget who I am and pretend I'm an ordinary guy who's spending an evening escorting a beautiful girl to a party.

We weave in and out of tables as we make our way toward the bar. My palm softly runs along Tatum's lower back when she suddenly stops dead in her tracks.

"What's wrong?" I glance down as all the color drains from her face. Then I follow her gaze that's trained straight ahead and land on a guy in a navy suit with a brunette on his arm.

"Adam's here," she whispers.

This time I get a clearer view of her ex. He's clean shaven and clean cut. While he wears a smile on his face, it's more forced than anything. One he's perfected over the years. His movements seem very choreographed and stiff, like he wouldn't know a good time if it smacked him upside the face. For the short while I've known Tatum, she seems fun and free-spirited. The complete opposite of this guy. What could she possibly see in him?

"He's coming this way," she mutters. Her spine goes rigid as she squares her shoulders, making herself appear taller. She runs a hand down her dress to brush away any imaginary wrinkles and I wonder who the hell this woman is.

"Hi, Adam. I'm so glad you could make it." Tatum's voice is bright, bubbly, and an octave higher than normal. "Lindsey. I'm glad you could make it as well." She gives her a curt nod.

Adam wraps an arm around Lindsey's waist and pulls

her flush against his body. My gaze is glued on Tatum as I watch her watch Adam and her mouth curls downward a fraction from his show of affection. Well, fuck. If my job is to make him jealous. Time to up the ante.

I run a fingertip over Tatum's soft cheekbone. When she glances my way, I cup her cheek and press my lips to hers. She squeaks out a surprise but doesn't stop me. In fact, a low moan rumbles in the back of her throat as she kisses me back. I break the kiss and slowly pull back and brush my nose against hers. She purses her lips to kiss me again, but I keep my mouth millimeters from hers. Her eyes flutter open, lips still parted. Desire swirls in her irises, and I know it's not because of Adam.

"I'm going to get a drink. Do you want anything?"

Her mouth closes and then opens, but she doesn't say anything and instead she nods. I drop my hand from her cheek. Twisting around, I hold it out to Adam. "Hi, I'm Connor. Tatum's date."

Adam's gaze, which flits from Tatum to me to Tatum and back to me, doesn't go unnoticed. Unsure of who I am and what I'm doing here, he hesitates before gripping my hand in his. "Adam." He nods to the woman next to him. "This is Lindsey." I squeeze his hand a little harder than normal, but I hold his gaze with a hard stare. I've met plenty of guys like him, ones who prance around like their shit doesn't stink. Hate to break it to him, but I see right through him and his shit stinks the worst.

Halfway to the bar, I spare a glance back and Tatum's posture is back to being prim and proper. I shake my head. I've seen the real her and this isn't it. When I return, Tatum is laughing at something Adam said, but it's not her normal sweet, bubbly laugh. It's stifled, like she's holding back. I've made her laugh, a real, genuine laugh where she's almost in tears from laughing so hard. This is not that. I pass Tatum her glass of wine. "What's so funny?"

"Adam was just telling us about how one of his clients filled in the wrong box on some paperwork." She releases another insincere laugh.

"You had to be there." Adam waves it off.

"Yeah. I guess so." I roll my eyes.

A middle-aged couple joins us in our small circle. He has salt and pepper hair while the woman has had far too many Botox injections to make her appear younger, but instead it makes her look plastic.

"Adam. It's so good to see you. I've been hearing a lot of good things about the practice," the older man says.

"Thank you, sir. It's just all in a day's work," Adam replies.

"Tatum, I can't believe you let this one get away," the older man says.

Tatum doesn't say anything, just gives him a tight-lipped smile. But I can see all the brightness inside her dim. Fuck. I've never seen her so defeated.

I hold out my hand to the older man. "Hi, I'm Connor."

"Senator John Ellis. I'm Tatum's father. This is my wife, Tamara." He gestures to the woman next to him.

"Nice to meet you both," I say.

Tamara's gaze wanders up and down my body like I'm a tasty treat for her to devour. It's a little unsettling.

The senator clears his throat. "So, what do you do, Connor?"

"Tonight, my only job is to be Tatum's date." I wrap my arm around her waist and tug her to me. Her warm body flush against mine feels like home.

Tamara reaches up and runs a painted fingernail over Tatum's hair above her ear. "Oh honey, you should have worn your hair down tonight. This neckline is too harsh for your oval face," she whispers, but not quiet enough for me not to hear.

Tatum's body tenses under my fingertips. My fingers clench into a fist. What kind of mother says that to their daughter? Instead of giving Tamara a piece of my mind, I direct my attention to Tatum. "I think she's the most beautiful woman in the room tonight."

Tatum's gaze lifts to meet mine. A small glimmer of adoration fills her eyes. Luckily, they announce for everyone to find their seats as dinner will be served and our table is far away from theirs.

With my hand on Tatum's lower back, I escort her to our table that has our names embossed on place settings. Outside of a wedding reception, I've never been to anything this fancy. And usually at weddings it's mostly to keep argumentative family members away from one another. I wonder if that's the same thing here?

I pull out Tatum's chair and she takes a seat. As I bend down to sit next to her, I whisper, "I don't know what you see in him."

"Who?" She turns toward me, crossing one leg over the other, and reaches for her wine.

"Adam. He's so full of himself." I scoot my chair in.

"What are you talking about? You met him for like five seconds. He's very confident. Self-assured."

"And completely self-absorbed. And what the hell happened to you when you saw him?"

She gasps in shock. "What did I do?"

"You became a different person. Prim and proper with a stick shoved up your ass. Like you had to be perfect. That's not the Tatum I know." I lean back in my chair and swallow a gulp of my whiskey.

"You think you have it all figured out." She twists so she's facing the center of the table.

I sit up and lean toward her so only she can hear. "Just be you. That girl has fire and passion inside her. Not the dull and fake person back there. Don't let anyone steal your sunshine."

Her blue eyes meet mine and the corners of her lips slightly tip up. I know whoever that person was in front of Adam wasn't the real her. That was the fakest personality I've ever seen, and I've encountered many fake people in my life. I saw through that shit immediately. Normally, their motives are for their own selfish needs, like they want something, or they believe they aren't good enough. So, I can't figure out why she'd do it.

For the rest of the evening, I make it my mission to make her forget all about Adam and let her be herself.

The server sets a Filet Mignon with roasted potatoes and asparagus in front of me and Tatum gets the Chicken Marsala. I cut off a piece a steak and put it in my mouth. I fight not to moan out loud. It's melt-in-your-mouth tender and coated in a rich and savory garlic butter sauce.

Cutting off another piece, I hold it out to Tatum. "You have to try this. It's so good."

She eyes the fork and then me. "You're going to feed me?"

"Yes." I wiggle the fork, coaxing her to open her mouth.

"Adam never fed me, let alone shared his food with me."

Bending down so my mouth is next to her ear, I whisper, "I'll let you in on a little secret. I'm not Adam. Now open up."

She releases a small laugh before her red lips part.

Then those same lips wrap around the fork before sliding off. It shouldn't be so hypnotizing, but it is.

For the rest of dinner, we eat our meals while continuing to feed each other small bites off each other's plate while conversing and joking around. This time I know her laugh is genuine by the way her eyes crinkle in the corners. When I glance two tables over, I catch sight of Adam staring back at us. Judging by the scowl on his face, mission accomplished.

THE HOLIDAY ESCORT

CHAPTER TWENTY

* ⭐ *

Tatum

Connor surprised the hell out of me during dinner. He was so attentive and oddly affectionate, not that I'm complaining. It just caught me off guard. Throughout the entire dinner, his hand would brush against my leg or my shoulder. He would lean in and whisper in my ear with mostly compliments, but sometimes it would be something that would make me laugh. His presence brought me a sense of calm. I forgot all about Adam and my parents and all the shitty baggage they carry.

Usually, when I'm at these types of events with Adam, I'm dragged around like arm candy as he talks to everyone of importance. But with Connor, it's different. His focus has been on me and only me. After we finish dinner, a small jazz band serenades the room with a smooth melody.

Connor rises to his feet and holds out an open palm to me. "May I have this dance?"

I flash him a wide grin before placing my hand in his. He leads me to the center of the wood floor, where several other couples gracefully glide as they dance. His fingers intertwine with mine while his other hand presses against my lower back, holding me close to him. The touch is simple but still causes butterflies to take flight in my belly.

"I never would have guessed you could slow dance."

"Can't have you knowing all my secrets." He twirls me around before hauling me back into his chest.

I chuckle. "I guess not."

Gently, we sway back and forth to the soothing sounds of a saxophone. There's something oddly comforting about being this close to Connor. His hand drifts an inch down, his pinky brushing at the curve of my ass. A heat of electricity surges through me from the simple touch. I press myself closer to him, loving how his body molds perfectly to mine. He's sweet and caring. He drives me mad one moment and makes me laugh the next. Right now, him holding me in his arms, there is nowhere else I'd rather be. Resting my head on his chest, I inhale a deep breath, the faint scent of his cedar and sandalwood cologne invades my senses. The steady thumping of his heartbeat under my cheek could almost lulls me to sleep. This is everything a perfect moment should be.

"I need to speak to you," my mom whispers through gritted teeth, startling me from my thoughts. She grips my elbow a little harder than normal. "Now."

I glance up at Connor. "Sorry. If you'll excuse me."

She drags me off to the side of the dance floor. My eyebrows pinch together as I rack my brain about what could have her so upset.

"Tatum Elizabeth. Explain yourself right this instant. Do you have any idea what you've done?" she seethes.

"Explain what?" I am absolutely dumbfounded about what the hell she's talking about. Connor has done nothing wrong. He's been a complete gentleman all evening. Unless Adam said something to her to get me back somehow.

"Your *date*." She jerkily nods toward the dance floor.

"Connor?"

"I'm sure that's not even his real name. Guys who do what he does wouldn't give out their real name. Do you not understand how this is going to look for your father's career, on me, on this family?"

Now I'm completely confused. "What are you talking about?"

"Everyone is talking. Everyone knows."

"Knows what?" I raise my voice higher than normal because clearly everyone knows but me.

"You hired an escort as your date," she whisper yells.

"Um. No. I didn't."

"Everyone is talking about how your date is your date." She uses air quotes around the last two words. "Were you that desperate you hired someone to be your date? Please don't tell me you're paying for sex. That's a scandal this family doesn't need."

"Oh my God. No. Why would everyone think I hired an escort—oh." Then it dawns on me. When everyone asks Connor what he does for a living, we've been telling everyone for tonight, he's only my date. Of course, they took that information and ran with it. It's amazing how the gossip runs rampant around here. I guess everyone needs something to talk about, probably to keep the focus off whatever scandal they have going on in their own life. "No. Connor's not an escort, and I'm not paying him for sex. He's actually my neighbor."

A wave of relief washes over her face. "Well, that's… good. This would have never happened if you let me set you up with Dr. Berkshire's son. Now, I need to go do damage control." She side eyes me before slinking off into the crowd.

I exhale a huff. For the fact that she would believe rumors about her own daughter than trust she wouldn't do something as absurd as hiring an escort is telling. When I turn around, Connor's no longer on the dance floor because why would he be, I left him. Instead, I find him at a small table chatting with Ledger. I stroll over to him and link my arm with his. The contact startling him.

"So apparently everyone thinks I hired you to be my date."

Ledger busts out laughing.

"Oh wait. It gets better. I'm also paying you for sex." This time, none of us can contain our laughter.

"Son of a bitch," Connor whines. "That was a missed opportunity."

"I wasn't going to pay you to be my date," I deadpan.

"But you did bribe me with cookies. So, if cookies were the currency, that would mean you paid me to be your date." A boyish grin fills Connor's face. "These people aren't wrong."

"It's not the same thing."

"Still have more cookies? We can work out a deal for sex." He wiggles his eyebrows.

I unhook my arm and playfully backhand his bicep. "I hate you."

"Hate sex. Even better." Connor flashes me a bright, wide smile. A part of me wonders what he would look like without the beard.

"I would have let Tamara and the rest of the gossiping socialites stew on that one for a while longer. It's more fun to watch them squirm." Ledger shakes his head before taking a sip of his whiskey.

Not that long ago, he was the center of the gossip mill, but mostly because he's dating Olivia. The thing I admire about Ledger is he never once backed down. He stood toe to toe with all of them to fight for Olivia. She definitely got lucky with him.

The rest of the evening carries on as normal, or as normal as these events can go. There were only two proverbial fires we needed to put out. One involved a socialite who had one too many wine spritzers and rumors of a cheating spouse surfaced. The other was an argument between two men and their business deal that went wrong. Luckily, Olivia and I were on top of it and got security to escort them out with minimal damage. But the real entertainment was Connor's escort debacle. He even ramped up his escorting duties by showering me with extra attention. Some women side eyed him while others slipped him their phone number. His whole I don't give a shit demeanor about this situation made me realize I shouldn't care about their perception of me either. Their minds are already made up regardless, including Adam.

From across the room I spot Adam talking with Mr. Findley, a local business owner. It's now or never. With my shoulders squared, I stride across the room until I'm standing next to the two gentlemen.

"Excuse me." I turn toward Mr. Findley. "Sorry for the interruption." Then I face Adam. "I'm over you."

His eyebrows pinch together but before he can respond, I spin around on my heel and strut away, feeling ten times lighter on my feet.

At the end of the night, after everyone has left, Connor dumped all the phone numbers given to him in the trash, stating there's no way their cookies are better than mine.

As we drive through our neighborhood, we make small talk about the event and laugh at how ridiculous some adults can act. When the conversation stops, the cab of the truck goes silent except for the low hum of electric flows between us. Or perhaps, it's all my imagination. Then he spares a quick glance my way and I know he feels it too. It's like we both have a million things to say but neither of us want to be the first to say them. Turning away, I stare out the window as the street lights pass by, needing to distract myself from the tension that's ready to snap like a rubber band that's pulled too tight.

My foot nervously bounces on the floorboard. The street lights offering very little distraction, so I break the silence. "Thanks for being my fake date. It was one of the best times I've had at one of these events." Not knowing what to do, I fidget with my purse in my lap.

For a brief second, he glances my way, then trains his eyes forward on the road. "It was my pleasure."

His tone is stoic. I'm unsure if he actually means it or if it's the polite thing to say. Even in the dim light from the dashboard I can see his jaw flex and tighten beneath his beard. I want to reach across the center console and run my hand over his cheek, soothing any of the tension. Instead, I stare out the window again as he pulls onto our road and then into my driveway. "What are you doing?"

"Taking you home." His hands grip the steering wheel.

"You don't have to do that. You're just across the street. I can walk home."

"What kind of fake date would I be if I made you walk home? Plus, I picked you up. I can drop you off." He turns to face me. "That's what a proper date would do."

"Yeah, like a whole fifty feet." I smile.

"It's the thought, not the distance, that counts." He shrugs.

After he shifts his truck into park, kills the engine, and steps out. He rounds the hood and opens my door. I hop down and with his hands on my waist, he helps me. I loop my arm through his and we walk side by side up to my front door.

Before unlocking the door, I whirl around to face him. His heated gaze is locked on mine and I suck in the corner of my bottom lip. The seconds that tick by feel like minutes. My lips part before I say, "Thanks again for tonight."

"Anytime you need a fake date, you know where to find me."

"Are you sure? I might hold you to that." Now I'm stalling because I don't want this night to end. A gust of wind flutters past us and I pull my coat tighter around me.

"I better let you get inside before you freeze."

I nod. But what I really want to do is grab him and kiss the hell out him. Invite him inside and show him exactly how much I appreciate him and what he did tonight. Confess he's the only thing on my mind. And that he's a big grumpy scrooge, but he's the sweetest person toward me. Instead of doing all that, I fish my keys out of my clutch because being vulnerable sucks.

"Wait." His cold fingers gently wrap around my wrist.

I glance over my shoulder and there's a brief pause.

He drops my wrist and instead grabs my waist, spinning me around, then his lips are on mine. It's soft and sweet but sends an electric jolt through my body. Forget being cold. His kiss just sent an inferno raging through me, awakening things I didn't know were buried. And it's entirely too short.

He pulls away a fraction, but he's still close enough that his warm lips graze mine. "I've wanted to do that since I picked you up."

A beat passes as I glance from his lips to meet his eyes. "But you kissed me earlier."

He shrugs one shoulder. "That was for show. This one was for real."

Everything screams I shouldn't do this. I shouldn't want him. He's not the guy for me. But right now, he's the only thing that makes sense. The only thing I want. And I'm exhausted from fighting it. Overthinking it. He's here. I'm here. And I'm just going to go for it.

I tug on the lapels of his jacket, hauling him to me, and slam my lips to his. He wraps his arms around me. I relish the way his large frame presses against mine, almost like a cocoon. His forearm rests against my lower back, just above the curve of my ass. The impressive bulge in his slacks presses against my belly.

"I could kiss you all night. Spend hours worshiping your body." His words are a whisper across my lips.

"I suggest we do that inside before our neighbors call the cops for indecent exposure."

He chuckles and steps away, but his hands never leave my waist.

My fingers shake as Connor presses his lips to the side of my neck. His hot breath mixed with the cool air sends shivers down my spine. He nips and sucks on my sensitive skin.

I release a slow moan. "If you keep that up, I'm never going to get this door open."

"So, the neighbors might get a show after all."

It takes all my willpower to concentrate on getting the door open. Finally, with a quick twist of the key, the door opens. Without any hesitation I grip Connor's tie and tug him through the open doorway. Once inside, he kicks the door shut and then his lips fuse to mine again. Fast and frantic, like the fate of the world depends on this kiss. He walks me backward into my living room, nothing but the warm glow of the Christmas tree lighting his path.

He pulls away, but his hands cup my cheeks. "I've never met someone as incredible as you. I never want this night to end."

"Let's make sure it doesn't." I press my lips to his as my hands skate over his shoulders, pushing his jacket down. My hands roam over his muscular shoulders and down his sculpted chest. He makes me feel protected. The way he touches me is soft and delicate, like he could never hurt me. It's everything that I crave. He's everything that I desire.

When he finds the zipper on my dress, he drags it down until it stops. The shoulder strap loosens and drapes across my bicep. Connor continues to pull the fabric down my body until it's loose enough to flutter to the floor. I step out of the dress and kick it to the side. His gaze wanders up and down my body, taking me in. Admiring me like I'm something to be cherished. Like he's seeing me for the first time all over again.

"Fuck. You're beautiful, Tinsel. So beautiful." He wraps one arm around my waist, tugging me to him. With this other hand, he threads his fingers through my hair and then his lips crash to mine. It's hot and sensual. Firm yet soft. I could spend all night kissing him just like this.

He breaks our kiss, pulls a blanket off the couch, and lays it on the floor. A sexy smile plays on his lips. He bends down and whispers next to my ear. "Have you ever been fucked under a Christmas tree, Tinsel?"

My breath hitches. I shake my head because I never have, but I want to. Right now. I want it so bad.

His hand skates over my waist and around my back, causing an eruption of goosebumps to sprout all over my body. He slowly lowers me to the plush blanket. His palms rest on the floor next to my head as he drops between my legs like he's doing a push-up until his large body covers mine. He's careful not to put all his weight on me. His beard scrapes against my heated skin as he presses open mouth kisses on my neck. I run my hands over the cotton of his shirt, feeling all his muscles flex and bow as he slowly rocks his growing erection against me. I spread my legs wider, wanting all of him.

He presses his lips to mine, then follows a trail across my cheek until he reaches my ear. His teeth sink into my earlobe, not hard enough to hurt but enough to send a blast of heat directly to my core. I never knew my earlobes were an erogenous zone.

"I bet you're soaked for me right now. Your tight pussy is begging to be stretched by my fat cock," he growls. His warm breath skates across the shell of my ear.

A shiver races down my spine and I buck my hips, needing him. "Yes," I pant. "Please. I need that. I need you."

"I like when you beg for my cock."

He sits up and I whimper from the loss of his warm body on mine. One by one he pops each button until his shirt falls open. It's like he's giving me a strip show and it's the hottest strip show I've ever seen. He drags it over his broad shoulders and down his arms. His sculpted chest with a light dusting of dark hair is on full display. The tattoo over his pec dances with each movement in the warm glow of the Christmas lights.

"Do you trust me?" His voice is soft.

I've only known him for a short while, but in my gut, I trust him. I trust him so much I think I'm falling for him. But I tamper down that thought. "Yes. I trust you."

Once his shirt is off, he tells me to lift my head, so I do.

The warm fabric of the sleeve drapes over my eyes as he wraps it around my head.

"Is that okay?"

My chest rises and falls in anticipation, and I nod. I'm in total darkness.

His lips brush against mine, the sensation causing my nipples to pebble. Then he whispers, "I want you to just feel everything. I want to make you feel good."

A cold draft flutters over me, the weight of his body is no longer on mine. The crinkling of plastic fills the silent room and a moment later something rests on my bottom lip.

"Open up and suck."

I open and the sweet peppermint candy slides between my lips. He slowly tunnels it in and out of my mouth, giving it a twist every now and then. When he's satisfied, he pulls it out. He trails the wet tip down my neck, leaving behind a line of sticky candy, but a second later his tongue runs along the path, licking it up. I arch my back and moan from the sensation. He flicks open the front clasp of my bra and the sides fall open. The cool air hitting my already sensitive nipples. He repeats the process as he drags the tip of the candy cane between the valley of my breasts. Again, the flat of his tongue follows the same trail. He moves his attention to my right breast.

"Fuck. I love your tits." He swirls the tip of the candy cane around my hard peak. "Your nipples are standing at attention, begging to be sucked."

"Yes." I moan and arch my back as he continues to circle the peppermint candy around my hardened nipple. While he sucks on one, he uses his other hand to softly massage the other. My hand flies up and threads through his hair. Since I can't see him, I need to touch him. His teeth sink down on my nipple and I moan. The slight sting is more pleasure than pain.

He trails the tip of the candy cane down my stomach, followed by his tongue. My body quivers from his touch and my breathing becomes labored as I wait for what he's about to do next. His fingers dip into the sides of my panties and I lift my hips. Slowly he drags the lace fabric down my legs, leaving me fully exposed to him. My body heats from the thought of his eyes on me.

He drags a finger down my slit, swirling the pad through my wetness. "Just as I thought. Drenched." He works his finger down until he reaches my opening and slides inside. I buck my hips, craving his touch. "My girl is needy." He continues to thrust into me with his finger. When he pulls out, he adds a second one, stretching me a little more. Then the candy cane is on my lips again. "Open."

My lips wrap around the candy, and he tunnels it in and out in sync with his fingers in my pussy. I can't fight the moan that escapes my throat. The double sensation is becoming too much for me to handle. He bends down and wraps his lips around my nipple. Everything becomes too much and I explode. My entire body trembles as my orgasm rips through me like a sonic boom. He pulls the candy cane away but continues to fuck me with his fingers. I scream out his name as wave after wave of pleasure rushes through all my limbs.

My breathing eventually evens out to shallow pants as I come down from my orgasm high. "That was... wow."

His beard scrapes across my cheek as his lips brush against the shell of my ear and he whispers, "I'm far from finished with you."

ONE TRICK PONY

CHAPTER TWENTY-ONE
* ⭐ *

Connor

Even in the dim light from the Christmas tree, I can see her entire body flush and fuck if it isn't the hottest thing I've ever seen. My dick uncomfortably strains against the zipper of my slacks.

I won't lie, I was annoyed when she thanked me for being her fake date. When it comes to her and the entire evening, I wasn't faking anything. A war waged inside of me on if I should kiss her or leave us to go our separate ways. But when she nibbled on her bottom lip, that was my sign I needed to kiss her. Now, I'm in her living room worshiping her like the goddess she is.

"Condom. In my bedroom. Nightstand. Right side," she says in quick breaths.

I jump up and race to her bedroom. With a foil packet

in hand, I unbuckle my slacks with the other. Once I'm back in the living room, I push them to the floor and step out. I kneel in front of her, tear open the wrapper, and slide it down my stiff, aching dick. I nestle myself between her spread legs and rest my forearm next to her head. With my other hand, I slowly slide the makeshift blindfold off her eyes. Her eyelashes flutter a few times as her eyes adjust to the dim light.

"I want to see you." I move my hand down to my cock and guide it to her opening. Slowly I push inside, taking my time, savoring her warm heat as it envelopes me. Her eyes go wide for a brief moment and her lips part as her body adjusts to my size, stretching her. Once I'm fully seated, I pause. "You're absolutely perfect. Everything about you is perfect."

Before she can respond, my lips are on hers. I don't want her to respond. I want those words to live in her head. I want her to feel perfect, cherished, loved. Because she deserves all of that. Even if I can only give her that in this moment.

I slide out of her and push back in. The glow from the Christmas tree makes her look like an angel. And for tonight, she's mine. Little moans and whimpers fall from her mouth with each slide of my cock. I pick up the pace, my grunts growing louder with each thrust. She lifts her hips, meeting every pump of my hips. I drive into her harder and harder, her moans spurring me on.

"Fuck. You're strangling my cock with how tight your pussy is gripping me." She clenches around me and I groan. I never want this night to end. Her hands wrap around my shoulders as if she needs something to keep her grounded. Her nails dig into my flesh, so hard I'm surprised she hasn't broken skin yet. I'll happily take whatever she wants to give me. The pain. The pleasure.

I'm here for her. I nuzzle her neck, sucking and licking her delicate skin.

I sit up on my knees and reach between us. While I continue to piston my hips, I rub little circles on her clit. With a hand under her thigh, I push her knee toward her chest and drive deeper and deeper with each thrust. Her breaths and pants become harsher and shallower.

"Oh Connor! Oh yes! Right there." Her body trembles beneath me so I know she's close.

I continue thrusting into her. Harder and deeper. All of a sudden, a friendly but robotic "Ho. Ho. Ho. Merry Christmas" sounds from next to the tree. I freeze. Once I think it has stopped, the voice is replaced with an upbeat melody of "Jingle Bells."

"What is that?"

Her head twists to the side, then back to me. "It's Santa. He's on a timer. I must have forgotten to turn him off." She flicks her wrist. "He'll eventually stop. But you can't."

"Apparently, Santa doesn't only watch while you're sleeping, but also when you're fucking."

She runs her hands up my thighs as a grin spreads over her lips. "Let's give him something worth watching then."

I drop her leg and bend down to kiss her. It's tender at first, growing more ravenous with each passing second. As the song continues to play, I thrust into her, hitting every beat of the music. My head drops to the crook of her neck. Her breath is heavy next to my ear as she softly moans and whimpers. I kiss at the sensitive spot under her ear, then whisper. "Come for me, Tinsel."

Her back arches while her pussy contracts around my dick as she screams out her second orgasm. Even in the low light I notice the blush that spreads across her cheeks. Her nails dig into my shoulders and I know I'll have crescent moon indents tattooed on my skin. A tingle starts at the base of my spine and catapults through my entire body and straight to my balls as my climax jolts through me.

"Fuck. Tinsel." I slam into her once. Twice. Then a jolt of pleasure erupts through me as spurts of cum fill the condom.

I rest my forehead against her collarbone, closing my eyes as I catch my breath. Slowly, I pull out and rest my cheek on her chest, the steady rise and fall almost lulling me to sleep. She runs her fingers through my hair. It's comforting. And fuck. I'm definitely falling for her.

"Wow. That was... wow. I didn't think it could get better than the first time. You proved me wrong."

"What did you think I was? A one trick pony?"

Her chest rumbles with laughter. "No. Frankly, I didn't know what to expect but it wasn't that. It was a pleasant and hot surprise."

"Well, Tinsel, there's more where that came from. Always." I press a gentle kiss between her breasts. "Also, I didn't have fucking to "Jingle Bells" on my holiday BINGO card, did you?"

She bites back a laugh. "Nope. That was a first."

"If we keep doing that, Christmas just might become my favorite holiday."

I continue to snuggle against her warm body, mostly because I never want to let her go. Fuck. I'm walking on thin ice. Pretty soon, I'm going to get too far and fall in. I need to tell her the truth, but right now I'm a selfish man and want to soak up every last moment I can get with her.

"I gotta dispose of this condom." With a push-up motion, I'm rising to my feet. The blanket floats down, covering her body. She grips the edge and tugs it higher over her chest. I pull off the rubber as I stroll to the bathroom to toss it into the garbage. When I return, Tatum's sitting up, leaning against the couch with the blanket still wrapped around her. She lifts the corner, inviting me in. I crawl under the blanket and hook my arm around her shoulders, tugging her to my chest.

Her hand runs over my stomach. "Truth or dare?"

I tense. "Like the game?"

"Yeah."

"You're serious?" I glance down at her.

She lifts her chin to meet my gaze and nods. "It's been years since I've played. Humor me."

Her sparkling blue eyes make it hard to say no. But I can't go with truth. I have no idea what she'll ask and I can't risk it. At this point, lying to her isn't an option. "Dare."

"Damn. I had a really good truth picked out." She taps her finger to her lips as she thinks. "Okay. I got it! Go outside and make a snow angel... naked." A mischievous smile spreads across her lips.

"It's like ten degrees outside. You want me to willingly throw myself into the snow?"

"Yes." She shrugs. "People do it all the time. They do the Polar Bear Plunge into Lake Superior. Or the Finnish tradition of jumping into icy water after a sauna. Some people even go surfing during a white squall in the freezing cold lake."

"They have dry suits when they do that, so that doesn't count. Unless, you have one of those? If so, I'll go snorkeling through the snow if you want."

She doubles over in laughter. "Too bad I just got rid of my dry suit. While I don't have a sauna, I do have a steam shower. If you do it, I'll have the shower steamy and waiting for you." Her eyebrows raise. When I don't answer, she continues, "if you don't take the dare, you have to answer the truth."

"How about we do it together?" I don't know how she does it, but she makes me feel alive again. I'll willingly do all these crazy and spontaneous things as long as I can do them with her.

She rolls her lips between her teeth. "Okay. Let's do it. I want to do something wild." She jumps up and the blanket slides down exposing her naked body. Then she's sauntering down the hallway.

I have a hard time collecting my thoughts. I'm hypnotized by all her silky smooth skin on display. When she disappears from my sight, I yell, "Where are you going?"

A few seconds later she's emerging from the bathroom. "Getting the steam shower ready."

I climb to my feet and I meet her in the kitchen. My gaze travels over every curve of her delectable body. My dick twitches as if he's ready for round two. I tamper down that thought. Every time I'm alone with Tatum, she's bursting with confidence. It's one thing I'm most attracted to about her. Yet, when she's around others, mostly Adam and her parents from what I saw, she loses fragments of herself. The people who are supposed to help her flourish, only want to knock her down. As long as I'm here, they'll have to get through me first. I'll always tell her she's perfect.

When she's within arm's reach, I wrap my hand around the back of her neck and haul her to me, claiming her lips in a soft and slow kiss. When I pull away, her eyelashes flutter open.

"What was that for?"

"I wanted to kiss you."

A small blush dusts her cheeks, but she quickly

recovers. "It's not getting any warmer outside, so we should do this."

She slides the patio door open as an icy blast of cold smacks our bodies. All my muscles tense as a visible shiver runs up her spine. Her arm stretches across her chest, covering her tits from the cold while I cup myself. She tiptoes onto her shoveled patio and I follow a step behind. We both turn with our backs facing the snow. I hold out my hand and she clasps her fingers around mine.

I peer down at her. "One. Two. Three." We fall backward. A wave of snowflakes flutter around us as we hit the snow. I clench my teeth together.

"Ahhh! This was a terrible idea!" She scream laughs.

I scurry to my feet and give her my hand to help her up. Once she's stable, I bend down and wrap my arms under her butt and lift. "Shower time."

I'm racing through the house with long strides until I reach the bathroom. She slides down my body as I lower her to the floor. Not waiting another second, she yanks open the shower door and steps inside. I'm trailing right behind her. When we're cocooned in the warmth of the steam, I wrap my arms around her shoulders, holding her to me. Her hands slide down my rib cage before landing on my hips.

"You never got to ask me a question."

"Truth or dare?" I ask, but then I answer for her. "Dare." The corners of my mouth twitch. "I dare you to spread your legs and let me feast on your pussy."

Wordlessly, she takes a step back until her knees hit the edge of the built in tile bench, then she falls to her butt. I lower myself to my knees, lift her leg over my shoulder, and get to work drawing another orgasm out of her.

After our shower we crawl into her bed. Her limbs are wrapped around me, with her cheek resting on my chest.

"What was your question? If I would have said truth."

She exhales a playful laugh. "What's your favorite sexual position?"

I slowly shake my head. I could have picked truth but jumping in the snow was more fun. Especially the shower afterward. My hand slides over her bicep, pulling her close. "Any and all of them as long as they're with you."

We continue to lay in the dark. A sliver of moonlight shines through the curtains. Eventually her breathing evens out, turning into soft snores. Her sleeping in my arms is oddly comforting. I never expected to fall this hard and this fast for her. I brush my thumb over the apple of her cheek. Her eyelashes flutter, but she doesn't wake. I press a kiss to the top of her head and whisper into the dark. "I'm falling in love with you."

Tatum

With one arm crossed over the other, I take a sip my cup of hot cocoa with extra mini marshmallows as I stare out my living room window, watching Connor shovel a path down his driveway and to the sidewalk. Any time there's more than an inch of snow, he's outside shoveling. I'm not complaining because then I get this view and I swear he purposely bends over right in my line of sight.

I had another amazing night with Connor. I don't want to jinx it and say I could be falling for him, but I could be falling for him. Gah! He's always on my mind. Even when I'm not thinking about him, I'm thinking about him. Earlier, I was flipping through the pages of a Minnesota Bride magazine, not looking for wedding ideas, but ideas for expanding our event coordinator business, and I saw an ad with a guy wearing a flannel coat. Immediately, I thought of Connor. Or when "Don't Let Me Down" played on a TV commercial, I thought of Connor. Even when he's not here, he's here.

Truth or dare last night was fun. I can't remember the last time I did something so wild and spontaneous. If I had to guess, it was in college and a group of us went skinny dipping at a closed park. When we saw the red and blue flashing lights everyone scattered like cockroaches to sunlight. Some people swam to the weeds, while others hid under the dock. The joke was on us when several minutes later a tow truck arrived and hauled my car away. After the park was cleared, everyone swam to shore and collected their clothes on the beach. Luckily, we followed a path through the woods and found some campers. After explaining what happened and a twenty-dollar bribe, they gave us a ride back to our friend's house.

While jumping in the snow wasn't as reckless, it was liberating. It was like the cold was expelling everything holding me back, Adam being the biggest thing. Then the warmth brought me to Connor.

As I pass the kitchen I grab a garbage bag from the pantry, then make my way to my bedroom. With the plastic bag in hand, I open my closet. I yank two hoodies off their hangers and stuff them into the bag. I continue rifling through the closet and then my bedroom for anything else that once belonged to Adam. Lastly, I pull open the nightstand drawer. A black picture frame sits face down on top of some books. Reaching inside, I lift it out and without turning it over, I drop it inside. Once everything is collected, I tie the top into a knot and deposit it into the garbage can in the garage.

When I return to the living room, Connor's no longer on the sidewalk but now in his driveway. He's the only person I know that can make shoveling look sexy. Parisa's car pulls into my driveway, drawing my attention away from Connor. Once she's parked, she stares across the street, eyeing my new neighbor.

Same. Girl. Same.

She spins around and I wave at her through the window, and she mouths "Wow". A few seconds later she's strolling through the front door, eyes wide, jaw nearly dragging on the floor.

"Holy shit!"

"I know. You should see him when he's chopping wood."

She tugs her coat off and hangs it up on a hook on the wall. "No. That's not it. Do you know who your neighbor is?"

"Uh. Yeah. Connor Tyler." I stare at her like she has two heads. I've been the one living across the street from him for three weeks.

"No. I'm pretty sure your neighbor is Connor James."

"And...?" Apparently, that name should be significant somehow, but I'm clueless.

"Connor James. The frontman for Onyx Stone." She says the last two words slow and deliberate, as if I should know who that is.

"The name sounds vaguely familiar, but other than that I have no idea who they are."

She tugs me to the window where Connor is still shoveling. "They're a local band who hit it big a few years back." She types away on her phone and pulls up a picture and holds it out to me.

I rip the phone from her hand and tilt my head, studying the picture. "No. That's not him. No way." Parisa stares at me, eyebrows raised. I glance down at the phone screen again. "I mean. They have similar features. Same build. But no way they're the same."

She taps the screen, enlarging the picture. "Remove the beard and they're the same person."

"Maybe it's his brother or his doppelgänger. They're more common than you think." I pull out my phone and search for his name on social media. Instantly, his profile is the first to pop up. Six-hundred thousand followers. He's pretty popular. "See. Look. Connor James can't be my neighbor. Here's a picture from two weeks ago with him on the beach." I read the caption to myself.

Toes in the sand and living every second like it's my last.

"There's no way he was in Mexico two weeks ago when he's been living across the street for three."

"It has to be a PR stunt to keep the paparazzi off his trail. That's Connor James. I'm going to prove it." She runs out to her car and comes back in with a bag. Pulling out her computer, she asks if I have a picture of him, so I send her the one from my home screen. Several minutes pass as she clicks and swipes on the track pad of her laptop. When she's done, she pivots the screen toward me. "See."

With her Photoshop skills, she removed his beard and then added a picture of Connor James next to it. "Holy shit," I whisper. I'm not even sure I said the words out loud. "That's not possible."

"You asked Connor James to be your fake date." A wide grin covers her face.

"I had sex with Connor James." I fall to the couch, my butt sinking into the cushion.

"Wait! Not only did you go on a date with Connor James, but you slept with him?" The cushion dips as Parisa sits next to me.

"Technically, we've had sex twice." I press my fingers to

my lips. I had sex with Connor. Connor Tyler. Or Connor James. A rock star. What the fuck is happening? Did I actually fall and hit my head while taking down boxes of Christmas decorations from the garage and this is a dream. "Pinch me."

"What?"

"Pinch me. This can't be real."

"Oh, this is real." She laughs.

I pinch my forearm and yelp. Well shit.

My phone chimes with a message. I unlock the screen to check it, and a text from Olivia pops up.

OLIVIA

> Ledger didn't want to say anything last night, but he's convinced your date aka your hot neighbor is in the band Onyx Stone.

I flash the screen to Parisa.

Her gaze meets mine, a wide grin on her face. "Told you."

After she leaves with the bag of toys I donated to The Lilith House for their annual Christmas toy drive, I pace back and forth in my living room, unsure of what to do. Is he really Connor James, the rock star? If so, who's Connor Tyler? Why didn't he say anything? I'm left with more questions than answers, and right now I want answers.

I shove my feet into my boots and throw on my coat, not bothering to zip it up. The cool air hits me as soon as I step outside, but it doesn't faze me. I march across the street until I'm standing on Connor's doorstep. I raise my hand and knock. My pulse thunders in my chest as I wait. Part of me wants to know his answer, but the other part doesn't. What if everything was a lie? What if he is a rock star? What will happen next?

Suddenly, the door opens, and his large frame fills the doorway. A black t-shirt stretches over his muscular chest. He stretches an arm up and leans against the door frame. The hem skims along his tapered waist and lifts on one side, exposing a sliver of his stomach.

Don't get distracted.

Somehow, I manage to drag my gaze up and meet his eyes. "I have a question, and I want an honest answer."

"That doesn't sound ominous, but okay. Lay it on me."

"Are you Connor James, the frontman for Onyx Stone?"

His eyes go wide for a moment. He drops his arm and crosses them over his chest. "Yes. There's your honest answer."

Holy shit. Connor James is my neighbor. I've been living across the street from a rock star. I slept with a rock star. But truth be told, that doesn't change the fact I know him as Connor Tyler. My grumpy neighbor who I've grown to like.

When I don't say anything, he spits out, "So what, you want an autograph to sell on eBay? A selfie? Maybe you want to tell whatever gossip magazine how you slept with Connor James? Give them every intimate detail for a few thousand dollars?"

I flinch at his words. Like a flip of a switch, his tone went from soft to sharp as a knife. But it makes me believe people have done these things. My heart breaks a little for him. "No. None of that." I fight to keep my tone neutral until I can determine how this is going to go. "Truth be told, I didn't even know who you were until a friend pointed it out. I don't even like rock music."

He barks out a humorless laugh. "That's right. Country fan."

I nod. When he doesn't say any more, I ask, "Why didn't you tell me?"

He blows out an exasperated sigh. His arms drop to his sides. "Do you got a minute?"

I nod again. Wordlessly, he steps to the side and out of the doorway to give me enough room to pass by.

IT WAS REAL

CHAPTER TWENTY-THREE
★ ★ ★

Connor

I guess the gig is up. I'm surprised I went undetected as long as I did, but it was inevitable that I would eventually get outed, especially with how many public appearances I've made. As I sit down on the couch, I run my hands down my face. She crosses her leg over her knee away from me and wraps her arms around her stomach, closing herself off. I can't say I blame her. Seconds tick by as we stare at each other.

"So, this is what I know. Your name is Connor Tyler. You're from California. So who's Connor James?"

I owe her the truth. I know this. She deserves the truth, so it's time to lay all my cards on the table since I know she's always been honest with me. With my elbows on my knees, I glance up at her. "My full name is Connor James

Tyler. I'm in the band Onyx Stone. I grew up in Harbor Highlands. When the band hit it big, I used Connor James as my professional name to help keep my life somewhat private. I didn't buy this house. It belongs to Grams. My grandma."

She nibbles on her thumbnail as she blinks rapidly, connecting the dots. Her hand drops to her lap. "Wait. Mrs. Hendrickson would mention her grandson, CJ, who went off to make it big in Hollywood. You're the grandson?"

I nod. "Yes. I needed to get away so when I heard she was moving into an assisted living facility, I volunteered to come here and pack everything up, fix it up a little, and then put it on the market."

She mouths "wow" before her hand covers her lips as she digests everything.

I hold my breath waiting for her response. Is she mad? Shocked? Want to strangle me? She isn't giving anything away, so I continue, "It was never meant to play out like this. Especially, you showing up at my door. The first time we met, I thought you were a fan, expecting something from me. But you weren't, and it caught me off guard." I drag my hands down my jeans before meeting her gaze. "You were real with me. Your feelings toward me were real. Even though you hated me, it was real. I craved something real. Just being around you made me feel like a person again, and not someone's pawn for their own agenda."

Her foot drops to the floor as she sits up in the chair. "So, let me get this right, you show up in town, are a complete asshole to me because it felt real. Then you had sex with me because why not?" She pauses as the air crackles between us. "You told me I was beautiful and perfect. Was that even real?" Her voice is low like she's afraid to hear the answer. Then she shakes her head. "Never mind. It doesn't matter. You did all this while you knew you weren't staying. Did I get that right?"

"Well… I mean…"

"Simple answer. Yes or no?" She glares at me.

"Technically, yes." I blow out a breath. "But it's not like that."

She leans forward. "Then what is it like? Please help me understand. We shared two amazing nights together, where we both said things. Things that I thought meant something. Like this could actually go somewhere. Instead, you're telling me that was never your intention. Were you telling me those things just to get me to sleep with you? You were just using me for sex to pass the time before you left?"

I reach for her hand so I can touch her, feel a connection with her, but she yanks her hand from my grasp. "No, that's not it. I meant those things. All of them." I sigh. "But also, I'm not staying. I was never planning on staying. I'm sorry I didn't tell you, but I didn't lie to you."

"It was a lie by omission."

"Running into you was never part of the plan. In fact, it made the plan even more complicated." I scrub my hands down my face.

"Well, I'm sorry to be a hindrance to your plan. It won't happen again."

"It's not like that. I don't know what you were expecting. For us to sleep together and suddenly we're what? Getting married?" I huff out a deep breath. "I never told you I was staying." I go on the defensive because I don't know what else to do.

"No, you're right. Silly me. I should have assumed you just wanted to fuck me and then leave," she seethes.

"Clearly, we weren't on the same page. We weren't even in the same book." She jumps to her feet. "It's not even important. None of this is important because you're leaving." She shakes her head. "You're worse than Adam."

I rise to my feet and stand in front of her, taking offense to the comparison. "I'm worse than the guy you were in a relationship with who fired you and dumped you for a younger woman? Yeah, okay. That makes a lot of sense."

"Yes! Because he never showed me how amazing something could be! I never felt I had to be perfect for you to accept me. For once, I felt like I could be me." She huffs out a humorless laugh. "Now look where that got me." Spinning around, she stomps toward the door and throws it open.

"Tatum! Wait!" I rush after her, but the door slams in my face as my fingertips brush across the door handle. I watch through the window as she runs down the stairs and jogs across the street, never once glancing back, and disappears inside her house.

Fuck. This wasn't supposed to happen. None of this was supposed to happen.

CANDY MAFIA

CHAPTER TWENTY-FOUR
* ⭐ *

Connor

I've gone over to Tatum's house a few times, but she never answered. I knew not telling her myself was going to come back and bite me in the ass. When you play with fire, it's inevitable that you'll get burned. And I had the matches in one hand and the accelerant in the other. I should have stuck with the plan and never got involved with her. Instead of getting the house finished, she's occupying all my thoughts. And it's all for naught. I'm leaving. I knew this, so I need to forget everything. Forget her. Unfortunately, it's going to be easier said than done.

The entire upstairs is finished, the only place in the house I haven't touched is the basement. And Grams liked to save everything, so this is going to be interesting. I flip on the light and descend the stairs. Nostalgia hits me as I glance around the open space. Growing up, every time I came to Gram's house, I would hang out in the basement. It was my own space. Dust flutters through the air as I swipe away cobwebs to get to a dark corner filled with boxes.

An hour later, I've opened half the boxes, most of them filled with blankets or old clothes. When I've made a dent in the stack, something white and shiny catches my attention and my heart rate doubles. Hurriedly, I lift boxes and move them to the side, until I uncover exactly what I thought it was. My Westone Pantera pearl white guitar. My very first electric guitar. I move a couple of the boxes to build a makeshift chair and sit. Resting the guitar on my lap, I strum a string and cringe. It's been a few years since this guitar has been played.

When I was a kid, I would always find something to bang a beat to and make my own music. When I told my parents I wanted to play music, they took that as piano lessons. I got to play music, so I wasn't going to complain. Except my piano teacher was brutal. Ms. Rurik. She was an older woman, probably much older in the eyes of a seven-year-old. Her hair was always in a bun so tight I'm surprised she had feeling in her face. At the first wrong note, she'd slap a ruler centimeters away from my hand. I was terrified she would actually hit my hand the next time. She was stern and kept me in check, but I wasn't getting a participation trophy from her. Looking back on it now, I can say she taught me persistence and discipline. By the time I was done with my lessons I knew how to play "Fur Elise" by heart.

When I finally worked up the courage to tell my parents I didn't want to play piano anymore, but instead I wanted to play guitar, they got me an acoustic guitar. They said it was quieter for me to learn on. But what I really wanted was the high energy, electrifying current of an electric guitar. Once Grams caught wind of my parents getting me an acoustic, she wasn't going to let that fly. She dragged me to the music store and told me to pick out whatever guitar I wanted, but it had to be on the sale rack. Again, no complaints from me. I was getting what I wanted. I spent an entire summer in this basement learning how to play "Every Rose Has Its Thorn" by Poison. From there on out, I knew I wanted to be a musician. Grams was there during that pivotal point in my life, so maybe she can help with this one.

I stride to the reception desk at Whispering Pines Assisted Living. An older woman with salt and pepper hair and a friendly smile greets me from the other side of the desk. I glance down at her name tag. Loraine.

I pull off my sunglasses and fold them over the neck of my shirt. While I don't suspect anyone will notice me here, I still want to keep a low profile, just in case. "Hi. I'm here to visit Mary Ann Hendrickson. I'm her grandson, Connor."

"Let me see if I can track her down." Loraine picks up the phone and makes a call. "You can sign in while I find where she's at."

"Thanks." I scribble my name, date, time, and who I'm visiting on a sheet of paper attached to a clipboard in front of me.

"Mary Ann is in the activity hall. It's down the hallway and on the right." She points behind me.

"Thank you." I turn around and stroll down the hallway she pointed to. Nurses and LPNs stroll past me, and I lift the collar of my jacket to stay hidden. I maneuver around an elderly couple shuffling their way toward the activity hall. The end of the hallway opens to a large room filled with tables and chairs. Christmas decorations fill every corner of the room. An electric fireplace is the focal point in the center of the wall. Flames flicker and dance as stockings hang from the mantle. It radiates a cozy vibe.

Quickly I scan the room and immediately spot Grams. She's the only person who still owns a hot pink track suit. Her back is to me, so as I approach she doesn't notice, plus she's too preoccupied by the game of solitaire in front of her. The scraping of the chair against the linoleum gets her attention as I sit down. She does a double take until a wide pink lipstick grin covers her face.

"Hey Grams."

"CJ? Well, hot damn. Look who finally pays me a visit. My favorite grandson." She holds her arms out and I wrap her in a tight hug. "I barely recognized you with that beard."

"Good try. I'm your only grandson. And what, you've only been here for like two weeks. Plus, I've been busy cleaning out your house."

"Three weeks. But who's counting."

I laugh. Grams may be eighty-eight years old, but she's still sharp as a tack and as feisty as the day she was born. It was her idea to go into an assisted living facility. She said she wanted to hang out with her friends all day.

I blow out a low whistle. "This place looks pretty swanky." I peer around the room. "You got a fireplace and an indoor garden. Everyone seems nice, too."

"It's not bad." She leans in as if she's telling me a secret. "But Tuesdays and Thursdays are my favorite days."

"Oh yeah? Why's that?"

"Thursday is cards. While they won't let us bet money, they do let us bet with candy." She reaches behind her for her bag. She glances over one shoulder and then the other before peeling open one side of her oversize black purse. A mound of butterscotch, peppermint, and strawberry hard candies sit inside.

"You hustler. What are you, the candy mafia around here? Got some lackeys doing your dirty work?"

"If you play the game, you better be able to pay." She pulls out a butterscotch candy, tugs off the wrapper, and pops it in her mouth. She nods as she holds her purse open to me. I grab one with the red wrapper and green top, colored to resemble a strawberry, because I haven't had one of these since I was a kid. I toss it into my mouth, the artificial strawberry is as sweet as I remember.

"So, Thursdays you steal unsuspecting victims' candy. What about Tuesdays?"

A gleam sparkles in her eyes. "Tuesday is bingo night. And I make sure to get down here early so I can get a seat in the front row."

"So you can hear them call the numbers?" I flash her a snarky smile. We've always had a close relationship. Out of all my relatives, she's my favorite.

"My hearing is just fine," she sasses. "Every Tuesday a very attractive young man, about your age, comes in to call the numbers."

"Oh! You come for eye candy." I laugh.

"Whatever keeps me going. Plus, I like to pretend I've dropped some of my bingo markers and he's always so gracious to bend over and pick them up for me."

"Oh shit. Grams' got game."

"He's a very nice young man. Helen told me he was her date for the Seniors Prom. I'm going to ask him if he wants to come with me this year."

"You cougar. He would be very lucky to have you as his date."

She waves me off, not wanting to be the center of attention. "Enough about me. Tell me what's new with you." She rests her hands on mine.

"I've been busy with the house. It's almost done. I scheduled a meeting with a realtor to get it on the market for you. And I met your neighbor."

"Which neighbor? The brunette who doesn't know how to keep her dog on a leash?"

"Tatum. The blonde across the road. She mentioned she always helped you with your Christmas decorations."

Her eyes light up like the star on top of the tree. "Oh! Yes! Tatum. She's such a doll, isn't she?" I smile and nod. "So, what happened? How did you two meet?"

I tell her about her coming over with cookies, running into her at Fir Meadows, and the snowstorm, while leaving out the sex details, her taking care of me with my foot, the charity date, and lastly why she hates me. Grams pulls away and rests her hands in her lap. She's eerily quiet for someone who generally has a lot to say.

"Connor James Tyler."

Oh shit. It's never good when you get middle named.

"If you hurt that sweet girl, I swear to God you won't see the light of day. And you'll no longer be my favorite." Her voice is stern as she glares at me.

Fuck. I scrub my hands down my beard. You never want to be on Grams' bad side. That's the wrong side to be on. "I know." I huff. "I don't know what to do. I never meant to hurt her, but it doesn't change the fact I'm leaving. It's inevitable. I need to get back to the studio. Back to my life." Even though I'm not one hundred percent sure it's what I want.

"I trust that when the time is right, you'll know what to

do." She rests her hands on mine and gives them a gentle squeeze. "And if you don't, I'll break out of here and hunt you down."

A laugh rumbles from my throat. Not because I don't believe her, it's because I know it's true. She looks innocent, but she can make you scared shitless with a single glance. "I better get back. I need to finish cleaning out the basement. But we'll talk soon."

"Oh, you better let me know what happens with Tatum. The gossip around here is good, but this is better."

"Love you, Grams." I rise to my feet and bend down to press a kiss to her forehead. She always tells me how it is and one thing I never want to do is let her down.

On the entire drive home, all my thoughts are consumed by Tatum and what it would be like if things were different. If I wasn't leaving. If we met under different circumstances. Would everything work out? Suddenly, the creative urge hits me and I step on the gas, needing to get home. Once I'm inside, instead of finishing the basement, I sit on the edge of the couch in the living room and pull out my guitar. For the first time in a long time, the words and melody effortlessly flow out of me.

SHIMMY DOWN HIS CHIMNEY

CHAPTER TWENTY-FIVE
★ ⭑ ★

Tatum

I'm sitting at my kitchen island organizing name plates into piles based on their table seating. Olivia sits next to me reading a contract for a New Year's Eve event we're organizing. Exactly like my life, I'm only going through the motions.

Read the name.

Put it in a pile.

Read the name.

Put it in a pile.

Read the name.

Put it in a pile.

My mind wanders to Connor, like it has every day for the past few days. I feel like I was played. Made out to be a fool and no one likes feeling like that. That's the thing that hurts the worst.

I genuinely enjoyed spending time with him. In and out of the bedroom. Ugh! Maybe I shouldn't have gotten so mad at him. He was only trying to protect himself, but at the same time it was at my expense. Why does this have to be so complicated? It would have been better if he had never come to town, then I could have stewed and moped to myself about Adam and being alone. Instead, Connor stormed into my life like a blizzard, disrupting every facet. And dammit, I miss him.

"Oh my God! What are you doing!" Olivia screeches from beside me.

I startle from her outburst and frantically glance in front of me in a panic. "What? What's wrong?"

She shoves me out of the way. "You've been putting the name plates in all the wrong piles. We need to redo all of them." She rips the stack of nameplates from my hand and sets them to the side.

"Shit. I'm sorry. I'll fix it."

She picks up all the piles I've started and reorganizes them. "What has gotten into you today? You seem distracted."

I blow out a heavy sigh.

She stops what she's doing, and twists to face me, leaning her elbow on the counter. "Let me guess. A certain grumpy rock star living across the street?"

I tap my nose. "What he did sucked, and I can understand why he did it, but I still wish he didn't."

"Alright, you know what? Your head's not in the work, so we'll do this later. Let's go to Porter's and be productive at drinking margaritas."

"I'm not one to turn down a margarita."

A short while later we're sitting at the bar instead of our usual table at Porter's since it's a relatively quiet night. Quiet as in there's actual stools available at the bar. Rylee, the bartender, sets two perfectly poured margaritas in front of us. Without hesitation, I lift the glass and bring it to my lips. The salty rim hits my lips first, but soon the tart lime takes over followed by the bite of the tequila. This is exactly what I need.

"Where's the rest of the crew?" Rylee's gaze flits between me and Olivia. "Usually when there's one or two of you, several more follow shortly after." She rests her palms on the bar. She's worked here long enough to know we're regulars and for the most part she's not wrong, but not tonight.

"We're just doing some sisterly bonding. And that bonding involves margaritas." Olivia wraps her arms around my shoulders and gives me a big squeeze. "Plus, she was distracted and fucking up our work, so it was best we leave the house." Olivia flashes me a bright smile while I push her away.

"I wasn't distracted." Who am I kidding? I was totally distracted. I saw it. She saw it. I'm sure anyone looking in the window, could have seen it too.

"Connor has you tied up in so many knots, it's like a bondage party."

"Lay it on me. This is kinda what I do." She pours herself a lemon water as she prepares to dole out her advice.

Rylee has become our resident bartender therapist. She gave Bennett advice to win Charlie back. She helped Van when he didn't know what to do about Hollyn. Maybe it's a rite of passage to get advice from Rylee. It's more of an unconventional way as she basically calls you out on your bullshit and tells you to make it right, but oddly, it works. Maybe she can help me out of my funk.

She quirks an eyebrow, waiting for me to say something. I swallow a gulp of my drink, choking down the liquid and tell her everything about Connor. How he moved in across the street. How we butted heads. Then there was a shift where everything changed, and it was like all it took was one tiny spark and a blizzard to fuel a night of steamy hot sex. That we're drawn to each other, but neither one of us want to admit it to the other person. How we had fun with each other at the charity gala and that led to another night together. Lastly, how all this was happening while he deliberately failed to mention that he was leaving. I don't tell her about who he is because while he hurt me, I still respect his privacy.

She stares at me and then glances down at my empty drink. Wordlessly, she grabs a shaker and proceeds to make me a fresh margarita. Her gaze meets mine. "I thought you would need this for what I'm about to tell you."

I choke down a gulp, bracing for impact.

"The way I see it. He doesn't owe you anything. You two had fun in and out of the bedroom, but I hate to break it to you. He's right. He never promised you anything. And trust me, I know, I've been through that. Does it suck? Absolutely. But you seem to be making this into something it's not."

I nod along, absorbing everything she's telling me. I hate to admit it, but she has a point. He didn't promise me anything. Truth be told, he doesn't owe me anything either. Damn Rylee and making sense. Apparently, I needed someone else to tell me what I already knew.

"Okay. But what should I do? I yelled at him and accused him of lying to me. I doubt he'd even want to see me again."

"You need to talk to him. And here's the thing, if you like him, why not enjoy what little time you have left together instead of sitting here pouring your heart out to the bartender? Even though my advice is gold. I really should charge extra for this."

I choke out a laugh. "But it's going to be so hard when he has to leave."

"Or you convince him to stay," Olivia interrupts.

"As much as I want that, that's not a possibility." I swirl the base of my margarita glass on the bar top.

"Why?" Rylee asks.

"He's got a lot of things he needs to take care of." I want to keep it as vague as possible.

"If that's the case, he's leaving either way. Why not spend that time with him instead of moping around wishing you were with him?" Rylee raises her eyebrows at me.

"She has a point." Olivia lifts her drink toward me.

"You're right. I would rather spend what little time we have together now and when the time comes for him to leave, I'll just figure it out then." I know it's going to be hard to say goodbye, but it's better to enjoy our time together now instead of cutting it short.

Rylee stands to her full height. "But let's think about the real reason. That's a lot of potential orgasms you'd miss out on."

"Yes!" Olivia points her drink toward Rylee. "You need to continue letting him stuff your stocking." Olivia laughs. "Or shimmy down his chimney."

"Let him roast his chestnuts on your open fire." Rylee nods.

"Oh! Oh! You can continue stroking his North Pole," Olivia adds.

"Okay. Okay. Point taken," I say between giggles.

"Last one." Rylee leans in. "Let him spread your

Christmas cheer." She wiggles her eyebrows, and we all fall into a fit of giggles.

From my purse, my phone rings and I pull it out. I stare at the screen as *Mrs. Fields* flashes at the top, which is odd since we're not the type of neighbors to call each other and definitely not at 8 p.m. I press the green phone icon. Her voice is frantic. All the noise around me dissipates. All I can do is nod as I concentrate on the words she's telling me. My heart plummets to my stomach. I end the call and jump off my stool.

"What's wrong?" Olivia asks, fear and concern lacing her voice.

I choke on the words as they fight to escape. "There was a fire at my house."

SANTA'S ON FIRE

CHAPTER TWENTY-SIX
★ ☆ ★

Connor

I pace from one side of the kitchen to the other, only half listening to the conversation with my agent on the phone. Something about getting my ass back to LA and into the studio to record our second album. This event. That event. Blah. Blah. Blah. All shit I don't care about right now. I round the corner and wander into my living room. An orange glow from the picture window catches my attention from the corner of my eye and I freeze. Oh shit!

"Spence I gotta go. Santa's on fire."

"What? Wait! Conn—"

Frantically, I press end and dial nine-one-one.

"Nine-one-one. What's the emergency?"

"There's a fire. At my neighbor's house." I finish

answering all their questions while I shove my feet into my boots and yank my coat off the hook. When they inform me help is on the way, I hang up and toss my phone onto the couch.

I race out my door, down the driveway, and over to Tatum's. Flames dance and flicker on the right side of her yard. The manger and the inflatable snow globe are a lost cause, but I might be able to save the Santa sleigh, reindeer, and a snowman. I trudge through the knee deep snow on the left. Yanking the decorations out of the snow, I unplug them and toss them to the side. Sirens blare in the distance as I continue moving through the snow to save anything I can get my hands on. Minutes later, red lights flash against the house's siding.

"Hey! You need to get out of there!" a firefighter yells from the truck.

When I notice the two lighted angel decorations, I yank them out and toss them to the side. She'd be devastated if she lost those. Someone else yells at me, so I make my way out of the snow as three firefighters work on extinguishing the fire.

An SUV flies down the road and slides to a stop. Tatum jumps out in a panic.

"Oh my god! What happened!" she screams, fear and panic clear in her voice. A firefighter holds her back to prevent her from getting too close. By the way, she's nodding, he's telling her something but I'm too far away to hear.

Tatum's hand rests over her mouth as she stares in disbelief as they work to put out the last of the fire. Smoke and the wrecked odor of burnt plastic swirls around us. Her gaze drifts my way, and we lock eyes. There're no words I could say to make this better. I wish I did but with how she left my house, I'm sure she wouldn't want to hear whatever I'd have to say anyway. Unable to bear her sadness any longer, I drop my gaze. I stroll back to my driveway as Tatum continues to talk to two men in uniform.

Once I'm inside, I watch as the last of the fire is extinguished. On the right side of her yard, there is nothing but black ash and patches of melted snow. She must be dejected. I know how much she loves Christmas and the decorations.

I continue to watch until all the fire trucks leave. She strolls through the aftermath of the fire, picking up pieces of melted plastic and tossing them to the side. She kicks at a pile of snow before she stops and her shoulders drop.

All I want to do is go over there and wrap her up in my arms and let her know everything will be alright. I want to tell her they're only decorations, and everything can be replaced, but I know they're much more than that to her.

I don't know how long I watch her, but eventually she gets in a vehicle and leaves. I flop onto my couch. I hate this for her. I hate it so much. Not only are most of her decorations gone, but now she won't be able to participate in the contest and I know how much that means to her.

I jump to my feet. I know she hates me right now, but this is no longer about me. She deserves the best holiday possible and I'm going to do my best to do that for her. My feet carry me down the hallway, and to the door that leads to the basement. There's one corner I haven't touched yet, so I hope there's something there. I pull the cord and a lightbulb flickers to life. Walking around the large open room, I continue to flip on all the lights. In a far back corner, I spot boxes upon boxes labeled *Xmas*. Bingo.

I step over other boxes and totes until I reach the corner. I peel back the cardboard flaps, searching for what

I'm looking for. With each box I find, I set it off to the side and continue digging for more. Several hours later, I have stacks of boxes I know will be useful for what I need. One by one I carry the boxes upstairs and plan out my execution.

TWO ORGASM LIMIT

CHAPTER TWENTY-SEVEN
★ ✦ ★

Tatum

After the fire, I was a complete mess. Olivia brought me back to her house because she didn't want me to be alone. Don't get me wrong, I'm relieved it was contained to only my yard, but I also lost over three-fourths of my decorations. A charred Santa and six melted reindeer won't win the decorating contest. I'm waving my white flag. I give up. Chalk this up to the worst Christmas ever. It even trumps the time when I was seven years old and found out that Santa wasn't real.

The following day, Olivia and Ledger drive me back to my house to meet the fire marshal. It was determined the cause of the fire was a faulty electrical cord that was draped across some hay in Jesus' manger. I swear I doubled checked all my extension cords but apparently one slipped by.

Over the next several hours Olivia and Ledger help me clean up all the charred wood, metal frames, and melted plastic. We toss everything into the back of Ledger's truck to bring to waste management. Afterward, they drop me off and Olivia tells me to get ready, and she'll be back in a couple of hours. She proclaims an afternoon full of massages, facials, and mud treatments, followed by mani-pedis is exactly what I need. Plus, it makes for the perfect Christmas present.

I stare at my empty yard, still in disbelief. The acrid smell of scorched plastic still lingers heavily in the air. Holes of melted snow, followed by twisted, ghostly remnants of once vibrant decorations fill in the rest of my front yard. This Christmas will be known as the one that went up in flames, literally, just like my life.

There's still enough time where I could rebuild my decorations but honestly, I don't have the motivation. Truth be told, I just want Christmas to be over. My heart clenches as I run a hand over a few of the plastic candy canes. Connor could have hurt himself, but instead, he risked his life to save what he could. For me. My hands fly up to cover my mouth as my heart expands in my chest when I catch sight of a silver wing. I race to the other side of the candy canes and pull out the lighted angel decorations. He saved them. A tear pricks the corner of my eye as I grab them and carry them up to the garage. Connor knew how much the angels meant to me and he saved them. I wipe the moisture from my cheeks.

From across the street, Fuck Xmas Frank glares at me with his one beady eye. Judging me. For everything.

"I know," I mutter under my breath. Then I finish cleaning up the last few surviving decorations, thanks to

Connor, and set them alongside the garage. When I'm feeling up to it, I'll make sure they still work. But that's for another day. In the meantime, I need to freshen up before Olivia arrives.

The air is laced with the soothing aroma of lavender and eucalyptus, while tranquil melodies play in the background. We're reclined in chairs, cocooned in white fluffy robes with cucumbers over our eyes, as the masseuses massage our feet.

I groan. "This feels nice." I'm doing my best to relax and not rehash the fire or the decorations, but it's hard. I continue to remind myself that everything can be replaced and to be grateful it wasn't the house.

"I totally agree," Olivia replies. "So…" There's a brief pause. "Have you talked to Connor yet?"

"And now it's ruined." I sigh.

"I'm sorry, but you know you'll have to face him. At the very least, thank him for catching the fire and saving what he could. He kind of put himself in danger for you."

"I know. Don't remind me." At the top of the list of things I'm trying to not think about, he's number one. Not only because my feelings are a jumbled mess, but because he could have seriously injured himself. I'd hate to be the reason why the frontman for Onyx Stone can't play anymore. Sorry everyone, he burned himself while saving my Christmas decorations. Or sorry everyone, he burned to death in my front yard. I swallow the giant lump in my throat on the last one.

Every second since the fire, I thought about what would have happened if he didn't catch it when he did. He risked his life to save what he could, including my nana's lighted snow angels. I don't know what I would have done if I lost those. Growing up, every time we went to my nana's for Christmas, I would spend hours playing in the yard just so I could admire them. When she passed away, it was the one item I had to have. Now, every year when I put them up, I imagine my nana is one of the angels looking after me.

"I don't know if I can face him right now. Or I don't know what to say. Thanks for not letting my house burn to ashes doesn't seem sufficient. And then there's the whole what do I do about my feelings for him." I peel the cucumbers from my eyes and roll my head to face her.

She removes her cucumbers as well and rolls her head to the side to meet my gaze. "You'll have to sooner or later. And I vote sooner because he's not going to be around for much longer."

"That's another thing I'm afraid of. I don't know how to tackle that. I was a jerk to him. Called him a liar. How do I tell him that I've changed my mind? All of it is too much to deal with." I roll my head and stare at the ceiling.

"Did the feelings ever leave?"

Ugh! I hate her. Of course they didn't leave. How could they? "After the fire, I'm just mentally exhausted and don't want to deal. Maybe it's best I stick with the out of sight, out of mind idea. Plus, if something happened to him, it would have been my fault." That's the biggest lie I've ever told myself. Out of sight only means that he occupies every available spot in my mind. It doesn't matter if it's 4 a.m. or 4 p.m., he's always on my mind. Luckily, he didn't get hurt in the fire, but what if.

"I don't know why you're torturing yourself. And stop using the fire as an excuse. No one got hurt except a few melted snowmen and Santa, but they don't count." She gives me a soft smile, wanting to lighten the mood, but I can't even offer her a fake one. "Anyway, I thought you already decided you were going to enjoy whatever time you had together and deal with the rest later." When I don't answer, she continues, "Fine, just let him leave, but I guarantee you'll regret it."

I roll my head to the side to face her but she puts the cucumbers back on her eyes and faces forward, essentially done with this conversation. Hell, I want to be done with this conversation. I hate putting my feelings on the line only to get dumped, like Adam, or most recently, lied to by Connor.

"I don't want to get hurt again and that will most definitely happen when he has to leave."

"Don't think about it. Just live in the now. You can worry about everything else later."

I suck my bottom lip into my mouth as her words swirl around in my head. I do miss his company. I'd be a fool if I cut it off early only to stand my ground. I can be miserable after the holidays. Honestly, I'm not mad at him. Sure, a little hurt he didn't tell me the truth but my feelings toward him outweigh the hurt. If all my thoughts are consumed by him, I might as well physically be with him, instead of daydreaming about it.

Olivia clears her throat. "Or you could convince him to stay."

A small giggle escapes me. "Big rock star stays in Harbor Highlands to be with the hometown girl. Those are things of fairy tales."

"Never say never," she singsongs.

For the rest of the afternoon, we spend our time at the spa, but I'm never fully relaxed. My mind wanders to a dream scenario where Connor stays in Harbor Highlands and we spend all our time together. The big question is, after what happened over the last two days, would he even want to spend his last days with me?

Once we're finished, Olivia drives me back home. When she pulls into my driveway, something is off. Something is different. Then it hits me. No more patches of melted snow. No more discolored snow. In fact, my front yard is packed full of Christmas decorations. My jaw drops as I slowly push open the door and step out. I scan my entire front yard. Plastic snowman, lighted reindeer pulling a sleigh, candy canes, two artificial trees, and a makeshift manger fill my front yard.

"Did you do this?" I eye Olivia as she stands next to me.

"It wasn't me." She shrugs.

Mrs. Fields walks by, and I call out to her, "Hi, Mrs. Fields. Did you see who did this?" I hike my thumb behind me.

Her gaze flits to my yard, then to me. "I saw the new neighbor. What's his name... Colby, Cody, Cannon..."

"Connor?" I ask.

"Yes. That's it. Connor. Green flannel. He spent his entire morning and afternoon working out here."

My jaw hits the ground. Connor spent his entire day decorating my yard for Christmas. Why would he do that? Especially after I yelled at him.

"Thanks Mrs. Fields," Olivia says as she waves goodbye.

"I need to find out why he did this." I rush past Olivia and down my driveway.

"Okay. I'll talk to you later. Let me know how it goes!" she yells to my back.

I flash her a wave over my shoulder without a glance back. My focus is on Connor's house. Without looking, I race across the road. A car horn blares, but I pay no attention as my feet carry me up his driveway. A few short steps later, I'm pounding on the door with my fist, nothing but adrenaline flowing through me. I continue beating until it flies open.

"What did my door do to you?" Connor's large frame fills the open space. The sleeves of his Henley are rolled up to his elbows. His guitar tattoo dances on his forearm as his muscle flexes as he rests it against the door jamb.

"Did you do that?"

"Do what?"

"My yard. With all the decorations? Was that you?"

"It's only a few decorations that I found in the—"

Before he can finish, I throw myself at his chest, clasp my hands over his cheeks, and slam my lips to his. It's desperate and needy. Because I am those things for him. I slide my tongue along the seam of his lips and he opens up. Our tongues softly caress against each other's. He wraps his arms around my waist, tugging me into the house. Once we're inside, he kicks the door shut and pushes my back against it. He rips my coat down my arms and tosses it somewhere across the room. Suddenly, my feet are no longer touching the floor as he lifts me up. I hook my ankles around his waist and moan when his lips crash back to mine. The coarse hair of his beard tickles my fingertips as I brush a hand over his cheek. Then I slide my hand over his temple and thread my fingers through his hair. He grinds his growing erection against my core, and I exhale a needy moan.

He breaks our kiss, his breathing heavy as he rests his forehead against mine. "Are you sure you want to do this?"

I peer up at him through my lashes and whisper, "I've never wanted anything more than this."

"I've never wanted anything more than you."

My heart erupts from his words. I don't care that I only

get a few weeks with him. Hell, I don't care if I only get a few more hours with him. I want to spend it all with him and I'll figure out everything else later.

My gaze flits from his eyes to his parted lips. The tip of my tongue peeks out and runs along the seam. Then my lips are on his again in a bruising kiss. It's as if I'm giving him a piece of me with this kiss. I run my hands over his shoulders and down his chest. His muscles flex and bow as he presses into me, forcing out a low whimper.

He pulls away, his lips millimeters away from mine. "I don't have any condoms."

"We'll figure it out." I press my lips to his because I want him too much to care right now.

"You were made for me, Tinsel." He peppers kisses across my jaw, nibbling and sucking on my skin.

I moan when he reaches the spot right below my ear. Shaking off the distraction, I drag my hands back down his chest until I reach the hem of his Henley, then I tug it up over his stomach. He stops kissing my neck and gives me enough room to yank his shirt all the way off. After tossing it to the floor, I frantically work to undo the button of his jeans. When I get them undone and pushed down as far as I can reach, which isn't very far, I cup his face and haul his mouth to mine.

He continues to grind his hard cock between my legs, hitting me in the perfect spot and causing me to squirm against him. I pull away from him. "We're both wearing entirely too many clothes," I say in breathy pants.

Without saying a word, he quickly kisses me and pulls away from the door. With me wrapped around him, he spins us around and stalks down a short hallway. When we reach a bedroom, he tosses me onto the bed and I release a squeal in surprise. I watch every bow and flex of his muscles as he shoves his jeans down to his feet. His impressively hard cock juts out, pointing right at me. I'll never grow tired of staring at his naked body.

Slowly, I drag my gaze over his torso, past his chest, until I meet his hooded eyes. Lust and desire are the only thing evident in his irises. I rise up to rest on my elbows as he crawls up the bed.

"Now only one of us is wearing entirely too many clothes." His voice is deep and gravelly and sends a fireball of heat directly between my legs. He slides my boots off my feet and tosses them to the floor with a thud. Next, he glides his palms up my thighs until he's at the waistband of my yoga pants. With his thumbs hooked under the elastic, he peels them down my legs along with my underwear. "Take your shirt off," he directs as he presses kisses up my inner thigh.

I do as he says and rip my shirt over my head. His beard scratches against my sensitive skin and I can't help the moan that escapes. While he continues to press kisses, alternating between each thigh, I unclasp my bra and toss it to the floor. When he reaches the apex of my thighs, I spread my legs wider, wanting his lips on my clit. Instead of giving me what I want, he rises to his knees and sits back on his haunches.

With a hand wrapped around his cock, he strokes himself once, then twice. My lips part a fraction. I'm unable to tear my gaze away from him gripping his cock, pleasuring himself.

"Touch yourself. Tell me how wet you are." He continues to leisurely stroke himself. Somehow, he grows harder with each stroke of his fist.

I run a hand over my breast, brushing over my erect nipple. I can't help arching my back and moan from the touch. His gaze lingers on my fingers, and I continue to trail them down my stomach until I reach my pussy. My heart hammers in my chest. I've never touched myself in front of someone else, let alone done it while they pleasured themselves at the same time, but it's kind of a turn on. I slide a finger down my slit and exhale a small whimper.

"How wet are you, Tinsel?"

I run my finger back up and my body jolts when I pass over my clit. "I'm so wet. My finger is drenched."

"You have me so hard just watching your body squirm under your touch. Keep going. Keep touching yourself."

I continue to rub tiny circles over my clit as I throw my head back, closing my eyes. The entire time I pretend it's Connor touching me. My moans and whimpers grow louder with each passing second. Suddenly, the bed dips and when I open my eyes, Connor's head is between my legs.

"Keep rubbing your clit."

Before I can respond, his tongue slides up my slit, and I moan. While I continue to rub my clit, he laps at my pussy. Each flick of his tongue drives me higher and higher. My body wiggles and squirms from both our touches. His hands grip my thighs to hold me still, but it's useless. A second later, a burst of white-hot heat floods my entire body and I explode.

"Oh! Yes! Connor!"

My hand falls away, but he continues to lick up my slit and his lips surround my clit. Before I can come down from my first orgasm, another starts building. Connor never lets up, in fact he doubles his efforts, licking me faster and harder. My hand flies to the back of his head and my fingers grip his hair, holding him in place. I lift my hips, needing more of him. With his lips wrapped around my clit, he sucks. Once again, I'm screaming out his name as a second orgasm roars through me. My chest heaves as I tug on his hair, pulling him from between my legs.

"No more. I can't take. Anymore." I pant out the words.

He chuckles and presses a kiss on my thigh before climbing up my body. "So, two orgasms is your limit?"

"Two back to back is my limit. But now it's time for you to get yours."

Sitting up, I push his shoulders, forcing his back to the mattress. I slide down his body before nestling between his legs. His thick cock juts out toward me and I wrap my fingers around him. A deep rumble comes from his chest just from my touch. Slowly, I slide my hand up and down his length a few times before sticking my tongue out and swirling it around the head. His cock twitches in my hand so I do it again.

"Fuuuck. Tinsel. Keep going," he draws out.

I run my tongue down the underside of his shaft and on my way back up I suck the head into my mouth. A bead of pre-cum sits on the tip and I lap it up. I stroke him a few more times with my hand before wrapping my lips around him and sliding down. His thigh trembles under my hand as he tries to keep his composure.

Connor sits up to rest on an elbow. His fingers brush a lock of hair from my face so he can have a better view. "Your mouth is fucking perfect. Your lips wrapped around me, sucking me. All of you is perfect, Tatum."

In tandem with my hand, I continue to slide up and down his cock. When I reach the head, I give my hand a twist before sliding back down with my mouth. I continue this motion, going faster and harder with each stroke. His hips jerk as his orgasm grows closer.

"I'm almost there." His fingers grip my hair as he guides me up and down his cock. I add more pressure with my hand. One stroke. Two strokes. On the third stroke his body jerks and he's roaring out his orgasm.

"Fuck. Tatum. Fuck."

He holds me still as he lifts his hips in short thrusts. Hot spurts of cum hit the back of my throat and I swallow him down. When he comes down from his orgasm I pull off him and wipe the corners of my mouth.

He yanks on my arm and hauls me up his body. Of course, I go willingly. My hand rests on his chest as it rises and falls while he collects his breath.

"Holy shit. That was... Holy shit." His arm wraps around me and his hand slides up and down my arm. "Yeah. We definitely don't need condoms."

My shoulders shake as I laugh. I run my hand over his chest. "Thank you. That was the sweetest, most thoughtful thing anyone has ever done for me."

"For the orgasms?"

I laugh again. "No, the decorations. You didn't have to do that."

"I know how much you love the holidays." Goosebumps prickle my skin as he continues to run his hand up and down my arm.

"I'm sure I'm going to regret this later, but I want to enjoy this for however long we have left together. I would rather have that than nothing at all. When the time comes, I'll deal with everything else."

"Did you know you're absolutely perfect?"

"You're only saying that because you get sex." Amusement fills my smile.

"Throw sex off the table and you'd still be perfect."

I press my lips to his in a chaste kiss. "Dammit. Now I want sex just for you saying that."

He wraps an arm around me and twists us around so he's on top, slowly lowering me down to the mattress. "Just

give me five more minutes. Then I'm all yours." He kisses
my neck, leaving a ripple of goosebumps in his wake.

"Wait."

He freezes.

"There's something I need to ask you."

THE BAND OF CHRISTMAS MISFITS

CHAPTER TWENTY-EIGHT
* ⭐ *

Connor

I hold my breath as I wait for what she has to say. This could go a million different ways and I'm not sure I know what it could be. As each day passes, she embeds a little more of herself into my soul. I know our time together has an expiration date, but I want to give her all of me until then. She deserves that.

"The other day at your house, you mentioned you needed to get away. Why?"

The mattress dips as I push myself up and move to lean against the headboard. She rises and does the same, wrapping the edge of the blanket around her chest. Being vulnerable is not my thing. Right now, it's like I'm standing naked in front of a crowded venue, instead of being naked in my bed. It's easy to mask my emotions in my music, but it's hard as fuck to face them head on.

I draw in a deep breath and glance at the ceiling. "I—I couldn't deal with the people anymore. I needed time away. Fuck." I drag my hands down my face. "There came a point when everyone only wanted something from me. A fan wanting an autograph. My agent wanting me to appear at an event. The label wanting a new album. I felt that's all I was good for. I was bitter and numb. I was alive, but only going through the motions. If that makes sense."

Her hand softly slides up and down my forearm in comfort. "I'm sorry Connor. I can't imagine how that must have felt."

"The realization that I needed to do something hit when I caught my then girlfriend sleeping with a member of another band we were touring with. Anyone's normal reaction would be to get mad, or to punch the other guy, but I just didn't care. I walked away. Grams needing help became the perfect excuse to leave. I told everyone I was tending to some family business and got the hell out of there."

"Has it helped?"

"It's been the best distraction. Or *someone* has been the best distraction." I wrap my arms around her shoulders and haul her to my chest. "I don't know what the future holds, but the present is pretty perfect." I press my lips to the top of her head.

"Like this exact moment, lying in your bed, naked," she giggles. It's soft and sweet.

"Naked is the best part." I press my lips to her shoulder and then nuzzle her neck, a spot that I know drives her wild.

She tilts her head to give me better access. "What are your plans once the house sells?"

And there's the elephant in the room just stomping his way through. The question is inevitable, but I was hoping I didn't have to think about it right now. "I guess I'll go back to LA. My record label wants to get started on a new album so we can do another tour."

"Is that what you want to do?" She glances up at me.

"Music is my life. It's in my veins. In my blood. I don't know what else I would do. I don't know what else I *could* do. Right now, the thought of playing in front of people gives me hives. Not stage fright or anything, but what comes after. I give them a song. Then they want another. Then they want an album. Or they want photographs and interviews. Or an appearance at their events or to be a guest on their podcast. Then it becomes a vicious cycle, and I don't want any of it."

"That must be so hard. Just remember, they want all that from you because you're amazing. I downloaded your album. It's been on repeat for the last two days." She beams up at me.

"Did I convert you to the dark side? You're a rocker now. We can toss out your cowboy boots?"

A laugh bursts out of her. "I'll wear the cowboy boots while waving the devil horns." She holds her hand up with her pointer and pinky fingers in the air while her middle and ring finger are folded down.

"You'd be a hot rocker chick. You could let your hair down and head bang." I hold up the devil horns and jerk my head to the imaginary music.

"I'd probably get dizzy and fall over." She giggles and rests her head on my shoulder. A wall clock loudly ticks several times before she says, "Thank you for the decorations. It means a lot to me."

"Of course. You probably won't win the contest, but at least you'll be in the running."

"Where did you get everything for my yard?"

I run a finger softly up and down her arm. "I went down to the basement figuring Grams must have something since you mentioned you've helped her decorate. That's where I found boxes of random decorations. Sorry they're a little dated. Grams keeps everything and never got something new unless she had to. She still has a Crock Pot that's twenty years old."

"No. It's perfect. But I want to get a closer look."

Once we're dressed, we head across the street to her yard and inspect my handiwork. Grams had some plastic snowmen that are mostly faded but still light up. There was an inflatable Santa, a blowup Teddy Bear, along with some stand up cut outs of a few gingerbread houses. In the backyard, I uncovered some old wood pallets that I nailed together to create something that resembles a manger. I also found Mary and Joseph, but only two of the Three Wise Men, so I had to create my own band of Christmas misfits. At the bottom of a box, I found an inflatable elf which could pass as a wise man once I wrapped it in a brown blanket. I also didn't have a donkey or a camel, but I found a Snoopy in a Santa hat and a lighted reindeer that could pass as acceptable substitutions. But most importantly, baby Jesus was missing so once again I had to improvise.

"Is that... a plastic snowman wrapped up in a Scooby Doo blanket in the manger?" Tatum steps closer, then laughs. "I didn't know Mary gave birth to a snowman. Or that Scooby Doo was a thing back then."

"Did you miss that day in Sunday School? Plus, Scooby Doo is timeless. Actually, that was my blanket growing up. I snuggled with it all through high school. I suppose it's time to pass it along." I wrap an arm around her shoulder and give it a squeeze.

"You're lying."

I lift a shoulder and let it drop. "You'll never know."

She shakes her head, but her wide smile never falters. "This is really incredible. Thank you. And you were able to save my nana's two angels. That means so much to me." She wraps her arms around my waist.

"I know." I press my lips to the top of her head. "It might be a far stretch on winning, but maybe you can get some sympathy votes. I'll vote for you, anyway."

She exhales a sweet laugh. Considering everything that's happened, I'm glad I can give her that. Even though I'm partially to blame for some of her sadness. I'll do everything in my power to make the last days we have together be the best possible. But fuck, it's going to be hard to say goodbye.

CAUGHT CHEATING

CHAPTER TWENTY-NINE

★ ✦ ★

Tatum

"I really have to go." I tug on the sides of his coat to pull him closer.

"Are you sure?" He kisses my cheek. "You don't seem to be in a rush." His lips skate down the side of my neck.

His hot breath mixing with the cool air sends a tingle down my spine and right between my legs. I fight back a moan when he sucks on my sensitive skin. "Screw it. They can wait five more minutes." I cup his cheeks and bring his mouth to mine, kissing him. His body presses against mine, pushing me against a tree. My tongue presses at the seam of his lips and he opens up.

"Where is Tatum?"

"She should have been here five minutes ago."

"She's never late."

Voices from the neighbors around the corner pull me from my Connor make out fest. Reluctantly, I pull away. "Ugh. If I don't get out there, they'll send a search party."

"She could be in trouble. We better go find her," a muffled voice says.

"Or trouble, aka my dick, could be inside you," he mumbles against my lips.

"Oh my God. That's cheesy." I push him away and he chuckles. "Game plan. I'll exit to the left. Give me a minute and you go around on the right. No one will know what we were doing."

"Because your smeared lip stick says you were doing what?"

"Ugh." With the tip of my finger, I rub at the corner of my lips. "How does that look?"

"Beautiful."

"Seriously. Did I get it all?"

He grips my shoulders, bending down, and stares into my eyes. "You are breathtakingly beautiful. No one will know you were making out with the asshole across the street."

My eyes soften. "You're not an asshole."

"Don't go telling other people that. Go. Get out of here. They sound restless."

"Okay." With his hands on my waist, he twists me around and playfully swats my ass. I glare at him over my shoulder, but he flashes me a sexy smirk and shrugs. My entire body flames red hot from that single look. It makes me want to forget the contest and spend our time melting a Tatum and Connor imprint in the snow.

For as long as I can remember, the Harbor Heights neighborhood has always decorated for the holidays. It's the neighborhood that trumps all neighborhoods when it came to decorating. Every year, everyone comes here just to see all the lights and fun decorations. After I saved enough for a down payment, I would not sleep until I found the perfect house in the Harbor Heights neighborhood. Once I signed the mortgage documents, I immediately got a seat on the holiday decorating committee and over the years I've moved up to chairperson. I do have to say, I've encouraged the homeowners to up their decorating game and each year they get bigger and more extravagant. Granted, a little bribery with prizes never hurts.

From Thanksgiving until New Year's we collect donations from visitors who come to visit the lights and all proceeds go to charity. A week before Christmas, everyone in the neighborhood gathers in a little park at the end of the cul-de-sac as we announce the winners. There are fire pits to keep warm, along with hot chocolate and a stand to make s'mores.

I step up to the podium next to my co-chair, Mrs. Fields, and glance into the crowd. Instantly, my gaze homes in on Connor leaning against a tree, hiding in the shadows. A smile tickles my lips as thoughts of our kiss minutes ago flit through my mind.

"Excuse me, Tatum?" Mrs. Fields leans in and whispers.

I lift my head to face her. "Uh. Yes?"

"You have a piece of bark in your hair."

"Oh!" I brush my hand over my hair and the piece of bark falls to the ground. "Thanks."

"You're welcome, dear." She flashes me a wink.

Why did she wink? Did she see us? I shake the thought from my head.

I clear my throat and face the crowd. "Thank you, everyone, for coming out tonight. We had such a spectacular display of lights this year. I've heard so many compliments over the past few weeks." Everyone in the crowd nods while others shout their agreement. I hold up the ballot box for the decorating contest and give it a shake as tiny pieces of paper rattle inside. "Without further ado, we'll get right to it."

"I never got to submit my vote." The deep timbre of Connor's voice carries across the park.

"Oh. Um. Since we haven't officially started yet, if you want to bring it up, you can enter it."

Connor pushes off the tree and saunters toward the podium where I'm standing. His gaze never leaves mine. If I had to guess, he's thinking less about the ballot and more about our kiss earlier. How do I know this? Because I'm thinking about the same thing. When he's standing right in front of me, I wordlessly hold out the box and he slips the paper inside. Slowly, he walks backward. Even in the low lighting his heated gaze bores into me, making my cheeks flush, even in the cold. All I want to do is grab his hand, tug him back to me, and finish what we started earlier. When did it get so hot outside? He winks then spins on his heel to retreat to the back of the crowd.

"Tatum? Tatum?" Mrs. Fields says.

My gaze flits to her, and she jerks her head at the box. "Oh! Yeah." My heart races, praying she can't read my naughty thoughts about Connor. I clear my throat and address the crowd. "Let's get to it."

I open the lock on the box and pull out a piece of paper. "One vote for the Tompkins family." As I call out the name, Mrs. Fields makes a tally. This continues as I pull out each piece of paper. "One vote for the Jeffers family." I reach my hand into the box and pull out the next piece of paper. I skim the words and my cheeks flame red hot.

You look so fucking gorgeous right now. I can't wait until this is over so I can rip your clothes off and bury my face between your legs.

My thighs clench together from his words. Quickly, I fold the paper in half and tuck it into my pocket. As I'm reaching into the box for another piece of paper, someone in the crowd yells out.

"Hey! She's cheating! She's hiding a vote in her pocket!" A roar of cheating accusations rips through the crowd.

"I'm not cheating! I promise!" I rack my brain needing something to say to divert from what it actually says. "Someone wrote on the card about how nice I look. Thank you, anonymous voter. That was very kind of you to say." My gaze wanders to Connor. Even from a distance, I can see the smirk on his face. Before anyone can ask any more questions, I continue with the ballot counts. Fifteen minutes later, all the ballots are counted and tallied. While I did end up with two votes, I'm pretty sure they were from Mrs. Fields and her husband.

"We have our winners! Second runner up and the winner of a dozen free cupcakes from The Sweet Spot is the Sheltons." An eruption of claps and congratulations fills the air as April comes up to collect her prize. "The first runner-up is the McCarthys. They win a gift certificate to the Pickle of the Month club. I didn't know there are so many different kinds of pickles." Another round of congratulations echoes around us as Danielle comes up and collects her prize. "And now for the grand prize winner... drum roll, please." When nothing happens, I glance at Mrs. Fields next to me. She jumps to her feet and taps her hands in rapid succession on the podium to mimic a drum roll. "The house with the best Christmas display and the winner of a weekend getaway at the Three Moose Lodge on the beautiful Lake Superior is the Smitty family!" The crowd erupts in cheers. Kelly jumps up and down, flailing her arms as she rushes up to the podium like she's a contestant on The Price is Right.

"Thanks everyone for another great decorating season. I can't wait to see what everyone does next year!"

The crowd disperses. Some gather near the fire pits, while others stand in line at the s'mores station. I'm helping Mrs. Fields clean up the ballots when I catch sight of Connor sauntering up to the podium.

Mrs. Fields glances at me and then to Connor. "I'll see if they need help with the s'mores." She slinks away, leaving me alone with my hot as sin neighbor.

He stops at the other side of the podium. "Damn. I can't believe I didn't win. I had my heart set on the Pickle of the Month."

I laugh. "Fuck Xmas Frank next to a Charlie Brown tree with even fewer decorations wasn't going to win anything. But A for effort."

"Dammit Frank. I knew he wasn't festive enough," he mutters under his breath.

While Connor's yard has been home to Fuck Xmas Frank for the past two weeks, earlier today we had to evict him. Connor had a hunch that a potential new buyer wouldn't appreciate him as much as we do. Instead of tearing him down, we very carefully relocated him to my yard with the use of a wheelbarrow. I figured he would fit right in with my hodgepodge of decorations.

"Maybe you can give me a consolation prize later." He rests his forearms on the podium and leans in. "Also, I do believe my ballot read 'You look so fucking gorgeous right now. I can't wait until this is over so I can rip your clothes off and bury my face between your legs.' That would be a win for both of us."

Heat creeps up my neck. How many times can I blush in one night? This has to be some sort of record. "What if Mrs. Fields read the votes?"

"Well, then she would think someone wants to bury their face between her legs. Who knows, might have made Mr. Fields' night. What do you say we get out of here, and I can get started?"

"As much as I would love your face between my legs, it's gonna have to wait. The celebration goes on for another hour, then I have to clean up."

"I'll stick around and help. Perhaps I could treat you to a s'more?"

Maybe it's his soft tone or the hesitancy, as if he's asking a girl out for the first time, but my knees go weak from the simple gesture. If the podium wasn't holding me up, I'd melt to the ground. "I would love that."

His lips tip up into a full smile as he holds out his elbow for me. I intertwine my arm with his and we walk side by side to the s'mores station. We find an empty log in front of the roaring fire. Connor gets us a couple of roasting sticks, marshmallows, graham crackers, and a chocolate bar from a nearby table. We sit side by side, thighs touching, as the orange glow from the fire cooks our marshmallows to perfection. After they're assembled, we eat our sweet treats in silence.

An hour later, everyone has left. We finish cleaning up and as we walk down the sidewalk, the first thing I notice is the for sale sign sticking out of the snowbank. I knew it was coming, but it's still hard to see.

"So, the house is officially on the market?" A heavy, somber feeling envelopes me.

His gaze follows mine until he notices what I'm staring at. "Yeah. Earlier today."

I don't say anything, mostly because I don't know what to say. It's like if we don't talk about it, maybe it won't be true. He won't actually be leaving, and we can continue to grow whatever this is between us. But it's all a lie. He is leaving. It's just that neither of us wants to say it. I tamper down those feelings. We're supposed to enjoy however many days we have left, and I can't enjoy them if I'm pouting. So, I change the subject.

"I have a date idea for tomorrow night. It's out in public, but it will be dark. No one will see you or recognize you. What do you say?" I peer up at him, a wide grin on my face.

"What is it?"

"Do you trust me?" I wrap my mitten covered hand with his.

"I believe when I used those words, an orgasm was involved. Is that what I can expect?" He pulls me to his chest and wraps an arm around my back so I'm walking backward.

"Perhaps something could be arranged. But after. No pre-date sex."

"What about after breakfast sex?" he counters.

"Now you're just being presumptuous that we're having a sleepover tonight."

"Or you're the one being presumptuous when all I wanted to do was to invite you over for breakfast in the morning."

The corner of my lips tip up into a smile and then a laugh bubbles out of me. "Oh, I'm sure that's exactly what you were thinking."

"No, you're right." He bends down, wraps his arms under my butt, and lifts me over his shoulder.

I wiggle and squirm in protest. "What are you doing?"

"I'm totally thinking sex, sleepover, breakfast, and more sex. Whose house?"

I giggle. "Mine. I have condoms."

"Good call." Then he's practically sprinting down the sidewalk with me on his shoulder to get to my house.

TAKE THE STAGE

CHAPTER THIRTY
* ⭐ *

Connor

"Where are we going?" My breath forms a delicate cloud in front of me.

After our night together, I couldn't stay long with her snuggled into my chest, even though that's all I wanted to do. Instead, I had to get up early to finish packing the last of Grams' things. That afternoon I got a text from Tatum, telling me to be ready at seven because she's taking me out on a date.

"It's a surprise, remember?" Her mitten covered hand clasps around mine as she drags me down the frosty sidewalk. The snow piled on either side of us glitters like diamonds from the streetlight. People bundled in scarves, knit hats, and cozy jackets shuffle past us, their laughter carrying in the wind.

Bending down so only she can hear, I say, "Like a sexy surprise? I like those. But we could do that back at my place."

She stops and whirls around, and I almost knock her over. Her hand rests on her hip as she narrows her eyes, but her sexy smirk gives her away. "No. This is something different."

"That's a shame. My idea would be fun."

She sighs but continues tugging me behind her. We come to a stop in front of Roasters. Another couple moves past us, up the stairs, and through the glass door. The faint sound of someone singing echoes out into the street.

I halt in my tracks. "Um. What is this?"

"Okay. So don't hate me, but also you don't have to participate if you don't want to. But I thought it might be fun to come out here and watch other people perform during open mic night. There will be a little of everything. Musical acts, comedians, and whatever else. Maybe it would make you less hesitant to get in front of people." Her big blue eyes plead with mine as she cups my hand with both of hers.

I glance at her and then at the double doors to Roasters. It might be fun to see people perform for a bit. She said I don't have to get on stage. I drop my gaze to Tatum. "Okay. But we sit in the back."

She squeals with delight and drags me up the stairs and through the doors. Off to the left there's an open area with tables that lead to a small stage. Colored spotlights shine down on a young man who's sitting on a stool. "Old Town Road" by Lil Nas X starts playing through the floor speakers flanking the stage. He pulls out two wooden spoons. Slowly, he taps the spoons against one hand. He does it again but rolls them over his fingers. Every movement from his palms to his fingers to his wrist, are all precisely controlled. He raps the spoons on this thigh to add a unique sound into the mix, then strums them down his fingers. I'm frozen in place, absolutely mesmerized by the movements and the sounds. When the song is over, the crowd rises to their feet and claps their hands. Next to me, Tatum enthusiastically claps. Her gaze shifts to mine, a face-splitting grin covers her face, then I join her.

We find an empty table at the far right of the stage. I pull out her chair and she takes a seat. Instead of taking the chair opposite of hers, I pull it around the round table and place it next to her. Once I'm seated, I wrap my arm around her back, resting it on the top of her chair. My fingers draw lazy circles on her shoulder.

The announcer steps up to the podium, he glances down at a piece of paper and welcomes the next performer. Over the next thirty minutes we watch a mime performance, which was more entertaining than expected, a couple of people read a variety of poems, and a woman played a very impressive cover of the "Shape of You" by Ed Sheeran on the violin.

I lean over and whisper, "That could have been you."

She throws her head back in laughter. I can't help the smile that covers my face just from her sweet sound.

"Not in a million years. There's no way I could have done that."

"You're underestimating yourself, Tinsel." Her gaze shoots my way and I wiggle my eyebrows.

The announcer calls up the next act and a guy who appears to be in his mid-twenties climbs up onto the stage with a guitar strapped to his back. The wood stool scrapes across the stage as he pulls it toward the microphone stand before sitting. His hands shake as he adjusts the microphone so it's at the perfect height. He clears his throat, the screech of feedback reverberates through the room. Quickly, he pulls away and winces. When the noise dissipates he grips the mic again.

I know exactly how he feels because I've been in his position many times. You'd think each time it would get easier, but it doesn't.

After he collects himself and regains his composure, he says, "I'm Nate and I'm going to play an acoustic cover of "Through the Darkness" by Onyx Stone."

My heart stops. Tatum glances up at me. I'm sure to see my reaction. When he strums the first few chords, a smile tugs at my lips. He hits the progression like a professional. The music flows through me and I feel at home. He plays the entire song and sings the lyrics without missing a beat. Holy shit, he's good. Fuck. He could replace me on the next tour and no one would even know. When he finishes, the crowd cheers and he returns to his seat a few tables in front of us. Two more acts perform before they announce a short break. Tatum excuses herself to use the restroom. I glance behind me and once she's out of eyesight, I push my chair back and rush up to the kid with the guitar.

"Hey, Nate." He glances my way. "Sorry to bother you. You were really fucking awesome up there."

"Thanks." His face lights up.

"I have a favor. Would I be able to borrow your guitar? I wasn't planning on performing tonight, but your song really inspired me. Plus, my girlfriend is here."

"Oh. Yeah. That's cool." He lifts his guitar case, sets it on the table, and unlatches it. He flips open the top and passes me his Martin Grand Performance acoustic guitar.

"Thanks, man." I run my fingers over the glossy natural spruce top. "This is a nice guitar. I have one of these at home." I throw the strap over my neck and stroll up to the podium where the announcer is chatting with another person. "Is there any chance I could go up next?"

He glances down at his paper.

"I want to surprise my girlfriend." Girlfriend. Fuck, that has a nice ring to it. "She went to use the restroom, so when she comes out, I want to be on stage."

"Yeah. I'm sure Harry and Judy won't have a problem with that. You can go up right now."

"Thanks." I flash him a wide grin.

My heart hammers in my chest as I walk up the two short steps leading to the stage. As soon as my shoes hit the wood floor, a spotlight floods the area, shining directly on me. I block my eyes with my hand so I can find my spot in the middle of the stage. Once my eyes adjust to the light, I drop my hand. All eyes are on me, but when I look out into the crowd, all I see is her. Tatum's standing next to her chair, a bright smile on her face. Her smile is all I need. I adjust the microphone. With my lips centimeters away from the windscreen, I say, "Hi. I'm Connor and I'm going to play a song that's dedicated to my girl. She's the hot blonde standing in the back. Give her a wave."

Everyone in the crowd rotates in their seats. They even move a spotlight so it shines directly on her. She drops her head in her hands in embarrassment, but when she glances back up, her grin is bigger than ever. Sheepishly, she waves her hand to everyone in the crowd. She moves to the table but doesn't sit down.

I clear my throat and strum the chords to "You and Me" by Lifehouse. The music consumes me and my gaze is glued on Tatum. I pretend she's the only one in the entire room. She's the only one I'm singing this song for. Her body slowly sways to the music, and she looks more beautiful than ever. She gave me the strength to perform in front of a crowd again, even though it's only about twenty people and not thousands. But for the first time in a long time, I love being on stage. I know it's because she'll be waiting for me when I'm finished, which is something I've never had before.

I sing out the last of the lyrics, feeling every note, and every chord deep in my soul. Then the note fades through the speakers. Slowly, I open my eyes, a hush rolls over the crowd before the entire coffee house erupts in claps and cheers. But my biggest cheerleader is at the back of the room with the brightest smile on her face, her arms raised above her head, clapping and screaming so hard for me.

Stepping off the stage, I hand the kid back his guitar. I thank him again for letting me use it. I make a mental note to be sure to repay the favor later. But right now, I only have one goal in mind, get to Tatum. When I glance up, she's staring back at me. But she's not only staring at me, she's seeing all of me. The real me. And fuck, it terrifies and thrills me both at the same time. I only want to go to her and wrap her in my arms. So, I do just that.

With long strides, I'm meeting her at the back of the room. She wipes at a tear on her cheek, but her excitement never leaves her face. Once I'm close enough, I tug her into my arms. Instantly, her arms wrap around my waist and hold me tight.

"I hope those are happy tears."

"The happiest. That was so amazing. And beautiful. I've never had a guy sing a song to me like that." She pulls away and glances up at me but keeps her hands on my waist. "Also, your girl?"

"Right now, you are most definitely my girl. And when we leave here, I fully intend to show you." I bend down and press my lips to hers. Her fingers clutch my shirt and tug me closer to her. I break our kiss but keep her close. "Should we get out of here?"

She nods. While we get ready to leave, a few people come up and tell me how great I did and I should come back again. They were genuine compliments, with no other intention behind them. No one wanting an autograph or a picture. Nothing. It was refreshing. It felt as if one of the many missing puzzle pieces from my life was put back into place. Slowly, I'm becoming whole again. And I owe it all to the girl next to me.

My phone buzzes in my pocket, and I pull it out and read the message. My heart stops as I read the words. I read it again just to make sure I'm reading them correctly.

Tatum rests her hand on my forearm. "What's wrong? Is everything okay?" Concern laces her voice.

"Yeah. Um. I got a message from the realtor. There's a buyer for the house."

ROAD TO YOU

CHAPTER THIRTY-ONE

Tatum

I knew it was inevitable, but it still hurts. The For Sale sign has been stuffed into the snowbank in front of Mrs. Hendrickson's house for only two days, and it already has a rectangular Sold sign across the front. The selfish part of me wanted it to stay on the market for an extra week, or month, or maybe forever. But I know Connor has a life to get back to. One that's two thousand miles away instead of two hundred feet.

It's Christmas Eve and instead of going out with my friends, I told them all I wasn't feeling well. It's not a lie, it feels like a string of Christmas lights is strangling my heart. As fast as Connor came into my life, he's leaving just as fast, if not faster.

A knock on my door startles me from my pity fest.

Climbing to my feet, I tug on the handle. I'm surprised when Connor is standing on my doorstep with a brown paper bag in his hand. When his gaze meets mine, the corner of his lips curl into a smile.

"What are you doing here?"

"I saw your light on, so I thought I'd shoot my shot and see if you were home. Hungry? I have Chinese takeout."

"Sure. I didn't cook anything, so this is perfect." I grab the bag from him and step to the side so he can come in. I stroll into the kitchen and set the food on the counter. A few seconds later Connor is following me. I pull out a couple of plates from the cupboard while Connor grabs the silverware.

"So, no plans for Christmas Eve?" he asks as he scoops some chicken fried rice onto his plate.

"Usually, we do Friendsmas. Like a friends Christmas, but I wasn't really feeling up to it. How about you? No family to visit?" I pluck a few pot stickers from the container and put them on my plate. Without saying a word, we pass containers back and forth like we've been doing this for years.

"No, but I stopped and visited Grams for a few hours. Told her the house sold. She called it a Christmas miracle. Then she went back to hustling everyone out of their candy stash." We both laugh, but it almost sounds forced. "Also, Grams says you can keep her Christmas decorations. She likes knowing they have a good home."

A weak smile pulls at my lips. I hate this. I hate that he has to leave. I hate that I have to say goodbye. I hate this entire situation.

He pokes at the food on his plate. "So, my flight leaves tomorrow at five. I'll have a quick stop in Minneapolis and then I'm off to LA."

My fork drops to my plate with a clatter. "Wait. You're leaving tomorrow? On Christmas Day?"

He stares at his plate. "Yeah. I figure it will be less busy on Christmas than after. I came here to sell the house, and now that it's done, I need to go back to being Connor James."

I shouldn't say it, mostly because I already know the answer, but if I don't, I can't say I didn't try. I inhale a sharp breath, ready to get it all out. "Or you could stay."

A moment of silence passes between us, and I'm actually scared to look Connor in the face. I don't want to see his expression because I'm sure it's just as pained as mine. He swivels on his stool to face me, his knees surround mine. He brings his hands up and cups my face, forcing me to meet his gaze.

"Fuck. As much as I wish I could, I can't. My band's in LA. My agent. My label. Everything."

A tear pricks the corner of my eye. I knew that was going to be his answer, so I shouldn't be surprised. Maybe because it's harder to hear it out loud. The tear runs down my cheek and he brushes it away with his thumb.

"You could always come to LA."

I swallow. Hard. I've thought about this a million different times and each time I come up with the same answer. "I can't. My sister's here and she has a new business that I said I would help her with. I can't just leave her to do it all by herself. Plus, what would I do in LA? Where would I work? Live?" I sigh. "It wouldn't work. At least not right now."

His hand drops from my face, and he twists his chair to face the counter again. "I understand."

"Let's just have this night together and think about tomorrow… tomorrow."

His head tilts my way, and a hesitant smile brushes his lips. "Tomorrow."

We finish our dinner while making small talk. I tell him about the New Year's party Olivia and I are planning. He tells me about the members of his band and how they all met. The conversation flows easily between us and I hate that it has to end. We talk about texting, calling, and FaceTiming each other, but it won't be the same.

I twist my chair to face him and run my fingers over his cheek and down his beard. "I'm curious what you would look like without the beard. I've seen a few pictures where it was shorter, but never fully gone."

"You want me to shave?" Goosebumps prickle my skin as he runs his hands up my jean covered thighs.

"Only if you want to. I know you've been using it as your disguise, but you're leaving soon." I lift a shoulder and let it drop, wanting to make it sound like it's not a big deal.

"How about this." His hands freeze, causing me to peer up at him. "I'll get rid of the beard, but you have to shave it."

I drop my hand that was on his cheek. "Wait. You want me to shave you? I've never shaved a beard before."

"But you've shaved other things."

"Well, yeah, but never that much hair."

He laughs. "I'm sure you can manage. Do you have an electric trimmer? That will work best for this." His hand runs over his face.

"Uh. No. What kind of woolly mammoth woman do you think I am?"

Another deep laugh rumbles from this throat. "Okay. Fair. Scissors will be fine."

Pulling open a drawer, I grab scissors and hold them up. "Got them. Let's do this." Spinning on my heel, I stroll down the hallway and Connor trails close behind. Once we're in the bathroom I direct him to sit on the closed toilet seat. In a basket under the vanity, I grab a new razor and a bottle of shaving cream.

"I'm sorry. All I have is vanilla shea butter. But I promise, you'll smell amazing." I shake the bottle.

"Fantastic. Then I'll smell like you." He smiles up at me and I can't help reciprocating with one of my own.

With my foot, I kick the dark gray rug off to the side to avoid getting hair on it. Standing between Connor's legs, I peer down at him. "Ready?"

"Always."

I drag a thin black comb through the course hair, using it as a barrier between the scissors and his skin. With the hairs pulled away, I glide the scissors across, cutting a section of hair off his cheek. Dark hair flutters down, some landing on his jeans and some landing on the floor. I continue to repeat the process with another section. Connor hooks his thumbs into the back pockets of my jeans as his fingers drape down. He holds still with his eyes closed, and I work my way around his face, snipping away. The entire time I'm trimming his beard, his fingers brush back and forth over my butt. The touch is small, but it sends goosebumps up my arms. When I get to his neck, I lift his chin and continue the same routine.

Fifteen minutes later, I'm setting the scissors and comb on the counter. I run my hands over his now shorter beard and hair clippings float to the floor. "Step one, done."

His eyes flutter open, but he never removes his hands. I uncap the shaving cream and squirt a dollop into my palm and smear it over. The razor scrapes across his face, leaving a wake of smooth skin behind. Over the next ten minutes, I shave, rinse, and repeat until his face is naked. When I'm done, I run a warm washcloth over his face, cleaning up any residual shaving cream and hair clippings.

I run my hands over the now smooth cheeks. "It feels so different. You look so different. Like ten years younger." I bite my lower lip and tilt my head. "I don't like it. Grow it back."

He wraps his arms around my waist. His fingers brush along the curve of my butt as he tugs me closer. "I can't just will it to grow back." He laughs. "Want me to glue the clippings to my face?"

I brush my thumb over his smooth cheek. "Yes. Do that." I smile down at him.

"Lucky for you, it grows back pretty fast. By tomorrow morning it will be a full beard again."

After he helps me clean up the mess in the bathroom, we spend the rest of the evening sitting in the living room in front of the Christmas tree sharing stories and learning more about each other, even though it's kind of pointless. Nonetheless I love this time with him and I will remember it always. I hope he feels the same way.

Finally, sometime after midnight, we both fall asleep on the living room floor.

I wake up to a set of lips on my temple. My eyelids flutter open and I'm met with Connor's whiskey colored eyes.

"Morning."

"Morning Tinsel. I have to get going. I have a few things to finish up and I need to get my truck to the delivery company before I take off. But I got you a Christmas present." He sets a small, perfectly wrapped box next to me.

I sit up and tuck my hair behind my ear. "You got me a

present? You didn't have to do that. I didn't get you anything."

"It's okay. You're the perfect present." He presses his lips to my temple.

I cup his cheek and guide his lips to meet mine. If I get one last kiss, I want it on my lips. He pulls away and rests his forehead on mine.

"I'll call you when I get to LA. We'll stay in touch. Call. Text. FaceTime. Carrier pigeon."

I exhale a humorless laugh. "I'll miss you."

"I'll miss you even more." He kisses me again.

It's a kiss that says everything that we can't say in words. He stands and I watch as he walks to the door. Then it softly closes behind him. I stare at the solid white door, waiting for him to come storming back through to tell me he isn't leaving. But as the seconds tick to minutes, he isn't coming back. I reach next to me, grab the small box, and set it on my lap. Sliding my finger under the taped flap, I break the seal. Slowly, I peel back the paper, careful not to rip it. Once it's off, I pull off the lid. Inside is a cassette tape shaped USB drive. Written in the Sharpie is *For Tinsel: You'll forever be a part of me.*

I jump to my feet, pull out my laptop from my bag on the chair, and take a seat. I plug in the USB and double click the icon. The music player pops up and I hold my breath in anticipation.

The deep timbre of his voice fills the room. "This is for you."

All of a sudden, a slow rhythm of a guitar starts playing. My heart thunders in my chest. I press my fingers to my lips. Then his deep voice floats through the speakers. Raw. Real. I can't hold the tears back any longer. He wrote a song for me.

NAKED AND HOMELESS

CHAPTER THIRTY-TWO

★ ⭐ ★

Tatum

My eyes are still red and puffy as I sit at my parents' house for Christmas.

Earlier this morning after Connor left, I laid on my living room floor and listened to the song on repeat for the next two hours. When Olivia called to ask me where I was, I reluctantly peeled myself off the floor and got ready.

Now I'm sitting at the counter with a glass of wine when I'd much prefer the entire bottle. Did I make a horrible decision by not going with him? Not begging him to stay? Sure, we can always talk on the phone, but it's not the same. Our schedules will never align and eventually he'll move on. Then all we will be is a memory. I swallow the last gulp of my wine as Olivia sits next to me.

"Who peed in your Louis Vuitton handbag?"

I tilt my head toward her, and she gives me a sheepish smile. I huff out a deep sigh. "Connor left this morning."

"I'm sorry, Tate." She wraps her arms around my neck and rests her cheek on my shoulder. "I know how much you like him."

"He wrote me a song. He put it on a USB in the shape of a cassette tape."

"He made you a mix tape! That's so sweet! Playlists will never beat the power of an actual mix tape."

"Well, sorta. It only had one song, but it was a song he wrote for me." I pause. "Am I making a terrible mistake by not going after him?"

"You two can always call each other and FaceTime."

I press my lips together and sigh. "But is that enough?"

She drops her arms to her sides. "If you're constantly asking yourself what if, then I believe you have your answer."

I nod. What if… What if I don't go and he's gone forever? What if I don't get a chance to tell him I love him? Because I do. I love him so much. My life has been sad and empty every second he hasn't been in it. If I don't get to tell him that, I'm going to regret it.

The chair scrapes across the floor as I shove myself away from the counter, then it topples over with the loud thud. "I need to get to the airport. I need to see him."

"What are you going to do?"

"I don't know. Go with him?" We've had such a short time together and I'm not ready to let that go yet. I'm not ready to let *him* go. For once, I'm doing something for me. It may be wild and spontaneous, but that's how he makes me feel.

Olivia jumps from her seat. "I'm parked behind you. I'll drive."

Ledger strolls into the kitchen. "What's all the noise?"

"Keys." She holds out her hand.

Ledger pinches his eyebrows together. "Keys? For what?"

"Keys! There's no time to explain now! A relationship is on the line. And if I don't get the keys it might be mine." She fishes in his front pocket until she's pulling out a key fob.

I race past a confused Ledger to the front door.

"Wait! Wallet!" Olivia hurls my wallet across the room, and I sandwich it between my palms mid-air.

I shove my feet into my boots, not bothering to zip them up, and yank my coat from the hook. I jump into the passenger seat and Olivia hops into the driver's side. She presses the ignition button, pops it into reverse, and steps on the gas. The entire twenty-minute drive to the airport I keep checking his flight, praying it will get delayed. Or cancelled. Anything to buy me a few extra minutes. Luckily, being Christmas Day, the roads are relatively quiet.

After breaking a few posted speed limit laws, Olivia comes to a screeching halt in front of the departure doors. I jump out and race to the automatic doors. I get impatient when they don't open as fast as I want them to. While the Harbor Highlands airport is an international airport, it's small with only two ticket counters and four gates. When I reach the counter, the only person in sight is a younger woman in a navy blue suit jacket. Her dark hair is pulled back into a bun at the base of her neck.

"I need... a ticket... for the... five o'clock flight... to Minneapolis." With my hands on my knees, I huff out the words while I collect my breath.

The clicking sound of her keyboard is the only noise in the atrium. "I'm sorry. It looks like that flight is full."

"Please. I need on that flight. I need to talk to someone on that flight," I plead. I'm here. I'm so close.

"I'm sorry. I do have an open seat on an 8 p.m. flight."

At the very least, this will get me through security. Then maybe I can stop the plane and tell him everything I need to tell him. "Yes. Yes. I'll take it." Pulling out my credit card and driver's license, I pass them across the counter. As she runs the card, my foot bounces on the tile. I need her to go faster. I'm wasting time. She passes me my cards and boarding pass. Before she can say anything else, I'm running up the stairs two at a time.

TSA scans my boarding pass and checks my ID. Once I'm cleared, I hustle to throw my coat, wallet, and shoes in the bin and push it through. After I go through the machine, I scan the gates to see if I can find Connor. When my tray rolls down the lane, I collect everything and race around the corner to the gates. I hop on one foot as I put a boot on. Then I do the other, all the while checking the screens. Gate four. Minneapolis. I run to the gate counter.

"I need to talk to someone on the plane. It's important. Please."

"I'm sorry. The doors are closed. We can't stop the plane."

My head falls. I'm late. I'm too late. I mutter a "Thanks" and slowly drift to the floor to ceiling window. The plane sits in front of me. I press my palm to the glass. He's right there. He's so close and yet so far away. The plane is pushed back from the jet bridge, and my fingers slide down the glass before dropping to my side. Tears prick the corner of my eyes. I amble back outside and to Olivia's car that's still parked at the curb.

Before I can sit down, she asks, "What happened? Did you get to talk to him?"

I slam the door and my face falls. "No. I was too late."

"I'm sorry." She rests a hand on my forearm.

"Let's go get my car. I just want to go home."

The entire drive to my house is a blur. All my thoughts were on Connor and how close I was. I know I can always call him, but it's not the same. It's not how it was supposed to happen.

I pull into my driveway and kill the engine. Right now, I'm just going through the motions. All I want is to get inside and bury myself under the covers.

I stroll up the sidewalk to my front door and freeze. The outline of a broad shouldered, muscular guy is sitting on my doorstep. Am I dreaming? Is this all a dream? He lifts his head and his gaze meets mine. My breath hitches. All the words I want to say die in my throat. Several seconds pass, neither of us saying anything, the current flowing between us saying it all.

Finally, I find the words I was looking for. "I thought you left."

"I almost did. I was steps away from the jet bridge when a devastating story about a family who lost their home to a fire on Christmas flashed on the TV screen. Instantly, I thought of you. What happens if you catch your house on fire again and I'm not there? Or who's going to steal your Christmas tree?" He glances up at me and I press my lips into a thin line, holding back the tears that want to race down my cheeks. He rises to his feet and in two long strides he's standing in front of me. "There's no snow in LA. What's going to happen to Fuck Xmas Frank? Who's going to make me chocolate chip cookies? Most of all, you're not in LA. And how stupid would I be if I left?"

Tears prick the corners of my eyes, and I can't hold

them back anymore. They slide down my cheeks while a smile lights up my face. "You would be pretty stupid."

A small laugh drifts from his throat. "I know. I can't have that." He reaches up and cups my cheek. With his thumb, he brushes away the tears. Instantly, I nuzzle into his warm palm. "I had a million excuses why I should leave but you're the reason why it's worth staying." His lips press to mine. Soft and sensual. He pulls away, but his lips are still touching mine. "So, what do you say? Spend Christmas with me?"

I scrunch my nose and look up toward the sky, pretending to contemplate his words.

"Well, don't think too hard."

A bright grin covers my face. "Yes! Of course!" I throw my arms around his neck and he wraps his around my waist. He lifts me up and twirls me around. When my feet land on the ground again, I rise on my tippy toes and kiss him. But quickly I pull away. "Wait. You don't have a house anymore. Are you only asking to spend Christmas with me because you're homeless?"

He throws his head back in laughter. "Damn. You're on to me."

I glance around the step. "Also, where're your suitcases?"

"Currently, they are on their way back to LA. So, I'm homeless and naked."

Now it's my turn to laugh. "Well, you're not homeless anymore, but I might keep you naked for a while." I grab his hand and tug him toward the front door. Before we enter, I spin around. "I have a confession. I went to the airport tonight to, I don't know, stop you? Go with you? All I knew is that I didn't want to be away from you."

"Damn. So, we could be on our way to LA right now."

"Well, no. I got to the airport, paid for an expensive ass

ticket, only to get to the gate to find out the doors were closed."

"Why didn't you call or text me?"

"I bailed on family Christmas pretty quickly and forgot my phone."

He nods. "Just imagine if I got on that plane. Things could be a lot different."

"I feel like we would have found our way back to each other. But this scenario has a lot less tears and moping. I'm glad it worked out this way."

His thumb brushes a loose strand of hair off my forehead. "Me too. Now let's get inside and I'll show you how glad I am."

A laugh bubbles out of me as he picks me up and pushes us into the house, slamming the door behind us.

Three orgasms later, two for me, one for him, we're lying in my bed. I inhale the comforting scent of Connor's woodsy cologne as his arms wrap around me. Lazily, I trace a finger over the tattoo on his chest. "I still can't believe this is real."

"Would one more orgasm prove that it's real?"

I press my lips to his chest. "There's no way I'm moving right now."

"You can lay there. I got the rest covered."

A giggle bubbles out of me as his chest rumbles beneath my cheek.

"I hate to burst this bubble we have, but what is your plan? Are you staying a few days longer and then we have to say goodbye again or—"

With his finger he lifts my chin, forcing me to look at

him. "I've never met anyone so strong and determined. Someone who pushes my buttons, but also pushes me. You're so beautiful inside and out. I strive to be a better person, a better man, for you. I love you. I love you so fucking much and I would be a fool to let that go. So, to answer your question, I'm not sure, but I'll figure it out. But I'm here to stay. I want to be with you, and I'll do anything and everything to make that happen."

"Aww. The grump doesn't have a heart made of coal after all."

In one swift motion, he flips me over so I'm on my back. I squeal out in half surprise and half laughter. Then he's hovering over me, his lips inches away from mine. "I pour my heart out to you and that's all I get."

"I love you. I love you so much. And whatever comes next... we got this. Together."

"Together." He leans down and kisses me. "I love you, Tinsel."

EPILOGUE

NINE MONTHS LATER

⭐

Tatum

I scream out Connor's name along with the rest of the crowd. The only difference is Connor tilts his head my way. The mic grazes his lips as he sings and gives me a wink. Swoon. I'm pretty sure my ovaries exploded for the tenth time in the past hour. Since Onyx Stone played at Porter's years ago, Connor convinced the band to play a small invite only party. Except it blew up into a large outdoor event in the parking lot of Porter's.

After Christmas, Connor stayed with me until New Year's when he had to get back to LA or they were going to kick him out of the band. We spent all of our down time talking, FaceTiming, and texting. He flew me out to LA practically one weekend a month and he was flying back to Harbor Highlands two weeks after that. One weekend while in Minnesota, he got an idea to buy an old cathedral and convert it into a music studio. As soon as he mentioned it to the rest of the band, they were all on board. Trey hooked him up and got him a great deal on the old building. While he didn't have a lot of time to assist in the remodel, I always FaceTimed him to keep him updated on the progress.

The band knocked out a new album and instantly they hit number one on the charts with their single "Road To You." Because of their success, they were able to convince the label to record at their own studio. When the band isn't using the space, Connor hired a manager to rent out the building to local musicians and even started a music center for kids. He said music changed his life, so he wants to make sure kids have the opportunity for music to do the same for them.

For the past month he's been home. Yes, my home is now his home, but soon he'll be gone for a year-long tour. Tonight is essentially the kickoff to the tour even though this show is more for fun. Next to me stands Nate, holding a Gibson Les Paul guitar signed by the band. Before the kickoff of the new tour, Connor asked me to find him at Roasters and pass along a backstage pass to the show at Porter's as a thank you for letting him borrow his guitar at the open mic night. Glancing over, I've never seen a bigger grin than the one plastered on Nate's face right now.

"How about I get my girl on stage with me? What do you say?" Connor's gaze shifts my way. The crowd erupts in screams. All my friends clap from behind me. Olivia and Parisa push me from our roped off area at the side of the stage. A roadie brings out a stool and hands it to Connor. He places it down next to him and pats the seat. Sheepishly, I stroll out onto the stage. I'm not the talent.

There's no reason for me to be out here, but Connor's boyish grin draws me in.

When we're standing toe to toe, he kisses me and then whispers in my ear, "Love you, Tinsel." Before I can say anything, he's addressing the crowd. "So, when I first met this beautiful woman, she wanted me to play a country song. Can you believe that? Country." The crowd boos and gives me the thumbs down.

I burst out laughing, then I steal the microphone from him and say, "In my defense, I didn't know he was the lead singer of Onyx Stone!" The crowd roars when I mention the band's name.

Connor snatches the microphone back. "So, since I wasn't going to play her favorite country song, I wrote a song for her instead. This is Road to You."

He directs me to sit on the stool next to him and I do so without question. I've heard this song over a million times now, either on the radio or on my own playlist, and I still get goosebumps. Right now is no exception. How can I not? He wrote a song for me. Even as he stands in front of a crowd of hundreds of people, every emotion he has for me is evident in his facial features. All I want to do is jump up from this stool and kiss the hell out of him.

Between verses, he moves to stand in front of me and we lock gazes. He mouths "I love you" and I do the same. Then he faces the crowd and continues with the rest of the song. When he's done, the crowd erupts with screams and hollers. A roadie runs out on the stage and takes his guitar and he flips a switch on the microphone. Slowly, he turns his attention to me, a sexy half smirk on his face. When he's standing in front of me, he runs his hands up my jean covered thighs and stops when he reaches near the bottom of my pockets.

Softly, so only I can hear, he says, "Life is full of

uncertainties, but there's one thing I'm certain of... Us."
He steps backward and reaches into his pocket. My heart
hammers in my chest. He's not about to do what I think he
is. Is he? My breaths become shallow as he bends down on
one knee. Cheers and clapping sounds from the crowd,
while my friends scream from behind me. His eyes meet
mine. "Marry me."

I stop breathing. Everything around me goes silent. It's
a question he doesn't even need to ask because he already
knows the answer. My lips split into a wide grin and I nod.
"Yes!"

He slides the ring on my finger. As he rises to his feet,
he wraps his arms around me and lifts. I clasp my hands on
his cheeks. His full beard is gone, but the stubble pricks my
fingers and I press my lips to his. Even with hundreds of
people around us, we're the only ones on stage. There's no
better place to be than wrapped in his arms. After what
feels like only seconds, he sets me on my feet. With his arm
still around my waist, he holds me tight as he grabs the
microphone stand, flips a switch, and brings it to his
mouth. "If you didn't know, she said yes. You all witnessed
it. She can't take it back now."

I throw my head back in laughter, then wrap my arms
around his neck and stare up into his eyes. "All my roads
lead to you."

He releases the microphone and curls his fingers
around the back of my neck. "And my road ends with
you." Then his lips are on mine, sweet and tender. The
crowd erupts in claps and screams, but it all fades away as
my soon to be husband holds me in his arms.

Road To You

The streets are full of people
But it's still a lonely place
When the sky is dark and gray
The light carries me to you

You're everything I want
Everything I need
The only thing that feels right
I didn't know then
All the roads lead to you

I'm hypnotized by your beauty
Drawn in by your soul
You make me want to fight
Fight harder than before

You're everything I want
Everything I need
The only thing that feels right
I didn't know then
All the roads lead to you

Now you're here in my arms
Once again I'm whole
Now the streets are empty
But I'm no longer alone

You're everything I want
Everything I need
The only thing that feels right
Everything I want

Everything I need
Everything that feels right.
I didn't know then
All the roads lead to you.
All the roads lead to you.

Thank you for reading Flirting with the Scrooge! Want more Connor and Tatum? Claim your copy of their fun and steamy bonus scene when you join my newsletter!

What's up next? Be sure to check out the Brews and Flings series! Not only will you see a lot of familiar characters from Harbor Highlands but you'll also meet a few new ones as the series focuses on Porter's Ale House. Guess what? Trey Wilson, Harbor Highlands resident bachelor for life, will be kicking on the first book in the series, Love Is Ale You Need.

A steamy friends to lovers, surprise baby standalone novel by romantic comedy author Gia Stevens...

We went from friend-zone to a fling. Now I have to tell him he's going to be a dad.

After my ex-husband left, I became a single mom, and I vowed never to date a guy in a suit again.

Then Trey Wilson entered my life. The guy who lives in

suits. He's charismatic, good-looking, and charming AF. Everything that can easily make any woman fall for him, including me.

So, I do the first thing that comes to mind… immediate friend zone.

The more time we spend together the boundary between friends and benefits blur. Eventually, one kiss leads to a night in bed. Then an afternoon quickie on the couch. And one time I'm left with a broken table.

But I know he's exactly like the others. They get what they want and then leave, leaving me to pick up the piece of my broken heart.

So before we get too deep, I need to put a stop to whatever this is.

Except I can't do that when the white stick shows two pink lines.

Get your copy of Love Is Ale You Need today!

ACKNOWLEDGMENTS

* ★ *

First and foremost, I want to thank everyone who picked up this book. I think I will forever be in awe that you want to read my stories.

I have to thank my husband. I don't know if I would have ever started writing without his words of encouragement.

A big shout out to Brandi Zelenka. You were there for me every step of the way and I don't think I could have done this without you.

To my creative team, you pushed me to put out the best book possible and I am so thankful to have you on my side. Thank you to my editor, Brandi at My Notes in the Margin. I tend to give you a hot mess and you make it brilliant.

Thank you to Katy Cuthbertson for all your work and support, especially your eye for commas. You've been a huge help.

Thank you to my beta readers Jessie Bailey, and Randi Gauthreaux. You gave me invaluable feedback to help make my manuscript sparkle. Thank you to my proofreaders Rachel Story and Tonya Fender. You've helped me out so much.

Thank you Enticing Journey Book Promotions for your amazing PR work. You made everything run smoothly.

Most of all thank you to all the bloggers, bookstagrammers, and booktokers for reading and sharing your excitement for this book. It means the world to me and I can't thank you enough. And of course, thank you to all the readers for reading my words. I hope I've been able to give you a fun escape for a few hours.

See you at the next book! Stay sassy!

ABOUT THE AUTHOR

* ⭐ *

Gia Stevens resides in Northern Minnesota with her husband and cat, Smokey. She lives for the warm, sunny days of summer and dreads the bitter cold of winter. A romantic comedy junkie at heart, she knew she wanted her own stories to encompass those same warm and fuzzy feelings.

When she's not busy writing your next book boyfriend, Gia can be found binge watching TV shows that aired five years ago, taking pictures of her cat, or curled up with a smutty book.

Visit my website for more information.
https://authorgiastevens.com

ALSO BY GIA STEVENS

* ⭐ *

Want to read more sassy heroines, swoony heroes, and fun and flirty romance books?

Visit Gia's website to find a complete list of all her books.

Made in the USA
Monee, IL
21 November 2023

46862684R00149